ULTIMATE SANCTION

SHADOW OPS: BRAVO

First Published in Great Britain 2019 by Mirador Publishing

First edition: 2019

A copy of this work is available through the British Library.

ISBN: 978-1-913264-43-7

Mirador Publishing
10 Greenbrook Terrace
Taunton
Somerset
UK
TA1 1UT

Ultimate Sanction

Shadow Ops: Bravo

Sarah Luddington

1

I WOKE LONG BEFORE DAWN, the sheets a tangled sweaty mess, the humidity of night pressing against my naked flesh because I'd forgotten to switch on the air conditioning again. Though the sweat might well have come from the dreams I didn't push to remember. Memories were bad enough; I didn't need to add to them with dreams.

"Run," I muttered to the empty walls. I untangled myself and rose, the darkness of Kinshasa never a complete pitch-black, unlike the nights I'd spent in the jungle over the last couple of years.

Living alone meant I moved easily around the room without tripping over discarded clothes. I wouldn't class myself as a neat freak but if an item had a home, not putting back in that home wasted time and energy. A habit I would never break after my 23 years in the British Army. The running gear had a home and I found it easily. I dressed in shorts and a vest, pulled on some socks and hunted down my trainers. While I dressed, I figured out which of my runs to tackle before the heat of dawn made running impossible for me.

"Seven kilometres should do it," I said, walking through my darkened kitchen. Light from my neighbour's back porch shone onto a wall of picture frames and one seemed to wink at me. A magpie attraction drew me to look, even though I knew it would be a jackdaw's beak plucking at my heartstrings again.

The picture showed me standing next to my corporal, his arm slung over my shoulder. He looks at the camera, in full DPMs, the Disruptive Pattern Material suitable for work in the deserts of Syria. I am looking at him.

Unable to stop the inevitable pain, I reached up to run a finger over the digital rendition of my friend while trying to ignore the expression the camera caught on my face. "Miss you."

I can't help looking at the younger version of me. The unmitigated longing in my face makes it hard for me to breathe. Flashes of memory. Flashes of seeing Jacob's long, corded limbs naked in the showers we'd shared, or rooms and tents over the years together, crowd inside my mind and make my heart beat faster.

The growl coming from my throat is low and dangerous. I force the images back in their box, where they never manage to stay for long, turn away from the wall of pictures and grab the house keys. My only house guest, a huge mongrel dog who came with the property when I bought it, lifts his head as I leave but declines my offer of a run. Hound doesn't run anywhere if he can avoid it. In fact, the dog doesn't really do anything other than put his head in my lap if I sit outside in the evening.

Forgoing the warm up, I opt for a gentle run to start, trying hard to keep my mind blank. By concentrating on each footfall, I gradually chase the ache in my heart away, put the memories back in their rigid containers, and stop thinking about the past or the future. By living in the present there is a safe numbness to my life which brings with it a sense of peace, perhaps even happiness, if you think happiness is no longer wanting something you can't have in your life.

The kilometres stacked up as I pounded along well-lit streets in the mega city of Kinshasa in the Democratic Republic of the Congo. I wove through the urban landscape, the roads quiet, the pavements empty, the air not exactly clean but better than it would be during the heat of the day. Summers here weren't desert hot, but the humidity could make them feel like hell.

I never thought I'd miss the deserts of the Middle East and Asia.

The burn in my muscles weighed heavy for a moment and I forced myself to slow down, having picked up the pace 5km ago. Walking up a hill made sweat slide down my back and another memory took the opportunity to leap out of the dark.

Unable to keep it pushed away, I stopped and closed my eyes for a moment indulging in the ridiculous fantasy.

Even after 3 years I could still recall every freckle on Jacob's face and shoulders. His soft brown eyes, pale but bright, like amber rather than something dark such as mahogany. The brown hair, always cut short, and naturally tanned skin. His hands and forearms I knew just as well, covered in fine hair, thick fingers and rough knuckles. Callouses from the hours spent on the firing range and working out in the gym. Five years we'd worked together in the Special Air Service. He'd come up from the Pathfinders, 12 years my junior and the moment he passed selection I had known I'd be unable to keep him away from my heart.

Within weeks our commanding officers realised we were a seamless team of two and every deployment found us working side by side. On a training exercise in Saudi Arabia I'd taken a tumble down a dune. The sand, hot and fine, suffocated me as I rolled down from the crest of the hill. I dropped 30 metres, the heat of the sand burning into my face and hands as I tried to stop the roll. We carried full Bergens, webbing, complete with magazines and water rations, belts and body armour. My assault rifle, the trusted L119A2 carbine, smacked me around the face making my tactical helmet slip so the next roll had the gun's butt hit my head. I had no control. I could hear Jacob scream my name but with a mouth full of sand I didn't stand a chance of answering, I could hardly breathe. When I hit the bottom the extra 30kg of weight I carried, the dizziness and the heat which left me sucking more sand into my body, made it impossible to move.

Arabian sand is like golden water. If the gods could find a way to make it look and move like water yet deny all those who needed their grace access to life by creating this mockery, then that's what we had in the desert. A mockery of water. It covered me. A prickly, miserable sensation of clinging sandpaper.

"Mac, shit, Mac, you okay?" Jacob's breathless question made me realise he'd raced down the hill after me.

"Sergeant, get your fucking arse back up this hill," barked our captain. The sadist had decided we needed more team discipline so forced us on a 10km forced march through the desert near the camp we were using as our OP. "And, Corporal Hayes, you are docked a week's pay for disobeying my direct order to remain in formation."

I watched Jacob's eyes flash with the need to give his CO the finger. I croaked, "Don't," and managed to lay a hand on his arm.

Jacob's expression darkened. "You okay?" He took out his water bottle and helped me sit up. The rest of the team were already doing double time away from our position.

I took a drink and watched them go. "That man is going to be the death of us," I muttered once I'd spat the sand out.

"Fucking rupert."

He was a prick, straight out of Sandhurst and must have licked some serious arse to get posted to the SAS so fast. He'd made it through our basic training, just, but the 22nd Regiment didn't like it when people played politics, so rumours were flying that his position in the team was probationary. We loved to gossip so this man's status as our CO meant we had little to no respect. A forced march like this in the desert wouldn't win him any medals from us.

"Well, we're going to be late back, so there's no point in hurrying now. Might as well take it easy." I poked Jacob in the chest. "But you shouldn't have come after me, you prick. You could have broken your neck."

Jacob snorted. "Yeah, I'm going to leave you in the sun to bake. Come on, old man. Let's get you up and make our way back to the OP at a sensible pace."

"He'll dock us another week's pay."

"That's going to be a problem," Jacob admitted.

I looked at him and recognised the blush covering his sunburned cheeks. "What did you do this time?"

He shrugged. "Might have found myself at a camel race when you went off to Turkey for that meeting with the Head Shed."

I sighed the sigh of a thousand martyrs. "Jacob…"

"Don't, alright, I know – I have a problem. Sorry." He actually hung his head.

I used his younger back and knees to push myself out of the sand. "Fella, you're a walking disaster area. We've had this conversation too many times to count."

"I know. Sorry."

"You want me to take over your wages again?" I asked. We'd been working on his gambling problem for a year now. I had the feeling it masked something worse, something deeper but I couldn't get him to talk it through. We'd gone into his bank and made arrangements for an allowance and everything over that he had to gain a signature from me. We'd cancelled the agreement a month ago, clearly that had been a mistake.

He nodded, thoroughly ashamed of having to be rescued. "Sorry, Mac. I never want to disappoint you."

I gripped his shoulder, the strength in him always surprising me considering he stood a good 10cm shorter than me. "You will never disappoint me." A wave of desire ripped through me, from nowhere, and I almost doubled over with the pain of denial that whipped up to chase it away.

The frequency of these moments, a sickening combination of lust for him and loathing for myself, left me raw.

I turned away from the sad puppy eyes. "Come on. Let's go." Rough words.

While we walked through the shifting sand, plodding because with every step we sank into the solid water, I wrestled with the ache in my chest, the need in my groin and the fear in my head. Jacob wanted women. He'd made that clear to me over the 18 months we'd worked together. He took them home, he fucked them, he behaved like every young squaddie since the beginning of wars, but I didn't.

I preferred not to think about sex. I didn't get close to the women in the clubs and bars, or the bases we worked out of all over the world. I liked women. I liked working with them, I liked being friends with them, but I didn't need or want sex. I wasn't very good at it and found the whole experience uncomfortable. I understood others gained a great deal of joy from the practice, but it wasn't for me. I worked. The SAS were my family, my life, my mission. I had nothing else. I wanted nothing else.

Jacob began to talk, he did that a lot, and I listened to the chatter about something one of the guys on base had told him about SEAL Team 7 and gradually the pain eased.

I'd become adept at lying to him, to me, and living in a world of denial so deep I'd never see the daylight over the weight of water drowning me on a daily basis.

"Mac?"

I logged back into the day, the heat almost felling me as we stopped. "What?"

"You okay?"

I smiled at him and reached up to grip the back of his neck, the only gesture I allowed myself despite Jacob constantly rubbing against me or slinging an arm over my shoulders. "Yeah. I'm with you, so I'm bound to be alright."

He grinned, his teeth very white in the deepening tan of his face. "I was saying – the girls on base are going to throw a party. We've all been invited."

The idea filled me with horror, but I'd get to spend the evening shooting the shit with some of the married women and that didn't sound so bad. The horror part would be watching some young thing throw herself at Jacob. I had visions of being his best man at the wedding, god father to his children and being their single uncle who never met 'the one'.

"Yeah, sounds good."

"You don't have to sound quite so enthusiastic," he said.

"Come on, we need to keep moving. You never know, we might beat them back."

"Unless you plan on whipping my arse to make me move faster that's never going to happen," he grumbled.

The thought of whipping his arse to make him do anything almost made me pass out the blood shifted away from my brain so fast. "Just walk, pest." I prodded him with the carbine.

He grinned at me and we fell into step together again, just like always. Life was good when I had Jacob at my shoulder.

2

NOW AT THE TOP OF the hill I began running again, either the dawn light produced more sweat or maybe… Perhaps… Tears made my cheeks so wet.

When I made it home my legs were shaking with the exertion. I'd beasted the last 2km so when I stood in my heavily gated yard and panted like a dog Hound looked at me like I'd gone mad.

"Yeah, well, one of us needs to be fit," I told him.

He lay the long muzzle on his huge paws and sighed at me in answer to my stupidity. He had a point. The dawn now coloured the African sky a pasty yellow as the haze of building traffic created more smog. I stripped off once inside my front door and wandered about naked, avoiding looking at any of the pictures I had up around the house.

In the shower I moved with difficulty, the muscles stiffening. I stared in surprise at my erection, they didn't happen often these days, and debated whether to do something with it or not. After the morning run with too many memories to handle I knew where my fantasies would go, so I ignored my cock except for a quick wash and left the shower.

Being forty-two and an ex-special forces operative meant my body had more than its fair share of aches and pains, but I kept limber and fit, even doing yoga on a regular basis with my neighbour. It helped prevent my joints from locking and I didn't drink much so I could keep everything under control. Keyword in my life, control. I had ruthless control over everything.

The only time I'd lost it had been the 6 months after I'd been thrown out of the Regiment. "No, Mac, we don't think about it." The sound of my snarling voice startled the grey dove on the tree in my garden and it rose in a woof of feathery noise. A surge of guilt hit me.

I pulled on a black pair of combats, a navy vest t-shirt and a loose-fitting forest green shirt over the top. I brushed my dark hair back, the grey more obvious now it was longer and brushed my collar at the back. Having shaved, eaten some fruit and toasted bread, and slugged some coffee, I left for work in the scruffier of my two trucks.

Driving in Kinshasa was a bit like doing the National Lottery with a gun to your head. It had a lot to do with luck. Still, I made it to the national museum in good time. I went through the security gate at the rear of the building, a long and high concrete wall with razor wire at the top and CCTV on the walls pointing in and out of the perimeter. It wasn't pretty despite the sanctioned artwork, but the general public didn't see it from the museum.

I parked in my marked spot. Not too far from the back of the impressive building but just far enough to make sure I didn't feel important. I noticed the vehicles of my colleagues as I stepped into the now unpleasant heat. Something made my back prickle and years of training made me drop to the ground, as if retying my bootlaces while I scanned my surroundings. Something whispered of blood and bones in the back of my head.

On the surface I could be in any car park, in any city, in the entire world. The new museum building was the pride of the DRC's rejuvenation programme. The world looked at Africa and saw nothing but peasants scraping in the dirt, starving and drinking dirty water, and the government of the Democratic Republic of the Congo wanted to stop all that. They wanted to be seen as a powerhouse for Africa in the 21st century. So, despite the endless cycle of Ebola, plague, malaria and who knew what else coming out of the jungle they wanted their showy pieces of bling in the city.

I didn't pretend to understand politics. The motivations of governments were a mystery to me and the one time I'd tried to fight against corruption in the British Government I'd been thrown to the dogs and discarded, told not to return to England on pain of imprisonment. Here in the DRC corruption was so rife it just came with the territory and at least they were more honest about it than those I'd tangled with back in Blighty.

The one big difference between here and home were the warring factions. In Britain we might face the IRA on occasion and the rising tide of Islamist violence, but we didn't have warlords. We didn't have child soldiers. We didn't have murder squads, at least not on the mainland. Here we faced threats in ways that necessitated my employment.

I headed up the museum's security teams.

There were three teams of twelve under my direct command. On rotation because we needed the building protected 24/7. We all did 4 days, 4 nights, 4 days off. I also had a team of reservists to call on if necessary. I kept them trained and disciplined. We weren't military but since I'd taken over the post, 2 and bit more years previously, we'd become a force to be reckoned with, much to the irritation of the warlords.

The museum held a secret. Not just the beautiful history of a magical land, but in its basement, there hummed the servers for the government. On those servers every man, woman and child had their details logged and the enemies of the government wanted that information. The smart ones knew wars couldn't be won just by bullets, not any more. They wanted access to the real intelligence. The facts and figures of daily life in the vast country. They wanted data. Information. The new gold. Though while they were at it, getting the gold stored here would also be a bonus.

Our job was to keep them out.

The prickling turned into a stream of almost unconscious information. I caught the movement of a young man wearing scruffy trainers and a football shirt off to my right, not the kind of kid who went to a museum or had a reason to be in the walled car park. The sense of being watched intensified, so when I reached into my back pocket for my phone, I kept low and close to my vehicle.

The number on speed dial answered within two rings. "Mac?" asked the heavily accented French African voice.

"Danny, I'm in the car park, you see anything on CCTV?" I asked.

"Hang on, I'm in the office." I heard him moving down the hallway, visualising the long slim limbs moving with his usual grace. "Um, the cameras aren't showing anything right now." A roll to the 'r' sound in 'right' made his accent exotic, almost a purr.

"Something's not right."

A pause. "Okay, what do you want me to do?"

He'd learned over the weeks and months we'd worked together that my instincts were honed to vibrate like a fucking tuning fork. "Break out the assault rifles, get the men in full tactical gear, webbing, the lot. I want everyone on point. I'm going to walk through the car park now. I'd appreciate over-watch from the west side of the building."

“Give me 2 minutes and I’ll be on the roof,” Danny said, already moving. We kept the assault rifles and other toys locked up but both Danny, who’d served in the French Foreign Legion and myself kept sniper rifles beside our desks and a handgun in the top drawer. It never paid to be lazy in the Democratic Republic of the Congo.

Unable to spend more time tying my laces I opened the door to the truck and climbed back in, on the pretext of looking for something. That crawling sensation became stronger and I half expected a shot through my windscreen. I kept slumped down in the seat and continued to keep the observational awareness of my surroundings high.

My phone rang but I kept eyes on while I answered it. “Yep?”

“I am in position, Mac. I see you in your rust bucket. Time to move.”

“You see anything else? Did you check the perimeter?” I asked.

He huffed. “I know how to do my job, Mac.”

Duly chastised I said, “I’m going to drive closer, keep a watch on my six, see anything let me know.”

“Sure thing, but you know the boss doesn’t like you parking in his spot.”

“Fuck him. Stay on comms. I’m switching to an ear piece now.” I dragged the ear piece and wire from the glove compartment and plugged one into my ear, the other into the phone. “Your one o’clock, Danny. There was movement there earlier.”

“Roger that.”

I heard him shift his position a little to accommodate my reference. The engine turned over and duly belched into life. I drove forwards, avoiding the chicane of concrete barriers masquerading as giant plant pots. When I reached the closest parking spot to the building I stopped. My actions would tell a half competent enemy I knew I was being watched but walking the 30 metres to the back door could have resulted in a bullet, so paranoia won over bravado. I’d survived 7 years in the regular army and 15 years in the Regiment for a reason and it wasn’t all down to luck.

The hardest part was leaving the relative safety of the truck and walking the 5 metres between me and the back door. I also needed enough time to punch in the security code.

“Can you get one of the others to open the door for me?” I asked down the line to Danny.

"Already on it. The door should only be open a little, from your position you cannot see it. Come on, Mac. Get your arse into the building, it's hot up here."

"You wanna try it?" I muttered.

He chuckled. "Didn't need to, my friend. I made it to work on time."

I growled. I was late but the run had been necessary, talking of which, my thighs and calves ached at just the thought of having to cover any distance at speed.

"Fucking hell," I cursed. I opened the door to the truck again and pushed one leg out, half expecting to hear or feel a bullet hit something.

Nothing happened.

I debussed and closed the door to the truck. The tingle grew so strong I shivered to try and shift the feeling off my back. The phrase 'I felt someone walk over my grave' came to mind. Five metres. I only had to cover that much distance. Seven steps. That would see me inside the corridor to the back offices.

If I ever had to face my execution then I had little doubt it would feel something like this. My heart raced, my palms were slick, and my stomach churned. All these reactions were familiar. I lived with fear in the field and I'd grown up with it every day of my rotten childhood, but the chemical cocktail made it hard to breathe in a calm cycle.

"If today is your day, Mac, then face it with at least a little dignity."

"Said like a true Englishman," Danny said. I heard the grin in his voice.

"Fuck you."

That just made him chuckle. One, two, three, four, five, six, seven, inside the door and it was shut. The light flickered on and I breathed again. No shot rang out. No screams. No violence. I'd say I felt like a fool, but I didn't. I felt like an operative who knew how to do his bloody job.

"I'm inside, Danny. I want the team assembled in the entrance to the front gallery," I said.

"On it, out."

The line went dead. I needed to get our comms unit in my ear so I could speak with the rest of the team. The back stairs were more comfortable for me than the staff elevator, so I worked the lactic acid build up in my thighs a bit more by sprinting up three flights. I strode into the office I shared with Danny, peered out of the window at the back of the building and checked the perimeter myself.

Nothing. Yet still that prickle chased itself over my back. I keyed in the code to the arms store next to the office and removed my Heckler and Koch MP5 and took a sidearm, the Sig Sauer P226. I grabbed my body armour, a comms unit with throat mic and set it up while on my way down to the impromptu meeting.

When I arrived, I found my team waiting. "Anything?" I asked Danny.

"Rachael just called, she says the CCTV is down," Danny stated, voice and face serious.

I nodded my acknowledgement of his words. "Looks like it's going to be a busy morning, gentlemen. I suggest we take our positions. We've done the training; we've faced tough odds in the last few months, so this isn't our first dust up. Remember, you are professionals. *They* are not."

"We don't know who, *they* are," said Kol.

"Does it matter?" I asked.

In the early days I'd made mistakes with recruitment, the different tribal allegiances making life more complicated and then there were the different religious groups as well. Nothing in Africa seemed to be a straight line, including the fought over borders.

Kol's face twisted and he shrugged. As a new member of the team he still needed combat experience and I wondered if I'd chosen wisely. His finger played with the safety mechanism on the SA80A2 most of the team carried.

"Any questions from any of you?" I asked.

"Do we call in reinforcements now or when we have contact?" asked Kol.

"On contact. Danny will make the call. Where are my medical officers?" I asked, knowing who they were but nodding at them when two hands went up. "Full kit in the right places?"

"Yes, boss," they answered together.

I winced. I hated being called boss. Being the only white face in the building made me stand out at the best of times, never a good thing for a soldier, and it made me feel like a colonial prick most of the time. Danny had laughed when I confessed to my dislike of the term. Apparently not all white men were bad, he'd reassured me and winked.

"Move out," I ordered.

3

"INCOMING!" I BELLOWED, DUCKING DOWN behind the concrete barricade. The stonework of Kinshasa's new museum shattered under the impact of the RPG showering those of us who fought tooth and claw to protect its contents.

"Fuck me," I muttered, spitting dust out of my mouth.

I'd opened it wide to prevent my eardrums from bursting at the moment of impact. The DRC might not be everybody's dream retirement but a life in the Regiment made much of the world too tame. This however, this was over the fucking top.

The impact seemed to shock the raiders, so we took advantage. "Return fire," I ordered. Each of my men proved their mettle by rising over the barricades and releasing controlled bursts at the enemy across the small plaza from their SA80A2 personal support weapon and the constant *rat-rat* bright muzzle flashes of the two Minimi light machine guns. The clink of brass hitting the hot tarmac and the smell of heated metal and gunpowder made the violence seem all too familiar.

In the 30 minutes since contact began, I'd changed magazines three times in the MP5. I had four mags left in my vest and we faced an army. It wasn't huge but they had more than twelve men on their team. Mounted on the back of a Land Rover being used as a technical, an M2 .50 calibre barked incessantly, but the operatives didn't seem to know what they were doing, it was going through belts far too quickly. Its noise though, that hurt more than my ears. I repeated the shake of my head to dispel the wrong smells and sights in my brain. This wasn't the desert; this was urban fucking warfare. I needed to get the pricks down off that improvised vehicle, then we could push the rest back once the regular armed police turned up or the fucking army, which is what I'd requested 30 minutes ago.

At the moment we were pinned down, only able to return fire when the heavy machine gun shut its fucking noise up.

Under these circumstances we couldn't win, but we could hold on until reinforcements arrived and that's what we were going to do, hold on, maintain our position and prevent the bastards from coming in the front.

A figure, white skin obvious in our surroundings, flashed through my peripheral vision. I paused, tried to locate him but lost the dark clad form in the gun smoke and small fires breaking out among the chaos. His body movements dragged at my memory, but it couldn't be right, so I discarded the thought before it threatened to overwhelm me far more than the current firefight.

"Medic!" screamed a man to my left. Two men from my position shifted, one of them the medic, the other his back-up. I'd trained them well and despite the mess, pride swelled inside me. These were good men at my side.

"RPG reloading, Mac," shouted Danny, my second.

"Send him over the bridge if you can," I shouted back. "I've no clear shot."

"None of us has," he yelled back. His dark eyes were wide, but he grinned at me, teeth covered in dust.

The dark clothed white man sprinted over open ground from my ten o'clock, rounds from the enemy AKs sending up sharp chips of pavement, missing him by whiskers as he continued towards us.

"Cover him," I bellowed, standing and spraying bullets until the Heckler and Koch clicked empty. I reloaded with oil slick precision and opened fire again just as the figure dived for the barricade and rolled without effort despite the long rifle in his right hand. He rose, turned, returned to me and took up position.

"Hello, Mac."

Time dropped away.

"Jacob?" I whispered. I had no time for the emotional reactions that tried to surface.

He grabbed the front of my vest and yanked me down behind the protection. "Good to see you."

"What the fuck?"

Jacob winked, lined up his Heckler and Koch 417, took a moment to find his target and despite the insanity surrounding him, dispatched the man with the RPG before he could release the rocket. Nothing remained of the man's face when he dropped behind his comrades. I retrieved my shit from where I'd lost it a few seconds before and managed to gather everything together again despite Jacob being beside me once more in a combat zone.

When he began picking off the raiders with the more accurate HK417 the enemy soon decided they had more important things to do than die, so they retreated. At least for the moment. In the silence that followed I stared at Jacob.

A thick dark blond beard covered his face and a deep tan made his amber eyes turn into something otherworldly. A scar, one I'd never seen before, tracked over his left cheek and vanished into the beard and one ear now missed a tip. My guess? Some silly fucker had tried to shoot him and missed. I bet he didn't get a second chance.

Jacob looked good though. A thought I worked damned hard to hide even from myself. The black t-shirt and dark jeans hugged the taut, muscular frame. A coiled raptor of a man.

"Good to see you, Mac," he said, eyes doing their own inventory.

"What the ever-loving fuck are you doing here?" I asked. "Did you know I was here?"

He grinned at me again, making his eyes crinkle in the corners. "We're in-country looking for some silly fucker and no, I didn't know for certain you were here. Guess the gods are shining down on me because the riot made returning to the FOB almost impossible."

The Regiment had a forward operating base in Kinshasa? I eyed the sniper rifle. "You often run around with that thing in your pocket?"

Jacob didn't say anything, but he rose with the ease of youthful knees and offered me his hand. "Come on, I need a drink. Anything to wash away the dust and gunpowder."

I took his hand, thick fingers, a rough palm, callouses everywhere and strong. It all registered, along with the spark of skin on skin contact waking more memories than were not comfortable or necessary. He heaved me off the ground and we headed back to the museum.

"What the hell are you doing here, Mac?" he asked. "Last I heard you were in Spain."

Three years ago, I had indeed been in Spain for a brief time. I'd been trying to drink away the pain of leaving the Regiment and leaving behind the one thing that meant more to me than the Regiment.

“Spain isn’t always the best place to keep busy,” I muttered.

Jacob touched my arm, drawing me to a halt. “I wrote to you,” he said, unable to hide his tension.

I couldn’t meet his gaze, though the burden further tightened my shoulders. “Sorry. You’ll understand when it’s time for you to leave. I didn’t want to be a weight around your neck.” I tried a smile to ease the strain between us, forcing myself to meet his amber eyes.

“You could never be a weight around my neck, Mac.” Those eyes were intense, disturbing in their scrutiny.

“Mac?” yelled Danny from the doorway to the museum. “We need you in here.”

I turned back to the building we protected, grateful for the release, and ran up the stairs. “What’s the problem?” I asked.

“The attack has damaged the electricity network in the building and we’re struggling to keep things stable. We cannot afford a problem.” His French African accent turned his English into a lyrical dance of sound and the dust made his sweaty black skin a strange grey.

“Shit, we need more bodies on the ground or they’ll break through with the next attack,” I muttered, running my fingers through my dark hair.

Jacob snorted. “Why are you guarding a museum? Let ‘em in and have at it, everything in here is old stuff anyway.”

Danny sucked air over his teeth and scowled. I punched Jacob on the arm. “Hey, I’m old and I happen to like preserving old ‘stuff’, which, you uneducated oaf, is important to the cultural history of a tormented but improving country.”

Jacob’s beautiful eyes widened, and he grinned. “You’re not old and okay, we preserve the old stuff.”

“We?” I asked.

“I’m here aren’t I? Set me up with a nest and I’ll make sure the fuckers don’t come back too fast,” he said, pointing at the HK417.

I studied him in the softer light of the interior of the museum. A vivid streak of something disturbing coloured his expression and I sensed something... *off*. I didn’t have time to think about it though because the lights flickered overhead. “Shit, we can’t lose the generator.”

Jacob followed my gaze. “What’s wrong with losing the electric? You’ve enough men to control the perimeter until you call in the cavalry. I'm assuming the DRC has cavalry?"

"You better not mean that literally," Danny muttered.

They sized each other up. I didn't fancy taking bets on either man; Danny had a vicious streak despite being a family man and it would match Jacob's attitude. "We can't lose the electric because we aren't just protecting old 'stuff' as you so elegantly put it." I turned my attention to Danny, a tough job under the circumstances. "Get hold of Rachael. She can fix just about any problem with this place. It'll be her saving this pile of stones while we try to keep them out."

"What you gonna do with him?" Danny asked nodding towards Jacob.

"Leave it with me." I clapped him on the shoulder. "Don't worry, he can be trusted." Danny huffed but followed orders and began yelling for people to organise themselves to help him defend our building.

It left me alone with Jacob. I found him studying me again. "You look… peaceful," he said at last.

I ignored him. Perhaps I looked peaceful to his eyes, but on the inside his appearance made me raw. I dragged him away from the front doors to the building so we could have a private word. "How many of you are there in-country?" I asked.

"Why?" Jacob replied.

"I need help defending this place, that's why." I shook my head and tried to assess his state of mind again. Three and a half years, give or take a month, had passed since I'd last seen him and something had changed. The young operator I helped train didn't exist in those shadowed eyes and hard mouth. "Can you reach your team and request help?"

"You left me high and dry, Mac, give me a reason why I should," Jacob said, crossing his arms over his broad chest.

"Why wouldn't you? We need to protect this place and the people inside it, that's the job, the mission, always. Protect and preserve life where we can – or has something changed in the Regiment I don't know about?"

Jacob's eyes narrowed. "How would you know if anything has changed? You dropped off the fucking planet when you left."

"I didn't leave. I was booted – remember?" I snapped. I didn't want this conversation, there were too many factors rattling around us like a slow-moving tornado of historical facts and assumptions ready to rip into a storm strong enough to break a man's heart and soul.

Colour tinted Jacob's soft skin above the thick beard. "I remember you walked when you could have fought. You left me." His eyes blazed for a moment, bright and hot, a challenge, a thrown gauntlet of unspoken anger. "I wrote to you, emails, text messages, left phone –"

I stared over his shoulder and tried to swallow past the lump in my throat. "186 text messages, 127 emails, 59 phone messages – most of which happened when you were drunk, 5 actual letters."

His palm hit my chest and I rocked back under the impact. "And you didn't answer any of them."

Thoughts swirled so fast nausea rose into my gullet. The shock of seeing him after that morning and the contact we'd had with the enemy threatened to overwhelm me. "I had to ignore you. For your own good. I'm a fucking albatross, Jacob. I would have taken you down with me. Can we please get on mission and leave this shit behind?"

Jacob shook his head, the shorn hair barely hinting at the umbra blond of his natural colouring. "We are not leaving this in the past, Mac." He drew in a sharp breath. "But I will let it lie for now. What's in this damned building that's so important? The more I look around the more I see things that make me believe that attack just now wasn't about destroying a museum."

He'd seen it, all the security we had in place. The CCTV, the metal detectors in front of the main doors. The armed guards, including me, the heavy barricades outside that doubled as flower beds, the thick concrete walls, heavy glass and thick metal shutters covering the vulnerable spots which even now were protecting us from the heat of the day.

"You're right," I said, walking him through the large entrance. "It's need to know only so the less people you tell about this the better. We aren't here just to protect the museum. When the government built this place, they put in large bunkers which house the government servers. On those servers are the details of every citizen in the DRC, there is a full census and that means people's religions and tribal groups, HIV status - everything. If those men out there get hold of that information, they will know exactly who to target for a fucking massacre reminiscent of Rwanda. On top of that are all the details of every fucking mine and government deal with trade partners. Whoever controls the information has the power. This latest spat is with a warlord who sees the value in the digital world, not just the value of what's dug out of the ground."

"Shit."

"Yeah, so are you going to help? Who are you here with and how many bloody guns have you got?" I asked.

4

JACOB SHED A LAYER OF bristling anger. "There is a four-man team, one spook and a rupert."

Standard formation, except for the rupert. "Good. Where are they?"

"I'm hoping they are back at the FOB. It's in Bandalungwa District," he said, mangling the foreign word.

"What the fuck are they doing there?" I asked. Then waved my hand. "Never mind, you can't tell me. How did you manage to get yourself separated from the others?"

The black jeans and a black t-shirt had seen better days, combined with a black shirt open at the front, I realised we dressed the same. "The team ran into a riot. I had over-watch, I couldn't get to them in time and I couldn't get through the crowds, so headed to open ground."

"The museum," I muttered. "Can you get in touch with your team?"

"Sure, I switched my comms off so I couldn't be tracked."

Why the hell would he be tracked? What on earth were they doing in the DRC?

Too many threads, too many holes, too many thoughts fraying and unravelling. I had to focus on the present, not our past. Those days were gone and perhaps it was for the best because whatever haunted Jacob left me vulnerable.

I moved away from him as he switched on his comms and reported back to his commanding officer. Peace, the long sultry days of the DRC, seemed a long way off right now and I wished for them to grace me once again.

"Mac?" Danny called from the stairs.

I jogged over to join him. "What's up?"

He stared over my shoulder at Jacob. "Who is he?"

"A good guy. We worked together back in the day," I said. "You can trust him."

Danny made a noncommittal noise in the back of his throat and focused on me. "Rachael has the generators purring once again. We have one man down with serious injuries to his face and hands. Another with a gunshot to the shoulder. He might lose his arm."

"Are they on the way to the hospital?" I asked. Concern twisted in my guts, these were good men and I'd lost two of them.

Danny grasped my shoulder. "It was not your fault, Mac. They didn't follow orders and panicked when put under pressure."

I tutted. "You know it doesn't work like that, Danny. I should have provided more training. This is on me."

"No." His dark eyes were hard, determined to drill it through my thick head. "They did not follow orders and your orders were clear, therefore they paid a price. This is on them, not you."

I grasped his thick wrist and nodded but didn't feel the responsibility lessen its weight on my shoulders. "Do we know who attacked?"

"It is as you feared, Mac. General Delta is closing in on the government. There will be a coup," Danny said. "I don't know how much longer we can stand against his troops."

"They aren't troops, Danny, they are a rabble militia and we stand firm until the government sends reinforcements. Delta will have to back down. He cannot hold the city. They are just testing us." I rested a hand on his HK MP5 and held his gaze, willing him to believe me when I didn't believe it myself. The complex warp and weft of Congolese politics left my head reeling. Did I support the government of this vast country? No, I didn't give a shit about politics but I did believe in protecting the information we had in this building because protecting that meant I protected the millions of people all over the DRC who didn't want to pick up a gun.

Danny nodded. "As you say, others will come to help us."

I patted his arm. "That's it. Believe in that. You never know, they might get bored and just fuck off."

He managed a soft grin that didn't reach his sad eyes. We'd had many nights drinking beer together discussing the Democratic Republic of the Congo and how it was slowly, tortuously, pulling itself apart. The DRC should be one of the richest countries in the world with its natural resources craved by China, the US and Europe, but everywhere people existed trapped in subsistence level lives and hounded by disease.

I shook myself free of the thoughts as Jacob strode over the tiled floor of the entrance lobby. "Lawson wants to see you, Mac. He says he'll help but he needs us back at the FOB first."

"Fuck," I muttered, glancing at Danny. "Can you hold everything together here without me?"

"How long?" Danny asked.

"An hour?"

His radio squawked, spitting French too fast for me track. Danny replied and I watched Jacob shift with restless energy across the floor, moving into and out of patches of sunlight, the shadows chasing him. A jackal of a man; poised and always hunting.

Danny's voice switching to English returned me to the present. "Men are coming, Mac. We will be safe for now."

I gripped his shoulder. "See, have a little faith. You'll go home to that beautiful wife of yours tonight, kiss the heads of those wonderful children and thank God for another good day at work."

A heavy huffed breath out told me he didn't believe a word, but he nodded. "That'll only work if Chica has forgiven me for getting drunk with you at the weekend."

"Mac," Jacob barked. "We need to go." He glared at Danny. I didn't like the look, the twisted expression of naked… something… I couldn't interpret it because we'd been apart too long. I opted to change subjects.

"We need to hide that damned rifle. Come up to my office. I'm not running around these streets with these guns. It's asking for trouble." I ran up the stairs, two at a time, Jacob on my heels. I lay money on his knees feeling considerably better than mine when I reached the top. We jogged down the corridor and I let us into my office.

"Strip the HK down and put it in this," I said, throwing a gym bag at Jacob. He caught the bag and walked over to my desk. A picture sat next to my PC. It showed the two of us, his arm draped over my shoulder as I leaned into his body. We were stood in front of a landy on a training exercise in Thailand. It had been taken just a few weeks before my life exploded and I'd been forced to leave the Regiment and, in the end, the country. It was the last time I remembered being truly happy.

He picked up the photo and I watched his thumb caress the glass as he stared at it. "I've missed you, Mac." The whisper of sound might as well have been a scream for all the effect it had on my aching heart.

"I've missed you as well."

He turned to look at me. "Three years is a long time."

"Yes."

"Why? And don't give me any bullshit about being an albatross hanging my career. We were a team, Mac and you left me." He jabbed a finger in my direction and his tawny eyes flashed in anger.

How could I tell him? How could I tell him that every day since I walked out of Hereford, I'd missed his laugh, the strength of him grounding me, his scent… I closed my eyes and willed the racing thoughts and needling confession to be still and remain locked behind glass walls too thick to break.

"I did what I thought was right by you. I'm sorry, Jacob. I never wanted to hurt you." I closed my fist over the handle of the day-sack I held and tried to meet his gaze but failed. The lies I'd told in the lonely, soft, dark humid nights rose to hit the barriers guarding my heart. I turned away. "We should leave, while the streets are quiet." Those lies were so much easier to manage when I didn't have to look him in the eye, when they just circled the memories like vultures over the corpse of our friendship.

He chose not to reply but I could see the need to defy the stupidity of my words. Instead he turned away and stripped down the sniper rifle.

I opened the door to the gunroom and stepped into my sanctuary. Out of the long list of arms I had requisitioned when I took this job, there were two Glock 17s with several magazines filled with 9mm rounds waiting to be loaded. I also removed the HK33KA3, it featured a retractable stock and a shorter barrel than the full-sized version, I could carry it under a jacket. They were used for close protection work mostly but right now I broke it down and put it in the day-sack with its mags. I left the grenade launcher; if we were in so much trouble that I needed to use a launcher on a quick trip across the city then it might be time to call it quits and just run.

Jacob came into the room and gave a small whistle. The tight confines meant I could feel his heat against my back, and he brushed my arm reaching for a fragmentation grenade. I smacked his hand away and tried to ignore the longing that brief contact set up in my flesh. It needed to feel more.

"No. We aren't blowing shit up, just going for a drive," I snapped.

"You're no fun," he muttered.

"I'm not meant to be fun. I'm meant to be a security manager for this museum," I said. "No blowing up my city."

We were far too close in this small room as I risked a glance into his face. Jacob stood shorter than me and had the wiry strength of a greyhound in his smaller frame. I resembled a bear, thick muscles not running to fat, grey hair lacing through the black I'd let grow out, so it now touched my shirt collar. Never one for facial hair I found my palms itching to touch his thick beard.

Jacob stared at me with a steady gaze, but I couldn't match his self-assured calm.

"We need to go," I growled.

"You never told me why you left. You never explained what charges were brought or for what operation. You left me high and dry, Mac. You owe me. There wasn't even any gossip. You just fucking vanished from my life, from all our lives." He didn't raise his voice, but I wanted to cringe away.

"Let it go, Jacob. I have. It's a new life for me here and I'm at peace with it." Almost, almost at peace except for this, except for lying to my best friend for years.

"Are you happy?" he asked.

Something shifted in his voice and I managed to look into those amber eyes. "I have peace, are they not the same thing?" I asked him, wondering where he was leading me in this ever-circling conversation. "We really have to go, Jacob."

He dropped his eyes at last, releasing me and I found the air necessary to breathe again. Without touching I managed to move past him and into the office. The air conditioning in the room rattled making the very necessary oxygen easier to inhale without Jacob's scent of musk and jungle sweat. I retrieved my car keys from the desk drawer, my wallet and something made me fish out my passport, stuffing it in my back pocket rather than my day-sack. I threw a bottle of water at Jacob, who caught it with barely a glance, and we left the office.

Jacob followed me in silence, and we exited the rear of the building through a side door. Due to the uncertain perimeter we kept the Glocks up and scanned our surroundings as we left the safety of the museum. Jacob moved with me as if we'd never been separated, watching our left flank and our six while I took right and point.

"The big Nissan," I said. The 4x4 pickup, more dust and dents than steel, sat in the sun, still only seven paces from the doorway. I unlocked the security system from a distance, and we slipped in, Jacob continuing to scan the almost empty car park while I started the engine and pulled out. The evidence of the gun battle soon vanished in my mirror while security teams came into the area from the government forces. They didn't prevent us from leaving. I needed to berate someone about that when I finished with Jacob and his team.

I wove through the sparse traffic on the main road and moved into the less salubrious area of Bandalungwa District. More than eleven million people lived in this city and not all of it was as safe as the area I lived in with its private security and high walls. The battered truck didn't stand out here, but our white faces did and so would the rest of Jacob's team.

"This is a strange place for an FOB," I said. "Very residential and hard to hide."

"Not my choice," he said, eyes still scanning.

He'd closed down on me. I could feel it, see it in the tension through his shoulders. The tick in his jaw.

The need to repair at least some of the damage I'd done by leaving made me talk, despite my almost equally strong desire to keep him at a safe distance. "I'm sorry," I said. "I should have stayed for a proper goodbye." I took my eyes off the road long enough to check he received the apology.

"Why didn't you say goodbye, Mac?" he asked, not accepting the apology. It left a nasty taste in my mouth.

The lights were against me. The truck's brakes screeched as I stopped. Women approached the vehicles selling melon and bananas, men sold watches and mobile phone cases. I kept the windows wound up, trying to maintain a quiet space.

"How could I say goodbye to you? We'd been brothers-in-arms for 5 years, Jacob. I couldn't…" Couldn't what? Confess to myself that in those 5 years I'd learned more about myself than in the previous thirty-four? That I finally began to have an idea that I wasn't the man my father beat me into being and those thoughts scared me more than any armed terrorist I'd faced. That maybe the brotherhood and friendship I shared with Jacob yearned to be something more, but I couldn't face what that might be so when I had to leave, I didn't just leave, I ran? Not for the first time.

I spotted a familiar figure on the street, outside a café, drinking a beer. "That's Bennet."

"Yep, Bennet, Shaw, Bradly, and Captain Lawson," murmured Jacob. "So you know us, all of us. Maybe you'll tell them why you left."

"Who's the spook?" I asked, ignoring the growl.

"Guy called Clark," Jacob said as I drew up just beyond the café. He opened the door to the truck to leave but I caught his arm. He looked at me in surprise, the skin under my fingers going white with the pressure.

"Tall guy, Indian looking?" I asked.

"Yeah, though Lawson said he's going to be a peer of the realm at some point, so we were ordered to be civilised." Jacob frowned. "Fuck, Mac, you've gone white, what's the problem?"

"What are you doing here?" I asked, unable to hide the urgency of my question.

"You know I can't tell you that without talking to Lawson. He'll tell you because he wants your help if we're lending you a hand. Though it looks like your team now have control over the museum."

"Does Clark know you've found me?" I asked.

Jacob relaxed back into the truck and looked at me. "What's wrong?"

Panic made sweat prickle over my skin where the air conditioning couldn't win. I licked my lips and tasted it. My hands trembled but whether from the need to kill or the need to escape I couldn't decide. The internal logic systems of my brain had been scrambled with Jacob's arrival, now I had to deal with Clark? That didn't –

The truck rocked up on its front wheels as the back window shattered and fire tore through the streets of Kinshasa.

5

MY HEAD IMPACTED THE STEERING wheel. I saw Jacob twist, trying to save his face from the windscreen. Screams erupted even as bricks and concrete rained down a monsoon of human detritus over the innocents filling the street. The world faded for long seconds where all I could hear was the internal noise of my body and the shattering cacophony of the explosion. Jacob yelled something but I couldn't hear a damned thing, and the blow to the head forced my world to tilt unnervingly to the left.

A strong hand grabbed the back of my shirt and shook me hard. "Mac? Mac? The team's been hit. Mac? I need you." Jacob's eyes were wide, and blood covered his hand where he touched his face.

"You've been hurt," I said, the words too quiet over the yelling and screaming. I reached for him, but he brushed me off and half fell out of the truck. With fingers stumbling in the simple task I managed to exit the vehicle as well and staggered into chaos. People were moving around in stunned silence or screaming in shock and pain. Blood coated dark skin, staining clothing. A young woman holding her arm in her other hand, rocked back and forth as her life drained from the wound. A child…

I turned my head away. I couldn't afford to register the dead and dying. The need to act, to do my job, had to take priority. Jacob lurched over the ruined remains of the café, calling for his team-mates, coughing up dust and smoke. Sirens began to bleed over the screaming, growing louder. I lifted a small child off the road and found a woman yelling for someone. She burst into tears as a mother's arms wrapped tight about the small body, which remained silent, large eyes unfocused and dilated in shock.

Another person, blood pouring from a head wound. A man this time. I ripped off a shirt from a dead body and pushed the wad of fabric against the head wound, lifting the man's inert hand and ordering him to hold tight. He blinked but didn't seem to understand anything else. I scrambled after Jacob until a sound I didn't expect intruded.

Concrete chipped up, slicing into my left hand and the *crack* of the shot penetrated the haze. More adrenaline flooded my system and cleared the tangle caused by the explosion. "Jacob! Contact! Get the fuck down," I bellowed over every other sound. A sergeant never forgot how to bellow. Another round sliced the air and just missed my boot. "Sniper fire."

Jacob scrambled to my position, grabbed my arm and together we dove back towards the truck. "Who the fuck is shooting?" he asked, eyes too wild, breathing out of control.

"Whoever wanted you and your team dead, we have to move. We're a danger to everyone else in the area." Another round hit the truck and glass exploded, showering another victim.

"My team, Mac…" Jacob's voice came out made of dust and smashed glass.

I gripped his arm. "We have to move. We have to run. Now."

"My team…"

"Dead, Jacob. We have no choice. If anyone is left alive in there the EMTs will save them, we can't. We are – shit!" Another round killed a tyre and the truck slumped. I wouldn't be driving home. The most urgent thing right now was retrieving the day-sacks and gym bags with the weapons in them.

I moved with caution and opened the door of the truck, reaching inside. Keeping my head down I grabbed the bags and pulled them out. Jacob slung the day-sack over his shoulders.

"Which way?" he asked.

"The shooter is high, they'll see us the moment we move."

"Give me the bloody HK33 and I'll find the fucker," growled Jacob.

I took hold of his face. "You will die before you get across the street. Listen to me carefully. The only way we can make this right is running. We then hunt the fuckers down. I promise you. We will hunt the fuckers down. Now, we run."

His entire body leaned into me. "Run. We run. Regroup. Then kill."

"Then kill."

For a moment he relaxed against me and a soft breath caressed my neck. I couldn't hold back the sharp intake of breath and shiver.

"Mac," he whispered.

"Move," I ordered.

Time snapped back into place and he pulled away.

I nodded. "We go to the alley." I pointed 5 metres to our left. "I'll give you covering fire."

"Moving," he said.

No more words. We both drew our handguns and chambered a round, the Glocks a comfort in our hands but completely useless against a sniper. I rose from behind the truck and turned to fire at my ten o'clock where I thought the shots came from. In the same moment Jacob lifted himself off the ground and raced for the alley. I released six rounds, the sniper got off two and I managed to locate their position.

"Northwest corner of the supermarket," I yelled.

Jacob shouted in return, "Move." He fired at the location.

"Moving," I said, acting on training I hadn't used for 3 years but remained a part of my psyche that would never leave. The sniper made a bid for me, but the shots were wild. Jacob's Glock barked and were not wild.

When I hit the alley, I tugged on his shoulder and he turned his back on the chaos of the street to follow me down the darkening and narrow stinking path. We wove through the rubbish, cats and rats scattering in our bow wake. The alleyway spat us out on a residential street, and I broke right. We hurried, but didn't run, down the street. People were reacting to the explosion. Two white men in this area of the city stood out too much, I had to move us further away.

"We need a taxi," I said, crossing the road and heading down a cleaner alley.

Escape and evasion in a city like Kinshasa were not difficult. The narrow streets joining larger ones, the mass of humanity and vehicles, along with the lack of surveillance made it possible to vanish. The colour of our skin made us vulnerable but when we hit the next shopping street, and a market hardly touched by the chaos of the explosion a few streets away, I managed to buy us a couple of hats. We reached the end of the market and I flagged down a taxi while Jacob watched our six.

"Clear?" I asked before ducking into the battered car.

"Clear. No one is chasing us." Jacob's face looked grim.

We sat beside each other in the back. Jacob's right knee bounced, rubbing against my leg and our shoulders brushed each time we checked our surroundings. The taxi man barely seemed to register our presence but drove with a relative confidence in the general direction of my home in the Zoka District. The streets here were quiet and I asked the taxi to drop us two streets away so we could mark the traffic to make sure we weren't followed back to my home.

We stood in the shadows and watched the taxi vanish, then watched the vehicles passing for a few minutes and checked the pedestrians, though these were few.

"Did you see the shooter in the end?" I asked.

Jacob shook his head. "He knew what he was doing. I couldn't see shit against the sun except for a dark figure."

"I'm surprised they missed at that distance," I said, walking towards my home now but remaining in the shadows of the walled off gardens. The humidity and shock of the last few hours were taking their toll. I ached with the tension and my head pounded from the explosions and stress.

Jacob grunted. "The bomb didn't miss though, did it?"

"You need to tell me what you were doing here. Who your team were targeting. Why you were blown to hell. I also need to know more about Clark."

"I should have been there, Mac. If I hadn't run into you…"

I gripped his arm. "Jacob, listen to me," I pulled him around to face me, "if you'd been there you would have died as well and no one would be left to seek justice for you because I wouldn't even have known you were in my city."

"Yeah, and who's fault is that, Mac? You dropped me like a hot fucking stone." He shook me off. "They were all I had left of my family. You certainly didn't give a shit about me once you were out." His amber eyes blazed a cold fury I couldn't match or temper.

My throat closed, halting the words I wanted to scream from the sky so he would not fail to hear my heart, but I didn't… I never had and he twisted away from me, storming ahead in the general direction of my house. A lonely figure of sadness and grief. I followed but didn't find a path through the maze in my head to give access to words locked in my heart.

I didn't even know if he'd listen to those words or smack me in the mouth for being a deviant bastard like my father had back in the day.

Leaden feet trekked behind the broken figure. When I caught him up at the junction we walked together, and his fingers brushed mine after a 100 metres or so making my heart swell.

"I'm sorry, Mac. This isn't your fault." The words were a soft growl of sound.

"It's been a tough day," I murmured, a totally inadequate statement to make under the circumstances. "Let's get you somewhere safe, where you can sleep and clean up. It'll help us plan the next move."

I stopped walking in front of my huge double gate. "This is us." I keyed in the security code and a small half gate to one side, slid open. In we walked.

"Wow," Jacob said, standing and looking at my home and its front garden. Beyond the small car parking area and separate garage sat my single storey house but the reason it stopped him walking was the assault on the senses. Colour raced over the wrap around porch and the front of the house, leaving only the door and windows clear of flowers and leaves. I had two tall trees poking out from behind the roof and many smaller ones I'd planted since arriving in the city. Hound ambled out from the shady spot under the veranda and made a half-arsed attempt at barking to warn Jacob off.

"Hound," I called. "Friend."

The huge mutt huffed, turned and ambled away, thick furred tail arching over his back.

"Hound? Original."

"He adopted me when I moved into the house. The previous owners left him behind when they moved, and the neighbour fed him until I bought the place a year later. I kind of feel he owns the place and I'm just living here on his sufferance. He's company though." I climbed up the three steps to my front door and let us into the cooler confines of the shadowy interior.

"You live here alone?" asked Jacob. The living room opened out onto the back garden, more flowers surrounded a lawn and vegetable patch.

"I've always been alone," I said, heading for the kitchen. "Make yourself at home though."

"Christ, this is weird," Jacob said, tracking me.

"What?" I knew what I found weird. Him, in my house, like some kind of fever dream. I handed him a cold bottle of water from the fridge.

"I just never imagined you in a house like this, with a dog and a garden." He took his Glock from his waistband and placed it with care on the kitchen counter. "It's all so domestic."

"I'm retired, it's supposed to be domestic. I like the garden. The dog likes staring at the night sky with me and the house is…" I looked around my simple but comfortable home. "My house is trying to be a home."

Jacob wandered over to a wall of photos I had up and had ignored before I left the house that morning. They were mostly of my days in the army. To be honest there hadn't been many days out of the army that were worth taking photos of or remembering. Jacob's face from before the scarring stared back at him from most of them. He touched one or two as if refreshing his memory of our time together as well.

"Maybe we should go outside," I said, his unexpected presence in my home making me uncomfortable. The level of intensity, the intimacy of having him here in the flesh, his scent filling my space, his breaths loud in the silence of my sanctuary. How often had I wished to tell him where in the world I'd chosen to settle?

"I need to call the Head Shed. I have to report my situation. The deaths…" Jacob's voice petered off and he seemed to fold into himself. "They only needed one more reason to bump me out and I guess this is it."

That shocked me, Jacob had been on track to rise high in the ranks, but his lost sadness made me hold my tongue. I chose to keep things in the present. "Who knew you were in that building? Why are you here in Kinshasa? I think it's time I had a little more information," I said, zeroing in my concentration on my companion and the present. "Gun battles aren't uncommon in the city, not at the moment, but an explosion like that? Something large enough to rip an entire building to pieces? That doesn't happen."

What kept Jacob upright and moving with restless energy seemed to just vanish in the space of a breath. He almost collapsed onto a dining chair and rubbed his hands over his dust and blood covered face. "We are here to find a scientist. She works for Porton Down as a geneticist. Apparently, she wanted to come to the DRC to work with the mosquitoes here, they want to use them to create a weaponised virus they're working on but won't tell us about. I think it's something to do with the plague or Ebola or something, but the virus is unstable in the open air so it's not a good weapon without being 'tweaked'. The malaria mosquito can be adapted to carry other vectors."

I moved into the kitchen area and began making us something to eat. "Wasn't she under guard or something? Don't the Porton Down lot send their people out with Paras or SBS or something?" It seemed unlikely they'd send the SAS for a long-term operation like that, but the Paratroopers were a far larger unit that could rotate platoons and the Special Boat Service did almost as much training work as active service.

"The scientists and their staff had a small compound in the actual jungle, a long way from any habitation. They were a secret. Very few people even in Porton Down knew they were there, and they only had private security." He screwed his face up. "Fucking cost cutting again. Rather than have the likes of us out here doing their job properly, or even training men who could do the job, they send a security firm who can't even look after the prisons back in the UK, never mind protect a top secret mission out here."

Private contractors. You get what you paid for and the British Government were selling contracts to the lowest bidder.

"An armed group came out of the jungle. Cut down the guards. Set fire to everything surrounding the labs. Killed the staff and snatched her and the other women to sell, but whether they know who and what she is we don't know. We just had to get her back. There's a man in the city who can contact the men we think are holding her. We needed to find him. The spook was supposed to help."

"Clark?" I asked.

"Yeah, you know him?" Jacob watched me as I went about making coffee for us.

Did I know Clark? "He's the one who got me bumped from the Regiment." Jacob knew nothing about the circumstances of me leaving, I'd worked hard to keep him ignorant of the entire debacle, more than ignorant, protected, I had to keep him and his career protected.

"That's it? I think I need more information, Mac."

I wanted to tell him, but where to start? It's not like I had any concrete evidence. Clark had seen to that 3 years ago. "Several of the jobs we did at the end struck me as off. People would escape, drugs or arms shipments would go missing. We got some of the missions completed but others just broke apart. I sensed something was wrong."

Jacob frowned and I sat next to him with the first aid kit and a damp cloth to clean his face up. "You never said."

“I didn’t want you tainted by anything I uncovered. I’d have shared the story with you once I had evidence, but I wasn’t going to share a suspicion that might place you in harm’s way.”

He captured my hand where it stroked away the dry blood and dust. “You didn’t have to protect me, Mac. I’m a big boy, always have been.” Those eyes, once so innocent were now harder, caged, but still able to captivate me.

“You had your career to think of, being in the Regiment meant everything to you,” I said. We were close together, sat like this, one of my knees between his so I could reach his face.

“Being with you meant more,” he said into the silence.

6

CONFUSED, I PULLED BACK, GIVING him the cloth to clean the wound while I fished out the oxygenated water and antiseptic. I struggled on with my theory. “There’s a cabal in MI6 and other parts of the security services, possibly other parts of the government, that have motives in either destabilising the government or making vast sums of money, I couldn’t work out which, and I couldn’t find enough evidence to go to the higher-ups. It didn’t stop them realising what I was up to though and Clark saw to it I couldn’t come after them anymore.”

Jacob cleaned up his face with more brutality than I’d have used. “Couldn’t the ruperts have protected you from Clark?”

I snorted. “You know what they can be like with SIS. We are just tools to use and discard. There are always more soldiers, too few good spies and Clark is very good at his job, the oily shit.”

“You think he’s the reason my team are dead, don’t you?” Jacob asked going still. I glanced into his face and froze with the bottle of oxygenated water halfway to his head. The coiled rage vibrating off him made me want to creep around him like a cat around a very dangerous and hungry dog. My heartbeat ticked up and I swallowed, his eyes zeroed in on the movement and I continued to hold still, I had to shift his energy away from violence.

“How do you do that?” I asked. I tried to soften my voice, keep it low and grounded but by asking a such a strange question I forced his higher brain functions to engage which would help bring him back from the brink of violence.

In the last 3 years something had happened to Jacob and it flipped him from the gentle soul I’d helped train into a compassionate but elite soldier, into a stone-cold killer. I’d worked with too many of those over the years.

“Do what?” he snarled, amber eyes razor focused on me.

“Flip so fast from one thing to another?” I asked, keeping the question purposely vague so he’d have to work to keep up with me.

He frowned and the energy cleared between us, turned into something softer. I breathed and moved again to clean the wound. The water fizzed as it hit the blood.

“In answer to your original question,” I said, “then yes. I think Clark is responsible and I have very little doubt the worm wasn’t in the building at the time of the explosion. He’ll be out there somewhere, and we need to find the fucker.”

“How?” Jacob asked.

I stood now and probed the head wound; it wasn’t too deep but could do with some stitches. “I’ve a few contacts that might be able to help but first I want us to talk to someone back home I trust to help us.”

“That would be good, Mac. I’m really tired though.” Jacob’s hand gripped the bottom of my thigh and his forehead hit my hipbone as he rested against me. The grunt I made at the contact shocked me. This was not the first time Jacob had rested against me while injured but having not been in daily proximity to him for so long it hit hard in places I couldn’t hide if he remained resting so close to my groin.

“Let me put a couple of stitches in this,” I managed to wrestle out of my straining throat. “Then you can bunk in the spare room.”

“I need a shower,” he muttered.

Of course, my brain went there the moment the words left his mouth. The tight body, naked, soaped up, warm water caressing…

“Mac?” he asked, pulling back a little and looking up at me.

I turned away. “I’ll find the needle.”

Walking away actually hurt and my hands shook as I rummaged for the kit I used to stitch myself up. I wasn’t keen on hospitals and didn’t entirely trust their cleanliness. The simple act of washing my hands again, threading the needle and returning to Jacob calmed me enough to be able to touch him. Just so long as I didn’t look into his eyes, I should be fine.

What was happening to me? When we’d served together feelings stirred inside me, needful emotions but I squashed them, hid them, buried them, blew them up… I used just about every mechanism out there to control the stray musings bombarding me every day while together, while we took on the world. Now though, now I seemed to have lost all control and while one part of my mind screamed at me that every thought, need and image coursing through my body was wrong, I couldn't stem the flow.

Being gay was not an option for me. Never had been. I could barely use the word aloud and tried never to think it. Long before joining the army at the tender age of sixteen I'd been taught being gay was bad. The day after I hit thirteen, it had been beaten out of me. Being soft, being a 'homo', being weak and gentle… None of those things were permitted by my father. No boy in his house would be queer. Compassion became a commodity I no longer understood, alien and scary, a weakness. The army, of course, couldn't ban homosexuality any longer but they hardly encouraged any feelings which might grow into more than brotherhood.

Until Jacob walked into the barracks as a new member of the 22nd Regiment not a flicker of sexual tension rose inside me around men or women. I had sex with women when they showed interest, but I rarely sought it out, dedicating myself to my work. I'd even had the nickname 'Monk' rather than Mac when us lads were released into Hereford's drinking dens.

I'd seen Jacob slink off with women. Being a handsome, charming, friendly and yes, deeply compassionate man, made it easy for him to find solace. When he did that, when he found companionship in a woman, I found companionship in a bottle of whisky.

Distracting myself again I asked, "You married yet?"

He jerked and the needle slipped, scraping against his skin. "Fuck, Mac."

"Sorry. Are you?" I asked, hoping against hope that he was and therefore freeing me from these deviant paths in my sick mind.

The emotional part of me, the part he'd nurtured over our time together, rose from the ever-widening corner of my mind and whispered, *It's not wrong, you know that really, it's not sick or deviant to love another –*

The soft internal voice almost squeaked in shock as I ruthlessly shut it down.

"No, not married, Mac," Jacob muttered. "Listen, there's something I need to tell you –"

I finished knotting the last stitch. "All done. Some of my best work. Come on, I'll show you the bunk and you can shower." I didn't meet his eyes and I didn't need to hear his voice any longer, I needed some peace in my house. Time to get my head on *straight* – which caused another internal bark of sarcastic laughter.

Mumbled words were exchanged. Jacob trying to talk to me, but the walls were firmly in place and so long as I didn't touch him, or look at him, I should be fine. I left him alone with the statement, "I'm going to make some calls, if you need anything let me know."

Full retreat proved the only option. The sensory attack of having Jacob in my house, the sanctuary I'd built for myself in this strange mercurial city, made holding on to the realities I'd used to keep the world at bay very hard. I simply didn't enjoy sex. Intimacy wasn't something I sought. I liked being alone. I had said it so often to myself that I almost believed the hard lie.

I went to a drawer in the kitchen and fished around in the back for a moment before retrieving an old Nokia 360 and charger. The phones were far more secure than the modern smartphone and without the necessary tech in the house for full cyber protection I let my paranoia have full rein.

Waiting for the phone to have enough of a charge to make a call, while still attached to the wall, I finished making a couple of sandwiches and returned to Jacob's room to leave them on the side while he continued to shower. I listened to the water for a moment, but my cock started to twitch again so I beat another hasty retreat.

By the time I returned to the kitchen the charge held enough to wake the ancient machine. The happy Nokia welcome made me smile. I remembered life before mobiles, and I remembered owning one of these and being far too damned proud of it. How times change.

The phone number I needed came straight to mind and I punched it in, adding the 0044 of the UK country zone.

Three times the phone rang the other end. "Brant, who is this?" asked a woman's voice, clipped and self-assured as always.

"Colonel, I don't know if you remember me, it's Philip Macalister here, I worked for you –"

"Mac? Well, there's a blast from our past. How are you?" she asked.

"Good, mostly. Can we talk?" I trusted Brant. Out of all the people I'd worked for, killed for, Brant had been one of the best. Her Unit 12 guys were, and are, the most elite soldiers the UK can produce and sometimes from other

SF operatives from around the world as well. Her technical team were pulled from the best cyber security in GCHQ.

"I have 10 minutes," she said, her voice now very focused.

"I won't waste them."

"I know you won't, Mac."

I grunted before giving her details of the last few hours. I finished with, "Jacob Hayes is safe. He's with me but I don't know where Clark is or how many of his men might have made it out alive. I dare not take Jacob back, that sniper wasn't interested in taking prisoners."

"Do you think you'll remain secure for the next 15 hours or so?" Brant asked.

"Maybe. If not I have somewhere else we can go that's secure. It's out of the city."

"Head there. Once there, text me the GPS. I'm on my way," Brant said, and the line went dead.

I removed the phone from my ear and stared at it in surprise. "Yes, ma'am," I muttered.

She might be right about moving away from the house. The sniper would have seen the truck and therefore the number plate. I kept it registered to an address on the other side of the city, more security than I probably needed but it didn't hurt, however, with some timely internet scavenging I could guarantee the people responsible for the bomb would find me and therefore Jacob. We needed a clean vehicle and we needed to move.

I returned to Jacob's room and knocked on the door. "Come in," came the reply.

A long lean length of naked flank and back met my eyes. The towel around his waist did nothing to hide the whip-cord muscles over his ribs. As I'd learned to do over the years we'd worked together, I forced my eyes to the ground, but now the army no longer had control over my life resisting the temptation made *everything* harder. I had no excuses for keeping him away, except he was straight. This thought gave me the strength I needed to look up.

"I've called in some help. Remember when you were injured in Yemen? You were out for 6 months and I was seconded to SIS Unit 12?"

"Yeah, if I remember rightly you did some mad shit with them," he said.

I hadn't told him much, I couldn't, but he wasn't wrong, I had done some ‘mad shit’ with them. “Yeah, well, Colonel Brant can be trusted and so can her team. I reported in and she’s on her way out to Kinshasa.”

Jacob’s eyes widened. “Wow, right. I ought to call the Head Shed in Hereford.”

“I don’t think that’s a good idea. She told me we need to move on from here, I have somewhere out of the city which is even more secure. Clark is good. He’ll know I’m here and he’ll know some news will filter back to me, even if he doesn’t know I’m already involved with you. He’ll send someone else to do his dirty work, so we need to leave. Neither of us needs another firefight today.”

Jacob sighed and dropped his gaze. “I’m so tired, Mac.”

“I know, fella. I’m happy to drive but we need to leave.”

He nodded and picked up his t-shirt. Filthy and bloodstained. I reached for his hand to stop him pulling it over his head. “I’ve some clothes you can wear.”

Shit, we were too close. He looked up at me and I swear his eyes dilated, his tongue definitely licked his lips. I swallowed hard, unable to drag my eyes away from the soft, glistening surface.

“Mac, I really need to tell you something before we go,” he said.

I jerked my eyes away, focusing on the bathroom door behind his head. “Later. Let’s get some kit together and move out.”

Jacob sighed and his shoulders slumped. “Sure. Move out.”

7

THIRTY MINUTES LATER I HAD two Bergens packed with clothing, ORP – ration packs, and some bedding for us. I grabbed the first aid kits stashed around the house, a box of frag grenades, flash-bangs, a couple of mortars and more rounds of ammunition. Well aware I shouldn't have any of these on the premises, they were all in a locked chest. Leaving without them though made me feel uncomfortable and prickly. I'd faced too many dangers in Africa over the years to go anywhere unprepared for trouble.

I loaded my other vehicle with these, the day-sacks and the gym bags with the larger guns. Next went water, a toolbox and another spare tyre. The roads weren't great outside the city. Purification tablets, a stove and finally I trudged over to my neighbour to ask her to look after the dog. I also asked her to deny seeing me or knowing me if anyone came looking. Her eyes were wide and fearful.

The last statement she made was, "God, go with you, my friend." Her elegant hand grasping my arm.

I didn't think God had ever gone with me anywhere.

When I returned to the house Jacob sat on the front porch with Hound's head in his lap. Both stared at me with big eyes and I swallowed the sentimental words that wanted to leak over them.

"Time to leave," I said, the words gruff, my shoulders tense. I walked past him, locked up the house, told Hound to return to his spot, checked his water and food bowls, then returned to my secondary vehicle.

"Bit nicer than the Nissan," Jacob murmured.

"I don't like driving it into the city," I said, starting the engine of the much newer Toyota. They weren't uncommon in the countryside, but it stood out as too expensive to be safe in the city.

“Is the dog going to be okay on his own?” Jacob asked, craning his neck to watch the animal vanish as we drove through the gates.

“He’s fine. As I said, he owns the house. He doesn’t like leaving it and my neighbour spoils him.”

“Seems a shame,” Jacob mumbled. I watched him lean against the soft padding on the side of the 4x4 and close his eyes. Within moments a gentle snore filled the inside of the truck. I couldn’t help the fond smile I allowed to soften my hard features.

Rather than indulge further in any fantasies about Jacob, I concentrated on leaving the city’s insane traffic system. I followed the N1 and the signs to Kasangulu, it would take several hours to escape into the countryside but once down near Kasangulu I could go right into the jungle and reach our destination. I had bought a small rural property from Danny’s parents as an escape from the city and its politics.

Thinking of Danny made me remember by responsibilities to my men from the museum. I’d become so caught up in the events surrounding my old team I’d almost forgotten the firefight and the injuries sustained by those under my command. An unforgiveable act.

I rang Danny, he picked up after three rings. “Where are you?” he asked before I could get a word out.

“I’ve had to leave Kinshasa.” The guilt nibbled at my ear making it hot and turning into shame. I should not have prioritised Jacob and the SAS team over the others.

“Why have you left, Mac? We need you here.” Danny’s voice held a note of recrimination I didn’t want to hear. It made me defensive.

“I’m sorry, but other things came up.”

“Like your friend?”

I glanced at the sleeping Jacob and swallowed hard. “Yes. His team was blown up. We were outside the building.”

“That was you?”

“Yeah.”

Silence for a moment before he asked, “The men?”

“All dead, Danny.”

“Shit.”

“Yeah. Listen, I know it’s asking a lot but I really need to help Jacob get through this. There's a bigger game at play and it's dangerous. Can you cover for me there?"

"It is not my job to cover for you, Mac." He spoke with deliberate care, as if to remind me of my role in the DRC and what I would lose by walking away. Or maybe I read too much into it – having Jacob returned to me confused everything so much and my drive, my *need*, to be with him drove all other considerations out of my head.

I gritted my teeth and tried to see this from Danny's point of view but I couldn't responsibly make that stretch. "I'm sorry, Danny. I have to leave the city, probably only for a day or so, please, look after the team, look after the museum and cover for me with the management."

Danny made a ticking and hiss sound as he sucked air over his teeth. "I am not happy about this, Mac, but I will do as you have asked. Though I will not lie for you. These are my men as well."

"Thanks."

He hung up without saying goodbye. Pushing Danny and my job at the museum away niggled at my guilt chip but the elation of being able to help Jacob outweighed anything else, even if it left a bitter taste. I could swallow that bitterness because the sweetness of being with Jacob sated a hunger I struggled to control.

WHILE I DROVE, I TRIED to concentrate on Clark's motives for blowing up the Regiment team, manage my grief for my old friends, and avoid thinking about Jacob. I failed on that last score. My eyes strayed to him with monotonous regularity. The new-to-me scar on his cheek and the slice off the ear tip, the broad shoulders, tight waist – all too clear in the snug t-shirt I'd loaned him – and the snug jeans over strong thighs. I watched his lax hands, fingers calloused, knuckles scarred, skin weather-beaten and rough. His fingers were blunt, nails short, back to those thick knuckles. He whimpered and those hands twitched, the densely muscled forearms tensing.

"Sleep, Jacob. You are safe. Sleep," I whispered.

I'd done this more than once over the years we'd shared our travels. He calmed, his breathing evening out again and I tried to concentrate on the dwindling traffic as night fell.

During the hours between midnight and dawn we reached our destination. I opened my car door, Jacob still gone from the world, and breathed in the warm but clean air of the jungle. The moist, earth laden air wrapped its warm arms around me after the cool interior of the truck. The farmland and forest were calm at night but full of the sounds of the jungle instead. The beating heart of this world was never still, never silent, unless something was wrong. I gazed up at the sky. After blinking several times, the stars began to spread, and the universe opened its arms and allowed me access to its depths. I heard the car door open and close.

Jacob stood at my side. His fingers brushed mine, forming sparks brighter than any of the thousand suns overhead. "I haven't slept that well in years," he whispered, preserving the sanctity of the night.

Rather than pull away, which I'd done almost as many times as stars overhead, I allowed my fingers to brush again.

Jacob reacted with a jolt and I felt him look at me.

"Mac, I'm gay," he said in the same soft voice. His fingers did more than brush, they tangled against mine. "I wanted to tell you before you left but the right time never came up and I… Coming out in the Regiment – well, it's not like there are many of us who admit it. I think Luke Sinclair was it before me. Then you vanished and I couldn't find you, but I couldn't keep the secret any longer. I had to be honest. I *have to be* honest. I can't live a lie to myself or those I care about any more. I just had to tell you, what you do with the information is up to you."

Of all the things I expected him to say in that moment, this was not it. This couldn't be real. This couldn't be happening.

Jacob was... Jacob and I could... Was it possible I could admit to being...?

My mind stalled.

He released his physical hold on me and returned to the truck. I just stared at the stars. I heard him moving behind me but turning would shift our reality on its axis. Nothing would be the same.

"Fuck," I whispered to the stars. "Fuck…"

I dare not move. If I moved the world would be different forever. My world would change forever. If I acknowledged Jacob's words the soul of me would change – had to change. How could it not? My fingertips still tingled from the brief contact. His scent still lingered in the thick air. I wanted to weep but didn't know how. I'd forgotten how to cry around the same time I'd learned that showing weakness meant the belt and being a 'faggot' meant you were weak. You weren't man enough to satisfy a woman.

Jacob was not weak. Jacob didn't fear his grief when something happened to move his heart to sadness.

I lived in fear.

I lived with aggression and loneliness.

I lived a lie because the truth might break me in a way my father's brutality managed to do so long ago.

The stars were distant, cold, untouchable.

Jacob was not.

A pulse of need made my groin stir and a small sound of protest escaped. A tight, agonised sound of confusion and longing. My heart ached, stomach clenched, throat tightened, and my breaths were laboured.

I whimpered, the pain so intense I couldn't hold it in any longer. I'd been stabbed, shot, tortured – I was a fucking good soldier who faced fear and acted anyway because that was my job and my training but this…? It would kill me.

I wanted to puke but how could I when my throat kept tightening?

"Mac?" Jacob's voice broke through the shifting quicksand under my world.

My knees buckled and hit the rich loam of the Congo.

"Mac?" The sound of the Bergens hitting the ground and rushing feet. A strong hand touched my back and I flinched away.

"Bastard," Jacob hissed, the grief and instant rage flashing hot bright between us. An arc of poisonous electricity. "I thought I could trust you. I thought you cared enough about me to accept me. Homophobia isn't something I can tolerate." The anger battered me.

I wanted to explain. I wanted to explain. I wanted…

God, I wanted.

A soft mewl of protest. A pleading sound of soul's agony begging for understanding because words were far beyond me.

"Mac? Explain yourself. For God's sake, have the fucking the decency to look at me, even if you hate me."

I doubled over. A tree felled.

"Mac?" Concern now. The hand again. The energy switching, knife blade quick. "Mac, I realise it must be a shock but…" He knelt at my side. The scent, the heat, the feel of him so comforting. My safe place. My friend.

I forced my hand to move. I'd climbed out of an artic crevice once, hand over hand, because our team lost a man down the hole and he broke his leg. This small movement, just incremental millimetres scared me far more than that brutal sub-zero climb. I reached for the back of his neck and the soft hair brushed my fingertips, the sweaty skin, the fabric of his t-shirt.

"Help," I managed to squeeze out.

Jacob, unknowing, pulled me into his chest. "Breathe, Mac. Just breathe. I'm here. I'll always be with you. I just need you to accept what I am and we'll never lose touch again."

"Help me," I whispered, tightening my hold on his neck.

His arms cradled me, pulling me into his body. He sat back on the ground and I collapsed into his strong arms.

"What's wrong, Mac?" he asked with a tenderness I remembered, craved in the dark seconds between breaths during darker nights.

The soft flesh of his neck rested against my lips. They tingled and I licked. The salt. The musk. The taste of a man not me. I jerked at the pain in my groin. Jacob stilled.

"Yes, Mac," he murmured. "It's all I've ever wanted."

My lips moved, was it a kiss? Was it a kiss? Was I kissing a man's throat? My lips moved again; my tongue darted out to taste again. He'd given permission. I had permission from someone I trusted.

He groaned and his hands tightened on my back, drawing me up to his face. He cupped my jaw and I stared into his eyes, lit by the starlight shining its benediction onto the dark centre of this complex continent. The beating of the universe running through the veins and arteries of a land more ancient than any I'd seen in England.

"Mac, just say yes for me and we can make this real."

His beautiful amber eyes blurred, and I growled, unable to speak using human language. I was elevated to using a language older than time, the language of protons, like drawn to like across the vast distances of galaxies to form stardust – to form us. He understood. His lips pressed to mine for the first time and held still. My eyes slid shut and I groaned, a sound dragged from that heated centre of the universe. He released me.

"More," I moaned.

"Anything," he whispered against my tingling lips. I'd never been more aware of them than in that moment and he claimed them and opened his, a light lick with his tongue seeking more. When was the last time someone kissed me?

My heart raced and my skin hummed. A wet kitten in his arms and yet also the strongest man on the planet. Our tongues touched, mine tentative, his confident, demanding – a heat-seeking missile of desire. I wanted so much more. Decades of fear spun away from me at the speed of a supernova explosion. I wanted this. I wanted it all. I wanted Jacob. We were made of stardust and gravity – pulling together the very stuff of the galaxy turning above our joined bodies.

His fingers were strong but gentle on my back. Mine were not, they clutched in a frantic need to keep this going, to never release this moment in case someone stole it from me forever. Forever… I was forever changed. It should terrify me, isn't that how people coped with change, by being scared? But it didn't. How could it?

I lay in the arms of the man I had always wanted.

Jacob shifted and pulled back enough to end the kiss. I whimpered and he chuckled. "It's alright, Mac. I'm not going anywhere."

Unable to form a coherent thought well enough to create a sentence I opted to nose under his jaw, the scratch of his beard setting off tingles on my nose and cheek.

"Shh, it's alright, Mac. I'm here. I'm here," he murmured, stroking my back. "But it's not very comfortable outside on the ground and to be honest I'm a little concerned about the bugs hereabouts so could we move inside? Maybe even use grown-up words?" The tender laughter in his voice brought me back from the brink.

I retreated from him in an instant. "Sorry." My hands dropped away, aching for him already.

He didn't let me go far, a hefty yank on my t-shirt drawing me back. "Don't do that. Don't assume I am pushing you away. I will never push you away. I would like you to look at me though."

A soft smile played on his swollen lips and when my gaze reached his eyes, they weren't amber, they were a deep honey. "Hello, Mac. Where have you been all these years?"

My cheeks coloured, the heat unmistakable, and his smile grew wider. "Running away," I admitted.

He laughed. "It speaks!"

I smacked his arm and managed to drag myself off the damp ground. Jacob offered me his hand, so I pulled him up and our chests bumped together. Standing I could look down into his face, at just over 6 foot I had at least 10 centimetres on him and it gave me a rush. His breath quickened at whatever he saw in my face and his tongue licked those soft lips. For the first time in my life I initiated a kiss with a man. I cupped his jaw, the beard sending sparks through my palm and pressed my lips to his, the entire length of his body yielded against me and his hard cock pressed against my thigh. My body hummed in acknowledgement of his presence. Rainbows exploded in my blood, I swear it.

The tough ex-squaddie had been reduced to thinking of rainbows as a way to explain the euphoria of having this explosion of freedom. I'd been imprisoned for decades and Jacob gave me a key of such simplicity it made me giddy.

"Bags," I growled when I let him surface for air.

"Yeah, okay, bags." He sounded breathless and a shiver of pride went through my body at the thought of making him weak for me. "Interesting house by the way."

A truer statement had never been uttered. In England it would barely be classified as a shed, maybe a small barn, but here it qualified for a house. Four walls of slatted wood over a simple wooden single storey frame. Two windows facing out, either side of the doorway. The windows were now glazed but they hadn't been when I'd taken over the place. The roof consisted of corrugated iron painted red and a small front veranda, also of wood, covered the front. It sat on a very solid frame raised off the ground about a metre, so when the rains came it didn't get washed into the jungle. There were two huge Iroko trees either side that the local community protected from loggers.

We lifted the bags into the house along with the box of ammunition. "Food," I said. "You need to eat." The interior remained dark until I managed to start the lamps I kept near the doorway. The small kitchen sat off to the left, the lounge to the right, a bedroom and what qualified as a bathroom at the back. Everything in the place was simple. A rug covered the floor, old paperbacks filled a bookcase, two rocking chairs and a small sofa qualified as lounge furniture. I didn't have a TV, but an FM radio and a CB radio sat on a table I used as my dining room. A film of dust covered everything, but dust covered all of Africa, except for the posh bits. This was not a posh bit.

"There's no hot water," I said. "And someone robbed my solar panels, so I don't have electric at the moment. We can buy some food in the morning from the neighbours but for now it's going to be simple."

"Can we cook and talk?" he asked.

"Okay."

I unpacked the Bergens and removed the water sterilisers, then set about priming the water pump for the well. Next came some of the ORPs; I chose the least disgusting, chilli-con-carne and grabbed the unopened whisky I packed as well. I tried not to drink, but damn, it had been a very long day and I deserved the burn. Jacob took the bottle off me and set about finding two glasses.

"First I need to know you're alright," Jacob said.

"Trying hard not to think too much," I muttered. I didn't want to burst the bubble created by our passion outside. I feared thinking.

The hand pump in this place took forever. I needed to replace those damned solar panels.

Jacob watched me. "Don't do that." His words were so soft I almost missed them.

My hand paused but I didn't turn to look at him. "Do what?"

"You're closing down again. Please, talk to me, Mac."

Why did he have to be so damned perceptive? Were soldiers like us supposed to be perceptive? Weren't we just bullets fired from a gun owned by the British Government and used by the security services?

The feel of Jacob's lips on mine, his fingers on my body, the groan I elicited from him by holding him close… These things reminded the quaking and lonely man inside the brutalised one on the outside that I needed this to survive, just as much as I needed food or water.

I braced on the edge of the metal sink. "My father…" I swallowed and tried again. Talking about him raised his ghost and I hated that fucking monster. "My father is an evil bastard. He beat me every time I showed any kind of weakness." I glanced at him and a sad smile of reassurance made my heart hurt. I had to look away, so Jacob reached for my hand. A gesture of tenderness. He rubbed his thumb over my knuckles. Old grief washed up on the barren shores of my memory.

"We have time, Mac. If it's too painful you don't have to talk to me. Let's just eat something and bunk down."

I snarled before managing to form words. "By the time I hit puberty I already knew that being a faggot would get me a beating so bad I might not walk away."

"Don't use that word, it's not right. It is not how I think of myself and it's not how you see me. Is it?" Jacob asked, the final question delivered with such a look of horror on his face my stomach flipped.

Terror shot through every cell in my body. I clutched his hands, now able to make eye contact. "No, Jacob. No, that's not how I see you. But…"

He studied me for a moment. "Christ, Mac. It's how you see yourself, isn't it?"

I swallowed the lump in my throat.

He disengaged his fingers from mine and cupped either side of my jaw, staring hard into my eyes, willing me to understand how important his words were. "There is nothing wrong with being gay, Mac. There is nothing wrong with the emotions and carnal needs we share."

Logically I knew he was right but what place did logic hold when the fear instilled in a young mind is never cured? Could I overcome the narrative that my father injected into me with a syringe made of fear and hate?

I studied my hands, they gripped Jacob's wrists. "I don't know if I can be the man you need."

"You are the man I want, Mac. You are the man I've always wanted. It's why I wanted to come out in the first place. Tell the world I'm gay so I could tell you and I prayed you'd respond. I could see the longing but…"

"Being gay in the SAS isn't really an option," I finished for him.

Jacob managed a chuckle and dropped his hands. "No, it's not the easy option."

"I guess there have been a lot of men?" I asked, half fearing he'd give me an answer.

He didn't quite meet my eyes as he said, "There have been enough for me to know I want you. Only you."

I nodded, accepting that as a sensible answer. "I tried to have relationships with women, before you joined the Regiment. They always seemed to know something was wrong, even though I managed to have sex with them. I don't think I'm very good at it." The heat on my skin added to my humiliation but Jacob deserved to know that even at forty-two I'd had less experience than the average bloke, gay or straight.

He came up behind me and encircled my waist as I tackled the water pump again. "Then we'll need to practice. A lot."

My turn to chuckle, then gasp as his lips suckled my neck. I shivered in his arms and grew hard. His hand strayed over my belly, over the belt buckle and cupped my cock and balls through my combats. I couldn't remember the last time I'd summoned enough mental energy to masturbate, even my sexual fantasies had to be straight. Just that morning I'd turned my body down, denying myself because of the illicit thoughts I had about the man currently wrapping his arms around my needy body. The sudden desperation of my body's denial made my hips thrust into his hand hard enough to cause pain.

Jacob made a satisfied hum because of my reaction to his stimulation and I realised he held all the cards now. He had the experience, the confidence, the drive to push us towards something new and potentially beautiful.

"I can't wait to taste you," he whispered.

My heart skipped several beats and fear diminished my lust. The need to curl up and hide made me pull away from him.

"Mac?" he asked in obvious confusion.

"Can we take this real slow? I… um… I'll go air out the bedroom and scare off the cockroaches." I didn't meet his gaze as I fled the scene.

8

JACOB HAD THE GOOD SENSE not to push me and I retreated to being the 'Mac' I'd always been around him because my beleaguered and confused state of mind couldn't give itself permission to imagine how this night might end if I allowed myself free rein.

We ate the chilli, moaned about the chilli, drank whisky and toasted our dead friends. After that Jacob's anger resurfaced. "How are we going to find Clark? It's not like we can go to the Firm and ask them to locate him."

"Brant's coming soon, she'll have an idea or two," I said, mind half on the conversation and half on the fact I needed to sleep but only had the one small double bed.

"Are Unit 12 really that good? If Clark is responsible for the death of my team and none of us saw him coming, how the hell are we going to fare any better?" Jacob asked, the rocking motion of his chair increasing.

"Unit 12 are the best," I stated. "Colonel Brant is one of the few people I trust enough to know if I die working for her, then I die in a good cause. She might not always give us all the information but for a rupert she's good. Unit 12 have some of the best minds from MI6, MI5 and Special Forces working towards protecting British interests around the world."

Jacob grunted. "What happens when a country doesn't agree with British interests?"

I managed a smile. "We're soldiers, it's our job to work for British interests regardless of whether it's right or wrong. I like to think we're morally right most of the time."

"Tell that to my grandfather," Jacob muttered.

"Ireland was never simple, Jacob, don't be obtuse."

He huffed. It wasn't the first time we'd discussed the rights and wrongs of our lives being spent by a Parliament that seemed bent on war more than peace. Sometimes I wondered why Jacob had joined up at all, never mind breaking his back to become an elite soldier. It's one of the things I'd missed most when I'd left him, a good argument about ethics and morals, sometimes I'd argue against my beliefs just to push him to think more deeply about his motivations. It had been my downfall with him really. Not only was he a tawny beauty of power and grace, but he had a brain as well and a strong moral compass.

I yawned. "Sleep."

We'd both showered – nothing more than a hosepipe with cold water – and when Jacob rose from the chair, he held out his hand. "Come, we'll do nothing more than sleep, but I want to feel you wrapped around me." In one simple move he'd taken away all my options.

Giddy, that's how I felt, knowing I could hold him, giddy. My belly fluttered like a medieval maid on her wedding night. I allowed him to lead me to the bedroom, the space barely large enough to contain a bed and two men, but what space did we need when all I wanted to feel was my arms around him?

He removed my t-shirt and I removed his. The smile on his face as his eyes roved over the surface of my body made me feel self-conscious. "What?" I asked.

Strong fingers tangled among the black and grey hairs. "I can't believe I finally get to feel all this," he whispered. A light brush ghosted over my nipple and I sucked in a breath at the intimate contact. He looked me square in the eyes and said, "When you feel ready to fuck me, it's going to be amazing, Mac. Right now, though, I just want you to hold me."

I nodded, struck dumb by the visual image of Jacob under me, or maybe over me, our bodies joined, him taking pleasure from me while I gave it willingly. My jeans dropped off my narrow hips and my cock strained at the surface of my boxers, but Jacob ignored both his erection and mine, instead he just pulled me onto the bed and we lay, facing each other.

"Can I kiss you?" I asked.

"If you do it won't stop there," he murmured.

I placed my hand on his backside, the snug boxers leaving little to my imagination, and yanked him into my body. "Don't want to stop." My lips and his joined, our tongues danced, our hips rocked, and Jacob slipped a thigh between mine to give me something to grind against. He pushed my underpants down and the feel of his calloused hands on my naked backside made me whimper and rock against him harder.

He pulled his mouth from mine. "That's it, Mac. Feel, take, I'll give you whatever you need. God, yes…" he arched as I savaged his neck, biting and licking. I needed it, all of it and I rolled over him, the skin on skin contact overwhelming me in ways a firefight never could. I had never felt this before, a connection so powerful I wanted it to devour every part of my being. Fire roared in my blood. Is this what sex should feel like? Is this what I'd been missing for so many years?

"Fuck, I always knew you'd be an animal in bed," Jacob moaned while my teeth savaged the thick muscle over his clavicle.

I needed more but I didn't know what I needed more of, so I tore at the boxers covering his hips and managed to get him out of them. A breathless chuckle left Jacob before my mouth took over his and swallowed every moan. The moment I freed him of the underwear our bodies locked tight and his cock touched mine.

The strange keening sound in the room came from me, it took long seconds to understand that, and Jacob's hands were now soothing not arousing. "Shh, it's alright, I've got you. This is going to feel strange and scary, but you trust me, right?" he asked, brushing sweaty hair off my face.

My hips still rocked against the taut body I wanted to claim. I buried my face in his neck and murmured, "Help me, please."

Jacob's tongue found my mouth and took over. His hand pushed between our bodies and that strong fist closed over both our leaking cocks. The first time his thumb brushed over my tip everything in me shuddered and I began to mindlessly fuck into his grip. It felt amazing, another man's hand – Jacob's hand – holding my cock tight, his pace matching mine and the velvet steel of his thick hard length just as overwhelming as his hand.

"Come for me, Mac."

Sweat slicked our bodies and the gathering storm inside me broke open and made me cry out at the tremendous agonised pleasure that roared through me. Jacob groaned low in his throat and the heat of his release hit my body just seconds after mine. His hand continued to pump, making us both shudder until

I whimpered the need for him to stop. Rather than roll away from me though, Jacob drew me closer and continued to kiss but with feather light care.

It took a long time for my heart and head to join forces again in this world and his gentleness had a large part in me coming down on the right side of dealing with my first time fucking a bloke. 'Fucking', who was I kidding? This wasn't sex. I'd had sex and it didn't feel like this.

"You alright?" Jacob asked, having wiped his hand on the bed sheet before touching my face.

I stared into those familiar amber eyes and knew I'd tumbled down a rabbit hole I never wanted to escape. He blurred in front of me and his head bumped against mine.

"Just sleep, Mac. We'll find words tomorrow. Hold me and sleep."

I sniffed in a manly effort to keep the swirling emotions under some kind of control and tried to find words to reassure him, but he didn't need reassurance. I needed reassurance and holding him close, in the dark night, seemed like the wise move.

THE SMELL OF COOKING BACON made me wake up. That and coffee. Two of my favourite things in the world. The third favourite, not in that order of course, stood whistling in the small kitchen when I dragged myself out of our bunk.

He grinned at me. "Morning, handsome."

I rubbed my hand through my straggly hair. "What time is it?"

Jacob handed me a tin cup of coffee, the heat almost too much. "11:30 hours. We slept well."

"Christ, I haven't slept that late in years," I muttered.

The burn of his hungry eyes travelled over my naked body and my cock stirred with surprising speed. "You gonna get dressed?" he asked.

I looked down at the beast who had suddenly become my best friend in the world. "No. Thought I'd shower and take you back to the pit to try something new."

Jacob laughed. A sound of such freedom and delight I stood there, coffee halfway to my mouth, just gazing at him while the sunlight threw hints of gold through the short tawny hair.

"Where'd you get the scran?" I asked to distract myself.

"Old guy next door. He tried selling me the chickens to go with the eggs, but I managed to convince him we weren't going to be here long enough." Jacob cracked an egg into the bacon fat and jumped back at the sizzle. "Go and sit, I'll serve you first as you don't like cooked bacon."

"I don't like burned bacon, Jacob. There's a difference. I can't believe you remember how I like my bacon." I sat on the chair, the cold wood making my naked arse smart.

"How many cups of coffee does it take to make me an irritable bastard?" Jacob asked.

"Four," I said, without thinking.

He came over with a plate of bacon and eggs. "That's how I remember what you like for breakfast," he said, dropping a kiss on my head. "Tuck in, there's plenty more." We ate in silence for a while.

"When is this Colonel Brant supposed to be coming?" Jacob asked after we'd both stuffed our faces for a few minutes in silence.

"Anytime now. I sent the co-ordinates yesterday." I chugged down more coffee and went for a refill.

"You really trust her?" Jacob asked.

"More than most. We need to get back to Kinshasa though if we're going to find Clark."

The tension behind me became a wave of sadness. "I need to find the bodies of my team. I have to report in. I should –"

"No, Jacob. Brant was right. Someone targeted the team and they'll come for you. Staying in Kinshasa without knowing who or what caused that explosion would have been a disaster and running was the right move. We stay here, regroup and go back with a plan." I approached him and for the first time since I'd woken, dared to touch him. The small caress to the back of his neck made tingles chase over my fingers and Jacob leaned into my thigh.

"I can't believe they're all gone," he whispered.

We deal in death, as elite soldiers. We cause it. We endure it among our friends, our family, but it always hurts. Or at least it should. When we stop caring about the bodies of our comrades it turns us bad and I'd seen it happen more than once over the years.

I sat and reached for Jacob's hand, still marvelling I could do such a simple thing and the sky wouldn't fall down on my head as punishment. "We'll get them, whoever is responsible. We'll get them."

We ate more food, showered and I was just about to drag Jacob back to bed when the growl of a hel shattered the peace of the small community. Jacob and I shared a single glance before we both grabbed our 9mm Glocks and Jacob ran out of the back door as I left the front. The trees started to dance, and monkeys screeched in protest while children seemed to appear from nowhere to watch the small dark olive hel appear over the horizon. I identified it as a Huey Cobra AH-1, the basic assault helicopter.

The dust it kicked up, along with the rubbish and noise brought out all my neighbours, most of whom complained loudly, and I didn't blame them. I watched it touch down. I kept the Glock at my side, hidden in the fabric of my unbuttoned green shirt, and saw the side door open. Twisting away from the rotor's chaos made it hard to see who exited the vehicle but both bodies were too small to be enemies.

The women's feet touched the ground and the hel rose, vanishing over the trees. Colonel Brant walked towards me, straightening up the moment the downdraft stopped being a problem. With her back ramrod straight and in fatigues, Colonel Brant, despite having no insignia on her, looked every inch the officer. A part of me relaxed the moment she appeared and made eye contact. The younger woman behind her appeared to be equally well disciplined. I stepped off my porch, tucked my Glock into my waistband and saluted.

"Colonel, it's good to see you," I said. The heels of my boots made a familiar click as I took a parade ground stance. I'd been free of all this nonsense for 3 years but the echoes of familiarity reverberated with eerie resonance.

Brant returned the salute. "It's good to see you, Sergeant Macalister. Where's your protégé?"

Jacob came around from the side of house. Not knowing who might be in the hel he'd vanished into the perimeter and kept eyes on. "Colonel Brant," he said, snapping off a salute.

"Lance Corporal Hayes, it's good to meet you and I'm very sorry for your loss." She held out her hand and Jacob took it in surprise.

"Thank you, ma'am."

"This is Sergeant Lydia Greenbrook. She's my…" Brant hesitated to find the right word to describe the young woman.

"Dog's body, ma'am," Lydia supplied.

Brant's mouth twitched in a smile. "I guess so, sorry about that."

"That's alright, Colonel, you bring me to all the right places," Lydia said eying the hut I called a house.

"We have coffee," I said by way of placating the young woman and she grinned at me.

"Now you are my favourite," she said. "Luke and Sam never give me coffee." She walked past me carrying a large Bergen that probably weighed more than she did.

9

BRANT HAD SHORT DARK BROWN hair, freckles and a wide face with deep crow's feet and tan on what probably should be pale Irish skin. Her lips were firm, but she smiled more than frowned by the looks of things and age hadn't robbed her of the elements that made her handsome rather than beautiful. Lydia clearly had mixed heritage and it gave her large dark eyes, long black hair and soft coco skin. If either Jacob or I swung that way she'd be in trouble, or maybe we'd be in trouble for even thinking we'd be good enough.

By the time I reached the house Lydia already had more technology unloaded from the Bergen than the entire village contained. Small fans whirred as she set everything up and Jacob began more coffee.

"Anyone want to eat?" he asked. Both women zeroed their attention onto him. "I'll make more bacon and eggs," he muttered.

"I want a full report, Sergeant," Brant said to me.

"Mac, ma'am. I don't deserve the rank. I was stripped of it." I leaned against the doorway to the bedroom rather than sit.

Brant's eyes narrowed. "If I read the file correctly, which you know I have, the SIS operative called Clark is the reason you were bumped. I suspect you were trying to make some noise *they* didn't like."

"*They*?" asked Jacob.

"Not sure yet, Lance Corporal but we're getting there," Brant said. "I want a full report." Her attention focused on me.

I gave her the facts as we had them, from the moment the firefight began at the museum. Christ, had that only been yesterday morning?

When I finished, Brant nodded. "I haven't told Hereford I was coming here to meet you and I haven't informed them Jacob's alive. I have called your family though, son. Your mother wasn't informed of your death so needless to say my call came as a relief once she realised I needed her to keep quiet and act like the mourning mother."

Jacob grinned. "Bet she's enjoying the subterfuge. I always thought she'd make a good spy. Bloody great liar my mother."

I had met Jacob's mother on a number of occasions, and I had to say, if I'd known my mother, I would want her to be just like Mrs. Hayes. Unfortunately, my mother left before I made it to my third birthday and my father decided it was my fault.

"She certainly has a way about her," Brant murmured. "So, Hereford currently think you are dead, Jacob. I'd like to keep it that way for the moment. The Head Shed in the Regiment are being difficult about giving me access to your mission parameters, but Lydia has managed to pull the relevant files from GCHQ."

Jacob glanced at Lydia and didn't bother hiding his surprise. "You can do that?"

"Give me a big enough lever and I'll hack the world," she muttered, quoting Archimedes while typing away on a virtual keyboard on my table. "Right, I'm in."

"In where?" Jacob asked sounding a little scared.

Lydia glanced up at Jacob and smiled with an innocence that made his eyes widen. "Hereford."

I had no sympathy. Unit 12 were part of the new Special Operations Concept, small teams designed to go in with maximum tech back up and no visible footprint to hunt down and defuse those who would further destabilise already unstable areas of the world. If they could prevent even some of the shit I'd helped create by being boots on the ground in an all-out conflict, they had my vote.

I sat beside the colonel and watched her screen as my military file popped up. "I can't search for Lance Corporal Hayes's without raising a flag because even I can't mask well enough to hide all my activity, but we can access Mac's and go into the mission through his because of the links to Clark."

More typing ensued and the final report on my attempt to prove Clark a spy-for-hire flashed over the screen. Jacob stood behind me, his eyes scanning the documents. I didn't bother reading it. I hadn't then and I didn't want to now – it would hurt too much. My entire life, one I'd been proud of after my upbringing, gone in a flash because I kept asking the wrong questions to the right people. The people with influence, money and something rotten to hide.

"If we piggyback –"

"You were court martialled?" Jacob said over Lydia while looking at me.

"No civil charges were brought," I said, the quiet statement a fact and a lesson in how to 'let shit go'.

"But why the fuck did no one tell me? Did Lawson know?"

Brant fielded the questions. "Mac didn't tell you because he was ordered not to and no, your CO didn't know. The dismissal became eyes-only because it involved an ongoing covert operation in Russia."

"Well, it fucking sucks," muttered Jacob.

Lydia returned to the task in hand. "Through this we can get into Clark's files, the ones he's sending back to The Firm anyway. Here's the latest." We all watched a report appear.

To say it was brief was an understatement. The report stated with even less detail than we'd given Brant the destruction of the Forward Operating Base in Kinshasa.

"He wasn't there," whispered Jacob. "This isn't real. It's not right. No one writes up a report like this after five men die on your watch."

"But he says he was there and escaped with his life because one of your friends protected him," Brant said, pointing to the last part of the report.

Jacob's fury lashed through the small house. Fortunately, I didn't own much to smash. "How fucking dare, he! I'll rip his fucking heart out and make him eat it." The low growl had a thread of grief and Brant rose to meet his anger.

"You'll have your chance, soldier. I can promise you that when we find him alive, you get first run at questioning him long before he can face justice in the UK," Brant said. Her conviction that she'd let Jacob off his leash when the time came settled the warrior and brought him back from the edge.

I remained calm, detached; allowing myself the luxury of rage over anything brought me too close to the path my father walked. I rarely indulged in alcohol for the same reason. My entire world had to be controlled, at all times. I glanced at Jacob, he represented the only person in this world I would lose everything for, including my control.

"We need to think with our heads, not our hearts," I said into the ensuing silence.

"Yes, we do, Mac. So, I want you two back in Kinshasa and I want Clark found, then I want the contact you were supposed to find for the Regiment, and I want them brought to me," Brant said. "At that point, gentlemen, we'll find out what the fuck happened to your team and we'll find out what to do next. The threats Hereford sent the team here to deal with haven't lessened, so we move forwards with the mission while the rest of SIS are sat with their thumbs up their arses wondering what the hell just happened."

I couldn't quite suppress my smile. I liked Brant, she rarely fucked about, didn't play head games unless she needed to manipulate her 'boys' because they were being difficult and never left us behind enemy lines with no back-up if she could avoid it.

Jacob and I cooked up the last of the food, cleaned everything away and locked up the small house. He drove, I slipped into the back seat, giving the colonel the front. For some reason I wondered if I'd ever see the place again or if my time in DRC was coming to an end. Whether I returned to Hereford or not, the night before I'd stepped over a line I could never re-cross. I'd held a man in my arms, been intimate…

The old rush of fear closed down the thoughts. A surge so powerful it turned my stomach but then I caught Jacob's eyes in the mirror. The soft brown, like melted demerara sugar in the shaded light of the truck's window, smiled at me and the fear washed back, stuffed into the closet I'd lived in all my adult life.

"I want to know what you're doing here, Mac," Brant said.

I glanced at Lydia. "How much do you already know?"

She grinned at me. "How much do you feel comfortable with me knowing?"

I rolled my eyes and Jacob chuckled. At that point I surrendered and gave Brant the full details of my work in the DRC. She nodded thoughtfully, asked some pertinent questions but seemed satisfied I'd done a good job training the men under my authority.

She then turned her formidable attention to Jacob. "And you – how have you been coping without Mac standing at your shoulder?"

Jacob looked at her for a moment, the traffic a little busier than it had been the night before. "Why? You interviewing me for a job?"

A ghosting smile flickered over her face. "Perceptive. I've worked with Mac before but not you, so yes, I'm making sure you aren't going to be a liability on this mission. Your file changes direction from perfect soldier to perfect pain-in-arse around the time Mac is bounced."

Jacob's hands tightened on the steering-wheel and his jaw clenched. I watched his eyes flicker to mine in the mirror. "Yeah, things were difficult for me after he left. I kinda lost my balance, ma'am."

"And you have it back now?" she asked, a softness to the question that surprised me.

He nodded once. "I fucking hope so." Again, our eyes met in the mirror and I gave him a smile. The tightness in his face released its choke hold.

"What do we know about the *man*, Clark?" she asked.

"Weasel," I said.

"Cockroach," Jacob muttered in the same instant.

"Let's try to leave emotions out of it," Brant said.

I sighed. "He's clever. Far cleverer than I am and dangerous. He sees things inside people that everyone tries to hide, and he uses it against them. On the surface he's handsome, charming, witty and very slightly submissive; this makes him ideal for underestimation. I don't think he's good with weapons because he doesn't need to be, he can call on mugs like us for wet work he wants done, then he can use it against us. He likes paperwork, keeps everything old school if he can because he doesn't want a digital footprint outside of the work he's supposed to be doing for The Firm."

"A lot of the information he has is in his head and nowhere else," Jacob said. "It's like he has entire servers of information up there. Some kind of mind palace I guess."

"It's going to make me redundant," Lydia muttered.

"So, what can we do to track him down?" Brant asked.

When a commanding officer asked for your thoughts you better have something good and it showed they respected your 'boots on the ground' approach to a problem. Brant liked her Chinese Parliament perspective to a problem, gaining insights from all those around her and divining the best way forwards with her team. It made us trust her.

"I think you should let Jacob and I visit a few people I know in the city. I'll tug on some contacts. Ask a few of my boys to do some snooping and see what shakes free. It could take a few days, but we'll find him if he's in Kinshasa."

"And if he isn't?" Brant asked.

"We track the fucker down to the ends of the earth," Jacob snarled.

"We go after his contact and finish the mission," I corrected.

"Good. Now I need to sleep," she said. The rest of the drive remained silent except for Brant and Lydia's huffed breathing.

WE RETURNED TO A HOTEL in the centre of the city, just a few streets from the museum and a place white skin didn't stand out too much. I kept the weapons locked in the back of the truck and took Jacob shopping to find him new clothes before checking in properly. Brant and Lydia shared a twin room next to ours. If either of them was surprised we were sharing a double they didn't say anything. It had caused me to panic when Jacob asked for the double room, but I couldn't stop him without causing a fuss and that would make things worse.

"You're quiet," he said, picking a deep red shirt off the rack which I knew would look amazing with the tawny hair and skin. How did I know this shit? I rarely noticed anything I wore, most of which were varying shades of grey or black. But Jacob? I noticed everything he wore, and he looked great in dark bold colours.

"Just weighing the options."

He stopped and watched me for a minute, head cocked a little to one side. "Bollocks, you're mithering over the room."

I hung the shirt back on the rail, then picked it up again and sighed. "I just..." The thought petered out, lost in the swirling confusion I inflicted on myself because of fear.

"What? You going to try squeezing yourself back in the closet? Mac, you are so far back in the fucking closet you could be in a different universe to everyone else."

"Narnia," I muttered.

"What?"

"The back of a wardrobe –" the look of mystery on his face made me smile. "Never mind, it doesn't matter." Jacob had never been big on books. "I just thought I'd have time to adjust to 'us' before having to tell other people."

"Did anyone notice or disapprove?" he asked.

"No."

He shrugged. "Then it's not a problem. Mac, you've spent your entire life hiding and fearing people will see you as something lesser because you desire men not women. It means you are always looking through a telescope the wrong way around. Assuming people can see something wrong, so you keep them at a distance. Be the man you were always supposed to be."

His words wounded me. "You haven't been out for long." Even I could hear the petulant tone.

He managed to supress the smile, almost, at my childish antics. "No, I know. At least I could be honest at home though. You've never had that freedom." He reached for my hand and I started like a wild horse being shown a halter. "Nothing we feel is wrong. Short of shagging in the street nothing we do is wrong."

"Not sure this lot will want to see your hairy arse anyway," I said, trying to hold his hand again. A strange elation clamoured through me. I held a man's hand in public. Unfortunately, the DRC was not a forgiving environment, so I wouldn't be making a habit of the tender gesture.

My reward though was worth the risk. His eyes shone the moment I laced my fingers through his, a gentle kindness in them I remembered from years before. "Hey, there's nothing wrong with my hairy arse. It's a nice arse."

I chuckled and warmth raced over my cheeks that the air conditioning couldn't fight. "Yep, it is a nice arse and one I'd like to keep private if possible."

"I certainly don't plan on sharing it with anyone else," he said, staring into my eyes.

Something passed between us in that moment and I realised we were making a silent promise to each other. I gave him a shy smile and he blushed. We paid for our goods and left the shops to return to the hotel.

My phone buzzed and chimed on the way back. "Danny," I said to Jacob by way of explanation even as I swiped the screen. "You have something for me already?" I'd rung him before the shopping expedition to start the process necessary to find Clark. Danny might be one of the good guys but his contacts from school weren't and he kept a tentative relationship alive with some of them to help keep abreast of the city's internal street politics. Being ignorant in Kinshasa usually resulted in death.

"I have something, but I don't want to give it to you," Danny said. The darkness in his voice made me stop moving on the busy street. Jacob watched me.

"Just spit it out," I muttered. I respected Danny but now he was a family man and tended to treat me as if he were protecting a wayward child.

"The general has him," Danny said. "That's the word on the street. If he's a white man who has caused the deaths of people belonging to the Congo, he will be forced to pay a heavy price."

I grunted. "So it's okay for the general to kill his people but not anyone else?"

"This is Africa, my friend, no one said life was fair in this place." Danny spoke with such sadness my anger dissolved. "I have an address where General Delta likes to take his enemies when he's in the city. After yesterday morning at the museum he is going to be angry and preparing to retreat to his strongholds in the north."

"What's the address?" I asked, keeping my voice tight. We'd need to get there quick, the general tortured before he killed if he wanted information and we needed Clark alive, conscious and able to speak.

"Mac, I don't think –"

"Danny," I snapped.

He sighed. "Yes, boss." The subservient tone grated on my nerves. "He's in the warehouse district behind the Avenue Colonel Mondjiba. I can text you the exact details."

"Thank you, Danny."

"Will I see you again, Mac?"

I paused. "They hit my people, Danny. I've a job to do. You can keep the museum protected. I've taught you enough."

"Go with God's Grace, my friend."

"You too," I said into the dead line. He'd already hung up.

I looked at Jacob, his eyes were bright. "We have a location?"

"We do."

He grinned. "Let's go find your toys and get this fucker."

10

WE RETURNED TO THE HOTEL and reported to Brant, she and Lydia would act as back-up. Lydia had sniper training, so she'd take over-watch. She called up the location on her laptop and we devised a quick plan. The location would not be easy to secure but if we could get in, locate Clark and remove him without bringing General Delta's men down on our heads, we would. If we couldn't, or we were forced to retreat, we'd leave Clark to his fate and go after the contact. We were already 24hrs behind the previous operation's parameters.

The warehouse district at the rear of the Avenue Colonel Mondjiba looked like every dog-eared warehouse district in every city from Los Angeles to Mumbai. Broken windows squatted on high breezeblock walls, a shadow of the broken dreams of those people who had lost their businesses or didn't care enough to replace the glass to keep the flies out. Weeds and small bushes sprouted in an attempt to pull guttering down, or rip into asbestos roofs and crack open concrete roads, all acting to end the dominance of man. These places were a masterful rendering of the post-apocalyptic worlds I'd seen in countless cities. A snapshot of humanity's future.

We drove into the area with care. Brant and Lydia took a different car and came in from the south. We knew the odds were not in our favour. We knew we'd be facing men with at least some training, perhaps there would even be professionals among them. General Delta had once been a special operative with Mugabe's forces in Zimbabwe. He'd not become a general by being a nice man.

"It's almost too quiet," Jacob murmured.

He drove the truck, leaning slightly on the steering wheel, hands lazy, eyes bright. I sat beside him, Glock in my right hand, near my thigh. We wore body armour and webbing with extra mags. We weren't in full fatigues, just street clothes so we could disburse more easily if necessary. With baseball caps on it meant our white skin was covered as much as possible. We turned left, following Lydia's directions. A stray dog nosed at a doorway to our two o'clock. It looked up at us, the blank stare of the starving in its dark eyes, tucked its tail and vanished into the shadows.

"Pull over," I said.

Jacob, body tense, did as instructed. We both checked our surroundings before exiting the vehicle. The warehouse squatted in the rising heat of the day to our one o'clock, the large doorway 50 metres from our position. There were no guards, no vehicles, no sign of anything including strays. Brant and Lydia would be arriving at the RV in a matter of minutes.

"This isn't right," Jacob said. "We've been given bad int."

"I hope you're right but I've a nasty suspicion something else is going on." I opened the door of the truck, no one shot at me. Jacob followed suit. He stepped out into the road. Again, no shot from a hidden crow's nest. We should have waited for the others, but instinct told me we were alone and didn't need the back-up we'd planned for, so I pulled out my phone as we didn't have a comms unit.

"Go ahead, Delta One," Brant said the moment the line opened.

"Zero, we have no company in the area. It looks like we're alone but approach with caution."

"Understood, Zero out."

Jacob glanced at me over the roof of the truck. "Clark either isn't here, or he's dead."

"Well, let's go and find out," I said. We picked up the HK33 and the HK417 and attached them to the lanyards already hanging around our necks, eyes working constantly to ensure our surroundings remained peaceful.

"I'll go across first," Jacob said.

"Roger that," I said, taking up a firing position with my back to the truck and the opened door to cover my flank. Jacob dropped his height, kept his weapon close to his body, eyes and gun muzzle moving together as one unit. He ran with a fluid precision a leopard would struggle to emulate.

I did 5 seconds on each compass point sweeping from the ground to the roofs of the warehouses and checking any changes in the windows. When

Jacob reached the edge of the target warehouse, he took up his firing position, dropping to his right knee and I raced over the road while he checked the street as well. When I took up position behind him, I tapped twice on his shoulder. Jacob turned, using me as his pivot point and headed for the door. I walked backwards, occasionally doing a 180 degree turn to take in my six. All remained quiet.

"No lock on the door, it slides but it's going to be nasty as we move it," Jacob reported. He pressed his ear to the door, but I could already tell the place was empty. "I'm opening the door," he said. If we were going to go noisy now would be the moment.

I heard the door groan and turned to cover the widening hole. Jacob stopped pulling it open at 50 centimetres and the muzzles of our weapons went first. Nothing happened. My skin crawled though at the smell tainting the thick air. It reminded me of a butcher's gone bad. I'd smelt it before in many warzones after the bullets stopped.

Jacob pushed the door open a little more, remaining on his right knee as I covered over his head. "Going right," he murmured.

"Going left," I mirrored.

We entered the warehouse.

It contained nothing in the first 35 metres. The wide concrete space had multiple dusty footprints. The light from the high, narrow windows coloured the room an ethereal orange which almost sparkled from the still shifting dust. Whoever had been here left only a short time before we arrived, the currents of air told us that story.

We both stopped, 3 metres into the interior, 30 degrees away from the doorway. "Fucking hell," Jacob whispered.

I'd lived in the DRC for just over two and half years and had never seen anything like this in any warzone, even under ISIS. All the nights I'd dreamed of this, this moment, coming face to face with Clark and I always thought I would be the one to end it. I walked towards the man who had ruined my career. They hadn't even allowed me to RTU, return to unit, by the time the bastard finished stitching me up and only my agreement to leave the country kept me from prison, so I owed this fucker… and yet even my darkest thoughts couldn't have created this vision.

Jacob started to walk forwards but while my eyes were busy on the vision before us, my subconscious had been working. The footsteps in the dust didn't just tell a story, they screamed it.

"Wait!" I shouted, the sudden noise making Jacob flinch and turn his weapon to our backs. We were both jumpy as hell.

"Wait," I said, remembering to breathe. "The dust. Mark the dust. I think it's a trap."

Jacob tore his eyes down to the ground and traced the marks. "Cover me," he said.

We were alone in the warehouse, we both knew it, but we had survived countless battles because teams as good as us did not make mistakes by being lazy. Jacob pushed his HK over his back and dropped to a press up position. "Damn, Mac. You've lost none of your skills. I can see a wire. It runs in a grid around the body, 15 centimetres off the ground. I'm going to track the system, see where it leads."

"Roger that, I'll keep eyes on."

Now Jacob had his focus on the wire he moved without effort to a crouching position. "Should we check for a pulse?" he asked without lifting his gaze to the vision before us.

"If he's still alive he's not going to want to be, so no," I said.

"Mac…" Jacob admonished.

I huffed. "Fine, you check him for a pulse and if he has one put him down."

"I'm going to be defusing the bomb," Jacob pointed out as he crab-walked along the wire to a dark corner of the warehouse.

"I'm not touching that," I said, pointing at the body.

I had a right to feel a little squeamish about touching the remains of Clark. He hung by his ankles from rough ropes that lacerated his skin, probably as he'd been struggling. There were no toes ending his feet and no fingers on the mutilated hands that dangled over the blood pool which contained flies and had a slowly hardening congealed skin covering it, the Devil's custard couldn't be fouler. To be honest we were almost assuming it was Clark hanging there, he'd had most of his face removed by a knife and chunks of his scalp. There were some body parts scattered about but not enough. His cock and balls were stuffed between his teeth, all too clear without the lips to protect them.

"I have six grenades laced together with some plastic and a simple pin pull mechanism. I'm going to remove the wire and separate the grenades. We should be able to take them with us, and the C4," Jacob reported from the dark.

"Is there a detonator for the C4?" I asked.

"No, they just wanted a bigger explosion," Jacob said. He sounded distracted, so I left him to figure out the IED.

I stepped over the wire, confident that if something unexpected happened and I stepped back into the wire it wouldn't blow us to hell. The flies were already making the most of their miserable host and the stink made me wish I didn't have to breathe. I'd seen some foul things over the years, but this had to rank in the top three of my nightmares. Working hard to keep my boots out of the blood splatter I leaned over and managed to place two fingers to the jugular pulse point. *Don't be sick*, repeated itself inside my head on a loop. I had to hope Clark hadn't been awake for the facial and genital disfigurement.

"Guess the old adage of harm being sent back ten-fold is about right," I told the corpse. Weird didn't begin to describe how it made me feel to see such a central figure in my downfall so broken. I wanted to pity the bastard for the last hour or so of his life, but I found it hard to have much sympathy and I wished I could have made him face real justice, then I might have been able to clear my name.

Jacob emerged from the shadows. "Dead?" he asked.

"Yep."

"Good, fucker."

"Yeah," I said, my anger with Clark older. "We still need to find the target though and we've lost our only lead."

Jacob grunted. "I've been thinking about that. General Delta is going to know everything Clark did, so Delta is going after our hostage, we have no choice but to assume that as fact. It means Delta is the one we have to track until we catch the dealer who knows where this scientist woman is and if General Delta finds her first we'll never get her back, Boko Haram must have her, it's what Clark assumed."

"Delta is going to go north again as soon as he can," I said. "He'll be moving towards their territory."

"Not if he thinks he can make a deal with Boko Haram through their intermediaries here. For all we know there's going to be an auction for this woman because she has knowledge that can end entire parts of the human race," Jacob replied.

He had a point. A man like General Delta didn't let something like fear of government forces prevent him from perusing something he wanted. The knowledge residing in a Porton Down scientist being captured as a human target was almost as dangerous as one of their damned viruses escaping. This scientist, Dilras Begum, would be worth a great deal on the open market even if Delta couldn't use her himself. It would raise his profile, perhaps even make the DRC's Government cede control.

"He has one hell of a head start on us, Jacob."

Jacob rested his hands on his weapon, the movement so familiar it made my heart constrict, like a love-struck fool. "We have to remove her from the table. Where would Delta go to feel safe? He'll send men after the target and if the target is a broker for Boko Haram then the target will simply sell to Delta and isn't in any immediate danger. They'll want to strike a deal."

"Unless Delta won't pay the price," I said.

"Worst case scenario Delta ends up with the geneticist either way, so we make him our new mission objective," Jacob said, sorting the priorities out.

I nodded. "We report to Brant, tell her about Clark, she can report to the local police. I want my name kept out of this."

Jacob frowned. "Why? I would have thought you'd work on having a positive relationship with the police."

"Once this gets back to Whitehall and if my name is attached to the police report the Security Services will come after me again. I can't afford to be on their radar. The target on my back is too large," I said.

"At some point I want that explained to me, Mac."

"At some point I will explain, let's just get out of here." I gave the body one more look and a mental 'fuck you' farewell.

11

BY THE TIME WE LEFT the warehouse Lydia and Brant were outside, parked near my truck. “Sitrep, gentlemen,” Brant said, leaning against the car with her MP5K in her relaxed hands.

“Clark is dead. You probably don’t want the details and he’d have talked,” Jacob said.

“Shit. Delta knows where to find Dilras Begum,” Brant said.

“Yep, we’re going to find General Delta now,” I said.

Brant pulled a face, a pensive pissed off expression. “I’m going to have to report this to Whitehall which means explaining what Unit 12 are doing on an unsanctioned mission the SAS were supposed to be dealing with. MI6 aren’t my favourite playmates right now.” She hung her head for a moment, rallying her resources. “Fine, go find Delta. We’ll report this to the embassy, keep Whitehall out of the loop for as long as possible. If Clark is dirty –”

“*Was*, ma’am,” I pointed out quietly.

“As you say, Sergeant. *Was* dirty, then who knows what else he told Delta. Right, new mission, find Delta, find the broker that may or may not exist. Keep the broker alive, take Delta out. I don’t want a general in the DRC having the information Clark knew. Do we know how long he’s been dead?” Brant asked.

Jacob did some fast calculations. “Bearing in mind the weather conditions I’d say less than an hour. The torture went on for a while, but we don’t know when Delta found Clark.”

“Clark could have given them anything,” Brant muttered. “Fuck.”

I had a moment of imagining the woman’s brain sifting the vast network of information she held to accommodate this latest twist in the game of politics she was forced to play as a senior ranking officer in a covert unit of SIS.

“We need to go, Colonel,” I said, dragging her back to the present.

"Of course. Keep me updated and try not to get yourselves killed. I need Lydia with me."

"Roger that," Jacob said, already heading for the truck.

When we climbed in, I took the wheel. "How do you want to proceed?" he asked.

"There's a chance Delta knows who I am, but Clark thought you were dead, so I think you should be a buyer the target wanted to sell to and I'm acting as security." I drove back into the traffic of the city and headed towards the N1 again.

"Where are we going?" Jacob asked.

"Matété, it's not the kind of district the tourists go and visit. There's a nightclub there General Delta frequents," I said, the tension in me rising with each rotation of the truck's wheels.

"You know of this nightclub how?" Jacob asked, giving me the side-eye.

I chuckled. "Yeah, lots of girls, and every service imaginable is on sale, including drugs but as we both know, girls don't seem to be my thing."

"Just checking," he mumbled.

"I never took you for the jealous type," I said, watching him as the traffic lights caught us again.

His eyes caught the light and turned a soft caramel. "Just don't like the thought of you playing elsewhere. Never have."

I laughed, this possessive streak coming out of the blue. "Jacob, you're being a dick. You know perfectly well there's never been anyone in my life but you and we've only just kissed. It's not like I move fast in the romantic department." I reached out and took his hand, the first intimate gesture we'd shared for several hours and it made my skin tingle. "I know about it because my job means I have to know about it. I had a police contact who gave me a rundown of all the places in Kinshasa I needed to be aware of if I wanted to remain in one piece."

"And this is one of those places?" Jacob asked.

"It's at the top of the list," I said. "Not the place you want to go if you're white unless you fancy finding a new and interesting way of committing suicide or have a great deal of money that you like spending on bad things."

"And I'm supposed to be a human trafficker going in there?" he asked.

"Yep."

"Shouldn't I be wearing a suit?"

"Nope."

"This is the kind of place our CO used to warn us about isn't it?"

"Oh yes."

"Fucking hell."

I grinned. "It'll be fun. I get to be the muscle."

"And I get to make sure they don't slice our ears off to wear as a necklace," he muttered.

"That's not Delta's way," I said, "he's more likely to take your balls."

"Don't remind me," Jacob muttered, probably thinking about Clark's balls.

I needed to be in the streets behind the Mosquée Al-taqwa so cut through the traffic, making Jacob swear. Traffic laws belonged to cities *other* than Kinshasa. We parked up and I left the engine running so we could take advantage of the air conditioning.

"Right, we need a plan," I said. "That's the club." I pointed to the gaudy entrance ahead of us on the other side of the road about 50 metres from our current location.

"Will it be open during the day?" Jacob asked.

"For the right price it'll be open all day, every day. It's not just a nightclub and Delta's not the only bad boy who uses the place to do business. It's something like neutral territory."

Jacob swivelled in his seat and watched the entrance. "So, we go in, ask for Delta and just offer to give him the money for the woman if he can get her back from Boko Haram?"

"No, I think we go in and offer to act as his emissary to some very big hitters in the arms race," I said.

"What?"

"We need the geneticist's location but to get the location we need to find your target. He might or might not be there. So we make the general show us to him or the other way around, and perhaps he'll play us off against each other. The man Boko Haram uses to trade prisoners only has power because of his contacts. If we have more contacts, more money, Boko Haram will want to deal with us and so will the general."

"Or take our balls for earrings," Jacob muttered. He reached into the back seat and hauled the large bag of weapons into the front.

"There is always that possibility, though I plan to keep your balls where they are right now."

Jacob snorted. "It's not much of a plan, Mac. I'd like to think we might stand a chance of going home."

"We don't really have much choice."

"It's hardly the seven 'Ps'."

I shrugged. "We don't have time or the facilities for a full plan or preparation."

"Which means we're going to have piss-poor performance." Jacob spoke with his eyes on the target building and despite his words I knew he had ideas bubbling away in that hind-brain of his, it always worked overtime.

"If it goes noisy, we just grab what int we can and get out. I'm not killing Delta unless it's easy," I said. "We can find him later if necessary."

"But Brant –"

"Isn't here and we are. Delta's going to be surrounded by well trained and heavily armed men. These guys aren't just gangsters playing soldier, they are soldiers and we won't be allowed guns," I said, plucking a SIG from Jacob's paws. "We take the Glocks, know we are likely to lose them, and we use our brains not our brawn."

Jacob grunted. "Sure, easy, I just wish we had the rest of the team as back-up."

"Me too, fella," I said. "Me too."

We studied the neon bright exterior in silence. A large brick-built place which might date from the end of French rule in the country. It certainly had the shabby elegance of a once mighty colonial haunt and this area of the city would have been an outlying village in the rich jungle and farmland of the original township. The colonnades now sported flashing lights entwined around the dirty plasterwork and bright signs declared in English and French that the girls were the best in the city. It reminded me of the worst of Soho or Amsterdam on a bleak and shabby day after some hideous world-shattering catastrophe.

I could almost predict the smell. Crack pipes, tobacco, sex, sweat, heavy cologne and perfume and the sweet smell of dope riding along on a hazy wave mingling with everything else. As night began to fall, we'd seen enough people arrive and leave to have some idea of the door security, so we tucked our Glocks into the backs of our jeans and went in search of trouble.

"You really do bring me to all the best places," Jacob muttered as we walked up the street.

"Wait until you see what I have planned for a second date," I murmured in return.

He chuckled and walked up the eight steps to the front door. A vast swathe of black skin covered in a t-shirt so tight and bright white I had to blink several times to prevent my retinas from detaching, stepped in front of us.

"What you want in here, white boy?" the booming French rolled around us and made me, at six-two, feel like a weasel in the claws of an eagle. The arms could barely cross over the vast chest. This man might appear to the uninitiated a threat equal to Hercules but one short sprint, a kick to his knee and the bugger would go down and stay there. Too many power shakes, testosterone and weights.

"I am here to see General Delta," Jacob replied in flawless French.

The dark brown eyes narrowed. "He has no business with white boys."

"I suggest you ask if he wants to do business. He is the power in the Congo, right? I am seeking the man who can offer me a real deal for what I want to buy and for who I represent, right?" Jacob asked. His eyes were harder than iron forged in the depths of Hell. In all the years I'd worked with Jacob I'd never seen this version. This was the man I glimpsed when he first arrived in my city, the one I hadn't worked with in the last 3 years. What had the Regiment done to him that I didn't know about?

I didn't watch Jacob any more than necessary. I kept my eyes on our surroundings. The heaving noise of some modern musical horror boomed over us, effectively silencing one of my senses. The lighting in there wouldn't help the other one either. I could already see the strobing white flashes and the prickle at the base of my skull warned me memories of conflict zones were surfacing from where I tried to drown them.

Flashing lights and loud noises didn't help the mind of an old soldier. They weren't helping Jacob either, evidenced by his index finger twitching with wild abandon as if squeezing the trigger on his assault rifle.

The bouncer sucked air between his teeth. "Wait here," he growled in French before retreating to a small cubby hole near the front door to the club.

"Fuck that," Jacob muttered, stalking off into the club.

"What?" I asked. "Wait." I strode after him.

The bouncer shouted but we were swallowed by the crowd. A heaving, sweating mass of limbs and libido. Women, who looked like they'd been rolled over by a glitter ball or six, touted for business, their dark toned skin shining in the flashing coloured lights. The men, some gangster style, some in suits more expensive than my house, many non-African, were in the business of finding the right fleshy glitter girl. The room stank of everything I feared and when the bouncer heaved into view in my peripheral vision, I grabbed Jacob and pushed him behind me.

"Hey," he snapped out.

"Bodyguard," I reminded him. I placed my hand on the butt of my Glock secreted under my shirt and took a ready stance. Left hand out to force the bull to stop and body twisted to the side making a smaller target.

The bouncer stopped as my silent instruction had requested. "You were not given permission."

I didn't speak.

Jacob said, "But I assume we have permission now?"

The guard scowled. "Follow me."

Jacob stepped around me and I followed, eyes working the room and trying to block out the noise. I could see violence written in hard eyes, hard mouths, tense bodies, all around us and not just the men. These were not good people and I realised I'd softened in the years I'd been out of the Regiment. Working for the museum, with good men and their families, had taken the brutal edges off me. I could still operate as an elite soldier, but I didn't *feel* it any longer. I was acting on years of training, but it didn't touch the instincts I'd had before.

Jacob, however, he moved through the crowd without hesitation. He gave them the impression he belonged in this circle of Hell. The coiled violence inside him made the air vibrate in his presence and when he met the eyes of dangerous men, they were the ones who looked away first. I followed in the wake of a true predator.

12

WE WERE LED THROUGH A red curtain and I muttered in English, "You know we could be heading for an execution, right?"

Jacob grinned. "At least I would be able to kill someone for murdering my people."

I fell silent. Is this what had happened to me before he came into my life, disrupting my only true love up to that point, the Regiment? Had I been this hard before he arrived? Had Jacob softened me, enabling me to return to the human race when I'd left the army?

There were strong reasons for me to pull the operation. Jacob was not stable. We were being provoked into actions that were reckless and we were operating in-country without back-up because someone had killed the back-up. I watched Jacob's back, strong, straight, tight, waves of eager violence coming off him.

A woman, dark skin slick, long nails vivid scarlet, along with the thick lipstick, pushed off the wall of the narrow passageway we walked down and draped herself over Jacob's left shoulder with a soft murmur in his ear.

He took her wrist with tender care, looked her in the eyes and smiled. "I am sorry but no," he said in soft French. "You are a beautiful woman, but women are not my thing."

Her eyes widened and I watched disgust flash through them. Jacob's smile twisted, and he shook his head. "Everyone is a fucking critic."

The bouncer led us through another doorway. The stink of crack pipes and unwashed bodies hit me before I reached the threshold and Jacob paused, his discomfort as plain as mine.

We crossed the threshold and found a vast room full of sofas, large soft chairs and a bar. Nude women walked about in heels high enough to end a man's life if used as a weapon and men leered at them, pulling at the decorative chains around their waists. Some of the women were draped over some of the men, while they sampled the wares. These were bottles of bourbon, white power, sticky lumps of tar and crystals. I saw pills scattered amongst them along with pistols. Both Jacob and I were still armed which surprised me but considering the company if things went noisy, we were fucked with or without the guns.

The sunlight, fading now, shimmered through large windows that were open to the breeze but shuttered, casting heavy shadows through the smoke-filled air. It stank of ganga now we were further into the room. Most of the men wore combat fatigues, some actual army but most fashion equivalents and many had ditched their shirts. The walls were once white but now held that horrible sticky yellow of nicotine, and wall hangings were everywhere, which must look great if you were high.

The bouncer we followed walked behind a leather sofa containing the man you knew was in charge. The sun shone on thick muscles, shoulders the size of a prize-winning ox and a neck to match. His dark skin came littered with scars and lots of gold, possibly Jacob's body weight in gold. Then there were the diamonds.

The big man tilted his head to listen to the bouncer while watching Jacob. He sucked on his teeth and I watched the room. The men surrounding the general were professional soldiers and we were in a space free of drugs even if bottles of beer covered the surfaces. Women seemed to be everywhere, many with glassy stares and my heart ached for the waste of such beauty. One though caught my gaze, her eyes were bright, responsive and despite looking no different to the other women, if covered in more clothes, she vibrated something... an awareness lacking in many of those around her, both the men and the women. A spike of worry tripped my brain and she found herself on the 'watch' list of possible dangers.

The rest of the list consisted of the general and the four men either side of him. They were sharp, focused, and not covered in women. There were also four men standing in a loose square which widened as we came in and held the Chinese Type-64. These were designed to be a suppressed weapon and showed that Delta had some serious fucking contacts. So, ten targets in the room with many other unknowns in unpredictable states of disrepair due to narcotics and alcohol. This wasn't the best plan we'd ever had, not by a long way – like a marathon distance…

When the bouncer finished speaking the general remained silent, watching Jacob, who stood in a puddle of tranquillity watching in return. The general smiled, a long crocodile creature that revealed gold teeth. "You think you can do business with me, English white boy?" He might look like an ox, but the man sounded like his education came from a far better British school than either me or Jacob had attended.

"Yes," Jacob said.

The general raised an eyebrow, waiting for him to continue, but Jacob remained mute. I ached to interfere to move things along, to get the fuck out of the building, but these men were sizing each other up and I couldn't afford to draw attention. The woman though, she shifted, sensing the same tug and pull of energy between the men.

In incremental movements the general shifted forwards, leaning his elbows on his knees and continuing to watch Jacob, who remained still.

The general grinned and pointed to the smaller man. "You, you are like the cobra, coiled and ready to strike at the slightest provocation. Sit, English man and talk to me about who you represent."

Delta flicked his fingers and a woman rose from a nearby armchair. Jacob moved towards it and sat. I took up position at his left shoulder, hands – relaxed – at my sides.

"I represent an organisation who wants someone you can find for us and we'll pay the kind of prices that will put you into power – permanently," Jacob said, keeping his voice soft and forcing the others to quieten down if the general wanted to hear.

"Why would you pay? If you are so 'all powerful' why can't you retrieve this person yourselves?" Delta asked not taking his eyes off Jacob's face. I had a horrible moment of Clark's fleshy skull superimposing itself and I wanted to puke.

Jacob leaned forwards, meeting the general stare for stare. "Why would we sully ourselves with Boko Haram? Of course, if you can't get what we are looking for our money can go to their cause rather than yours." A hiss went through the room. The Islamic extremists were not popular among those who wanted to make real money in the DRC. Boko Haram spread hate like a virus and violence like confetti. A man like the general would not want to give them more leverage in a country he needed to keep secular in order to gain power.

The general's face twisted into a sneer. "You are threatening me?"

Jacob sat back and shrugged. "No, I am merely informing you of how important this person is to us."

"This woman is generating a great deal of interest," Delta said. "I thought to keep her for myself." We hadn't mentioned gender, so we knew Delta had information from Clark.

"If you do keep her, we will be displeased," Jacob said in the same quiet voice.

The tension in the room notched up.

The general's sneer turned into a frown and I itched to grab the Glock. "And who exactly do you represent, white boy?"

"Room 39."

Most of the people in the room laughed, not understanding. The woman who watched me not Jacob visibly blanched and the general grew very still. "Why would they want you, white boy?" General Delta asked, matching Jacob's quiet and now intimate tone. I had a sudden flash of the DRC's future with this man in charge, it looked scary. He wasn't just violent, he had a brain and the education to match, if he took control of the government and its information very little would stop him becoming another African dictator. In his early thirties, he had the time to make it happen. Maybe Brant's idea of putting him down would be the wise move after all.

Jacob cocked his head a little and said, "They use me because they trust me, and I can move around this world without the same level of scrutiny other races provoke."

The general chuckled. "It's still a white man's world."

"For the moment," Jacob shrugged, "but it won't be forever, and I plan on belonging to the winning side. It might be wise for you to court their services as well."

"What use have I for North Korea?" the general asked.

"The same use you have for the wealth of South Korea, I should imagine. If you help us find our target and negotiate a peace, we will view it as an act of friendship. When the time comes for us to act, which it will, our friends will be protected," Jacob said.

I wanted to stare at him in disbelief. If I didn't know any better, I'd swear he actually worked for the North Koreans. The woman I watched instead made it clear to me that she believed every word.

"I want US dollars and the transfer fee should also be in US dollars. Boko Haram might be jungle rats gone mad, but they have power in the regions they control, which does not come cheap."

"Of course, and I can offer weapons as a sweetener," Jacob said.

The general nodded and sat back. He gestured to the woman I'd watched throughout the negotiations. "Drinks for my guest." He ordered this without looking in her direction and with a click of his fingers. The utter contempt in her gaze might be hidden from her 'employer' but not from me.

Jacob asked for water and I decided it might be wise to find out a little more about the impromptu waitress. I left my post and followed her to a bar in the corner, making certain to stand so I could keep an eye on Jacob. He talked to the general about arms shipments.

"Can I help?" I offered, speaking English.

Her dark eyes lifted to mine and she smiled. "I only speak French," she said in French.

I arched an eyebrow. "We both know that's bollocks," I said in English once more.

The eyes, almond shaped and highlighted by the least amount of makeup possible, narrowed. "Fuck off." Her accent had an unmistakable burr even in those two words.

"CIA?" I murmured.

She drew in a sharp breath. "I have no idea –"

I placed a hand on her arm. "I understand. Meet us? Please? Perhaps we can help."

The general bellowed about her flirting with the help, meaning me, and she slid away. I'd either made a terrible mistake or we were about to find an ally in all this mess. Either way, it would mean movement towards our goal. Jacob referencing Room 39 made me twitchy, but anything about North Korea made me twitchy. It did make me wonder how much Jacob still kept to himself about the original SAS mission and he performed his role with too much ease, the entire set up turned my guts into a washing machine on fast spin.

The woman gave Jacob his sparkling water and took the general's empty beer bottle, returning to the bar and me. As she brushed past, she whispered, "Romero's Lounge, 23:00 hours, bring your boss, I don't deal with lackeys."

I almost laughed. "Oh, she'll love you," I murmured. Romero's Lounge happened to be in the hotel we'd already booked.

The woman's eyes widened a little, but she returned to her post with the beer in hand. I returned to Jacob. "Then we meet tomorrow and you bring Boko Haram's envoy."

The general nodded. "Until tomorrow. For now, you are welcome to enjoy the best Kinshasa has to offer, on the house of course."

Jacob smiled. "Of course, General Delta."

IT TOOK ANOTHER 30 MINUTES to clear the building and my nerves made each one stretch out to last at least an hour. By the time Jacob managed to field the many offers he had from the women, sweat must have stained every atom in my being and the moment we were out of sight of the doorway and back in the truck with the air con going, we both slumped.

I checked my watch. "Come on, we've a long night ahead and I need to speak to Brant."

Jacob rested his head against the window of the passenger side. "Damn that was hard work."

I mulled over the rights and wrongs of what I wanted to say but decided straight forwards would be best. "Why Room 39? You didn't even blink. Why didn't you tell me you knew for certain Boko Haram had her?"

Jacob rolled his head enough to look at me from the side. "You don't trust me?"

I gripped the steering wheel, the need to be honest warring with the need to keep my lover happy. Common sense overrode the romantic. "I don't trust what you've become, Jacob. I watched you. The moment you walked through that doorway I no longer knew who you were. It shocked me."

He reached out and clasped my knee. "I'm the man you knew."

I turned to face him. "No, you aren't. I'm not sure where he is but I only get glimpses of him. Your team is dead. Clark is dead. We have to find a woman who is being held by Boko Haram and you are dealing with a man who scares me as if he is nothing more than a mosquito that needs squashing but you'll do it in your own time."

Jacob rolled his head back and closed his eyes. "Would you rather have me panic and get us both killed?"

"No, I'd rather feel like I can trust you."

I watched his jaw tense repeatedly. "I need to speak to Brant."

I huffed, saddened by his lack of communication but not really surprised. The *wrongness* inside Jacob fed into my anxiety, a spreading awareness the man I knew struggled under a weight morphing and controlling him, twisting him into something unnerving. When he'd made love to me the night before the world aligned with the planets and stars to create the perfect template for my future. Now the real world wanted its payment for such peace.

I sighed and made a decision. Still watching the door of the club, I began to speak about why I'd left the Regiment.

13

"THE LAST TIME WE WERE in Syria on an active op with MI6 tagging along in the shape of Clark the money we were supposed to give to the rebels fighting ISIS came up short, by a lot. I confronted Clark and he denied knowing anything, pushing the blame firmly onto our team. I reported it to the Head Shed back in Hereford. We all know some money goes missing when we go on these missions, but we'd lost thousands. Someone from Whitehall sent me an email I couldn't trace, telling me to forget about the missing money and I'd be compensated for my memory loss."

Jacob turned to me again. "SIS tried to bribe you?"

"*Someone* in SIS tried to bribe me. They need boots on the ground. Regiment and probably Paratroopers who they can trust because we're the first inside any conflict region in the world. Even before the Americans most of the time." I kept my tone measured but my heart raced. The moment I confessed all this Jacob would be implicated, would know about my downfall and therefore his career could end as abruptly as mine if anyone found out.

"You didn't take the bribe?"

I looked at him. "It was a lot of money. I thought I could trace it back, use it to implicate them. Keep you and the others clean…"

"That was beyond naive."

I still gripped the wheel but looked down between my knees feeling weak. "I know. It gets worse. The money kept coming and Clark began actively using me on missions to move drugs, guns, and more money to various groups inside the countries we infiltrated. People left our custody, though he knew not to trust me with that, and people weren't where our int put them. I kept records of everything. All on what I thought was a secure server."

"Jesus, Mac. Why didn't you ever tell me any of this?"

I glanced at him. "Why do you think? I didn't want to risk your career or your life. I loved you, Jacob. Even though I knew I could never admit it aloud, I loved you and wanted to protect you, but I also loved the Regiment and don't want it used like this. I don't want good men giving up their lives to a few corrupt ruperts and spies in Whitehall. I collected all the evidence I could and went to Benjamin. I thought he'd believe me."

Jacob laughed, a brittle sound of horror gone bad. "Really? You honestly thought he was the best rupert to talk to? Mac, he might be a damned good commanding officer as far as it goes but the man is Company through and through. He'd never believe you."

I nodded. "I know that now. The moment I walked into his office I knew I'd been had. I'd sent an email after the job in Somalia when we retrieved those British sailors from the pirates –"

Jacob chuckled making me stop. "I almost kissed you on that trip when you dug me out of that fucking swamp."

"Wish you had," I confessed before returning to my story. "I walked into Major Benjamin's office and Clark was there, with his boss Franklin. They had intercepted my email and knew why I wanted the meeting. Clark must have suspected something. All the evidence I'd collected was gone but the money in various off-shore accounts remained."

"They set you up?"

"Yep. They were clever though. Made sure I wasn't RTUed, made very sure I would never be trusted by anyone or permitted to speak to you or the team again. They even managed to take the money while giving me my freedom. They fucked me completely without locking me up or giving me a way to fight. If I said anything to you or the others, they'd take your careers as well. They made that very clear."

"So Benjamin is corrupt as well?" Jacob asked.

I shook my head. "No, he was ordered out of his office while Clark and Franklin took me apart. I couldn't stop it, couldn't control it, and knowing I could walk away with my freedom rather than face life in Belmarsh prison, it seemed the best I could hope for, they also threatened to take you down as well if I didn't co-operate," I added, the words a final and damning confession.

"Mac… I would have stood by you," Jacob whispered, taking hold of my shoulder and turning me towards him.

I couldn't meet his gaze. "I know. That's why I couldn't see you, speak to you, warn you. I dared not contact you in case they were watching and it drew unwanted attention." I managed to look in his face at last. "I couldn't risk you finding out or being implicated just because I had crumbled and reached out for the only good thing left in my miserable life."

His hand snaked around the back of my neck and he drew me close, pressing his soft lips against mine for the first time in far too many hours. Losing him had cost me far more than losing my reputation. I groaned and clutched at his wrists where his palms cupped my jaw. The kiss turned heated, desperate and Jacob growled in need. The taste of him drove me crazy and I suddenly wondered what his cock would feel like in my mouth. How it would taste. If the skin over the head really was soft against my tongue. Would I like the taste of him? What if I didn't? What if I puked the moment he stuck it in my mouth?

Jacob drew back. "Okay, what happened, Mac?"

"What?" I asked, panic taking over. I wanted to retreat. I really needed to retreat. I started the car. He reached across the console and switched the engine off.

"What happened just now? You were matching me then you vanished, and it felt off, different. What happened?"

My cheeks burned. "I wanted to suck your cock but then I panicked."

He laughed. A sound so free of artifice that it made me grin. "I tell you what, old man, I'll suck you off first and give you what you need, then we'll swap if you're ready."

"Doesn't seem fair."

"You taught me how to survive in a desert, Mac. I think it's fair if I teach you how to give head."

The weight of the evening with General Delta and my confession lifted and we were just two men who cared about each other. Jacob stroked my chest. "I need you to understand that nothing, not even this stupidity, will ever come between us, but you might not feel the same way when I tell you what I've done."

"You believe me? That I'm not corrupt?" I asked.

He bumped his forehead against mine. "Mac, you are many things, but not corrupt. Bloody stupid perhaps, but not corrupt."

"You understand why I left you?" I asked.

He drew back, a weighted sadness in those soft eyes. "I understand but you should have trusted I could handle it."

"Yeah."

"Yeah."

My phone rang. "Brant," I said when I fished it out of my pocket.

"You know Lydia might be able to find the evidence you lost," Jacob mumbled as I picked up.

I glanced at him as I said, "Ma'am."

"Are the local police here just stupid or plain corrupt?" she snapped down the line.

"I'm guessing they don't want to investigate who killed Clark?" I asked.

She huffed. "Even the fucking consulate is being quiet about the repatriation of his body. Tell me you have a lead?"

"We have a couple," I said. "Jacob's Oscar winning performance has ensured we have a meeting with Boko Haram's man on the ground doing the negotiation for the scientist and we have a meeting in an hour with you at Romero's Lounge, possibly with the CIA."

Jacob frowned, not understanding. Brant made a happy noise. "Come and get us."

ROMERO'S LOUNGE HAPPENED TO BE a top end bar in an exclusive, very white, hotel in the best part of the city. I'd been there once before with Danny and his black skin stood out almost as much as my working-class background. Brant, however, looked like she owned the place despite being in jeans and a shirt, while Lydia ghosted her in full soldier mode.

Jacob and I were also guarding our commanding officer's back but not from possible assassins, more from drunk overpaid business types who saw a challenge when she walked in. The next man who offered to buy her a drink would find themselves pushed through the very expensive fish tank behind the bar.

There hadn't been time for Jacob and I to continue our conversation, so I still didn't understand where he was coming from with this job, but my foolishness at least rested easy for the moment.

Fifteen minutes after the designated time the tall woman from the club walked in and I realised there were times women could be more attractive with their clothes on rather than off. The short and almost transparent dress she'd worn in the club had turned into a cream linen suit, offsetting her rich dark skin tones.

"Wow," Lydia murmured.

"Don't you have enough trouble with Aria?" Brant muttered.

Jacob and I exchanged glances not totally in on the comment but catching enough of the drift to understand Brant's tolerance for the gay community in the army stretched further than most.

The woman's eyes focused on me and I found I wanted to take a step back as she stalked towards me.

Gazelle on the Serengeti, meet lion – try not to get eaten.

She pointed a long slim and very sharp looking finger at me. "You almost blew my damned cover. Who the fuck are you dick wads?"

Brant raised an eyebrow but remained quiet. I coughed. "Sorry, but your cover just isn't good enough to fool everyone."

She growled and I swear I lost a layer of skin from her glare alone. "Don't fucking push your luck, limey."

Brant decided to save the rest of my skin. "Colonel Elizabeth Brant, British Military Intelligence – Unit 12. You are?"

The woman's eyes swept Brant up and down, for her part, Brant didn't shift or flinch, she remained relaxed as she leaned back against the bar.

"Miri, CIA. Working General Delta while trying to keep the fucker out of my panties," she said, holding out her hand for Brant. "Do the British want him dead? My lot won't let me kill him, if you do, I'm changing sides."

Brant chuckled. "We can always do with good operatives. Let me buy you a drink. I can promise these boys won't try to get in your pants. They are far more interested in each other's though I can't promise to protect you from my young sergeant."

Lydia smiled and flashed her big brown eyes at Miri. "Hi."

Miri relaxed. "Hi, yourself."

"I thought testosterone was more potent than oestrogen?" Jacob muttered to me.

"Want to share with the group, Lance Corporal Hayes?" Brant asked over her shoulder.

“Um, no, ma’am. Thank you, ma’am,” he said.

“Wise choice.” She turned her attention to Miri. “Why have the CIA embedded you with General Delta of all the evil bastards in the world?”

“You may well ask. My parents were from Rwanda, it means I have the right accent in French and English, and the right skin tone and bone structure. I was born in the US though, shortly after they were taken to safety during the Hutu and Tutsi slaughter. My parents are from both, so they left before the killing started because they were already in danger. When I joined the Agency, they finally had their paws on an asset they could train to monitor the region on the ground. General Delta is dangerous and clever, he deals with the Russians and the Chinese, so – naturally – the CIA wants to know if he’s worth their bother as well. I just want to kill the bastard.”

We all shared a long look behind Miri’s slumped back as she slugged back a vodka and tonic. “Fuck I’m tired of this shit,” she whispered.

People who worked for the CIA were never this forthcoming – unless you counted those they’d pissed off like Sam Locke who ended up working for the Regiment and Unit 12.

“Okay,” Brant said, drawing the word out. “What can you tell us about General Delta?”

“I’ll give you everything I can, but I want you to promise you’ll end that fucker,” Miri said. There were tears in her eyes and I glanced at Lydia who moved to place a hand on the other woman’s arm.

“Why don’t we go somewhere private and have a chat? I know what it is like to feel alone in-country,” Lydia said with a level of empathy I didn’t find comfortable.

Brant’s expression was grim. “I think we need to call it a night, gentlemen. We’ll reconvene at 08:00 for breakfast. Don’t be late.”

The English women flanked the taller American and whisked her off.

“Do you think…?” Jacob asked, his face a dark mask.

“I think, but don’t want to, so let’s not.” I waved at the bartender and ordered two more beers. We sat, shoulders and thighs touching, on barstools and drank in silence for a while considering Miri’s obvious sense of overwhelming grief.

Nothing in the world would make me consider her weak for breaking in front us, I dreaded to consider what she had endured, but I wondered if she’d broken too deeply to be of use to our mission. I also recognised the cynicism in that thought.

In the last 3 years I'd softened from the brutal man created by a life in the British Army. Jacob began the process of softening me but leaving the SAS finished it and to be honest it felt good. I liked not thinking about how to kill first and ask questions second. I enjoyed having uninterrupted sleep, apart from the nightmares, and keeping fit within my body's limited parameters rather than trying to match men 15 years my junior.

The men, my previous brothers-in-arms, who had died needed their justice, I knew that, but a part of me didn't want to have to be the one who served that justice and I didn't want to drag Jacob through it either. I glanced at his face, the coiled coyote still there inside him but at peace for the moment. The more delicate bone structure than mine looked too pronounced, he needed to eat more, and the dark shadows under his eyes spoke of many waking nights over an extended period. He wore a cloak of barely controlled violence and exhaustion so deep he didn't even recognise it as enervation any longer.

I placed a hand on his arm. "Hey, we should hit the road and sleep at my place."

Jacob blinked with heavy eyes. "Yeah."

I frowned. "Or we could rent a room here and just crash?"

"Yeah. Your place would involve walking and driving," he said and yawned. "Can we afford this place?"

"I can," I told him. Jacob and money were never in the same place at the same time for very long. Whenever we'd been sent on missions together the Head Shed would give me the money, not Jacob. He'd 'lost' more than twenty thousand dollars on one mission in Belize of all places. "Come on, we need sleep."

"I killed them," he whispered as I slid off the bar stool. I froze, he stared into the fish tank behind the bar his eyes distant and a long way from the present. Only my presence kept him tethered to the world. I sat again.

"Where?" I asked, preserving our quiet bubble. The noise of the bar itself and the rest of the hotel faded as our bubble built a thicker skin, holding our secrets safe.

"Where else? Syria. All the world's shit happens in Syria. And we weren't even supposed to be there." He ran his hand through his short hair and tugged on the beard. "I fucking hate that country. So many dead."

"What happened?" I asked. Jacob had killed many, many people. It's what we did, we were soldiers, licenced killers and trained to know the difference between the enemy and the friendlies but sometimes we made mistakes and I wondered if Jacob had made one and it weighed on his soul too heavily.

"They sent us into Baghouz," he said.

My heart pounded in my ears.

"Since you left, I've been sent into that country more times than I can count. All because of my Arabic and I don't look English enough to cause a problem." He glanced at me, his expression haunted. "I don't look English enough, Mac."

He didn't look Arabic but the soft brown of his hair and eyes, the naturally swarthy skin and fine bone structure did look exotic.

"I'd seen some sick horrors. I thought I couldn't see any more. I thought I'd become immune to it, you know?" he asked, as if seeking something I couldn't give – redemption, understanding, sympathy. Trying to help him now I just nodded. In many ways, leaving when I did, I'd been saved from at least some of the worst horrors and we weren't supposed to be in there during the early days of ISIS's rise and virus-like contamination.

He continued, looking at me, into me. "I was on point. It was dawn. The town stank of the dead, of sewage, of foul misery. We had to clear a small part of the town that morning, a main residential street and a square which terminated the street. Do a sweep of thirty odd houses and businesses. Every building looked like it had black freckles all over the white, many had holes in their roofs, almost no glass in the windows and several with no doors into the street. We saw no one. Not even a dog or a chicken but they'd have been eaten, I guess. Whenever the shooting stopped the women and children would leave. We'd help corral them into the trucks. They'd go to the internment camps. The black crows. They weren't women any more, they were crows feeding on the dead, ravens, rooks… After doing a sweep of each house, making certain we weren't going to be blown up, we were all strung out, sweaty, tense, on the edge – you know?"

I nodded again, my throat too tight for words. If I'd been there, he would have been behind me. I would have protected him, shielded his mind from what came next.

"The plaza at the end. A fountain, dry; trees, dead; paving stones smashed; a gibbet rose from the centre. Two bodies hung there. Two naked boys, young men. Women in black watching as four of their coven hung on the feet of the boys to weigh them down, stop them thrashing – who the fuck knows. I yelled a warning, raised my gun. One of the women turned towards me, shouted, 'They are sodomites, this is justice in Allah's…'" He stopped and drew in a breath made of dust and bones and blood and bullets.

"I fired. I kept firing. I shot them all. Nine women were in that plaza killing two gay boys. I killed them, Mac."

I sat in silence, absorbing the information, thinking through the implications from a Regiment perspective and then from a humanitarian perspective. I finally considered how Jacob would feel. It took too long.

Jacob shifted on the stool, threw back the beer and ordered a double whisky. The moment it hit the bar I placed a hand on his arm again and held it down.

14

"WHAT YOU DID WAS A war crime," I murmured.

"Yes." He stared into the liquor, eyes the same colour.

"And yet you are free."

"My men backed me up. Said they were armed. They almost RTUed me, instead they bumped me back to lance corporal. Sometimes I think returning to my unit or leaving the army would have been better."

I didn't want to comment on that, we'd be diverted off the important topic. The one that might bring Jacob back from the edge. "Were the women armed?"

He shrugged. "Not with assault rifles if that's what you mean. Or do you count the rope around the boys' necks? The knives? And yes, they had small calibre weapons among them, but they weren't raised towards us."

"If you were faced with the same decision again what would you do?"

Jacob folded in on himself and a tear slid down his cheek to vanish into the rough beard. "Christ, Mac…"

"Tell me."

He glanced up at me, warring with himself to meet my gaze, the battle painful to watch. "I would do it again. After what I've seen there. After what I've experienced. They… they are evil. How can they be like that?"

I didn't have an answer. When I'd been in Iraq and the early days of Syria, I'd asked myself the same question, how could so many good people turn on each other? There were no answers for a simple soldier, there was just the job, but sometimes that job was just plain shit.

I squeezed his arm. "Drink that and I'll get us our room key from reception."

"Mac," my name sounded like a plea.

"It's alright, Jacob. It's going to be alright." But as I walked out the bar, I wondered how I could fix this.

I paid for a room for the night, a good suite with a bath, and returned to the bar. Jacob still sat on the barstool staring into the whisky but didn't seem to have moved. I approached him with caution, highly trained men on the edge weren't exactly predictable, and placed a hand on his back. He didn't even blink.

"Come on, let's go to bed," I said.

The other customers stared at us as I took his hand in mine and led him through the hotel to the elevators. Even 3 days ago I wouldn't have done it, I'd have gripped his arm instead, but that man no longer existed. This new Mac held his lover's hand when comfort was needed. Jacob didn't speak during the entire journey and remained mute in the suite.

I must admit I barely glanced at the expensive and roomy interior as I sat Jacob on a white damask chair. The bathroom though warranted a moment of awe. A huge bath, with clawed feet sat in the middle of marble room. Large white towels were everywhere, and it had a separate shower big enough to wash an entire battalion of sweaty grunts.

While the bath ran hot, I returned to Jacob. He sat with his elbows on his knees, head in his hands, rocking just a little.

"Hey, let me get you ready for a bath," I said.

"I just see them, the boys. If we'd been quicker to reach the plaza they would have lived, would have loved and those women would be alive."

"Nothing can change what happened and it will take you many years, if ever, to come to some kind of peace with this, but you will learn to live with the grief. We all learn to live with the grief, or we leave humanity behind and turn into something else. Whether it's the bottle or the rage, we find ways out. I'm not going to allow that to happen to you." While I spoke, I unlaced his boots, then pulled his shirt and t-shirt off.

"I've been holding it together for months, but the edges are crumbling, and I don't know how much longer I can survive," he whispered.

I led him once more by the hand into the bathroom. "Take your trousers off, Jacob. We're having a bath."

He blinked. "How can you look at me? I can't look at myself."

"Is that why you grew the beard?" I asked.

He nodded.

"Okay then, we'll make a decision about that another time. Right now, you need to sleep, so – get your kit off." I tugged my clothing away from my filthy skin and threw it into the corner of the room, naked and very far from turned on, I helped Jacob step out of his jeans and into the hot water. Behind him now, I drew him down and between my legs, resting his back on my chest. The tub made it easy for us to fit and I took the expensive smelling soap into my large hands. With great care I started to wash his chest, neck, shoulders, arms. Not doing very much, just being with him. Kissing the damp hair sometimes and rubbing my cheek against it. My heart ached for him, it also burned in anger for him. The company commanders were not supposed to send in armed men with women and children still present in places like Baghouz. The Syrian Army should have cleared it, not our boys.

I soon realised Jacob wept. I let him. I held him and murmured soft words of such tenderness they could have been born in the Arabian deserts of old. The time of mystery and magic. When Babylon thrived and magical carpets swept the sky clean. I loved this tender, broken man with all my heart and soul.

He turned in the water and clung to me, quaking with the tears wracking his body.

"Come on, sweet boy," I whispered as they began to ease. "Come on. We can sleep now."

"I'm so sorry, Mac."

"I know."

"I never wanted to let you down. Everything I did when you left, I did to make you proud even though you weren't there."

Christ, that hurt. "I'll always be with you now." The lump in my throat made my usual deep burred voice a bear's growl of sound. "Let's go to bed before we fall asleep in the bath."

Jacob sat forwards and I rose. He stood but on shaky legs, so I helped him out and dried him off, trying to stroke those corded muscles dry without raising the beast between my thighs. It didn't work. Patting beads of water off Jacob's smooth skin proved to be one of the most stimulating experiences of my life. I traced the scar of a bullet over one hip, another from a blade of some kind, burn marks from an IED that had scarred us both when we'd collided with it in Iraq.

He didn't seem immune to my care either and I remembered my earlier need to taste him. My attention drifted south and stayed there, watching his cock swell, just from my presence.

"You can take whatever you wish from me. If you can still find me… if I haven't…" Jacob's words were stuck but I had the feeling I knew what he asked because there were tears on his cheeks again.

I stroked them away and raised his face to meet mine. "I will always want you."

I placed my lips on his, an affectionate gesture rather than passionate. He wrapped his arms around my neck and opened his mouth to deepen our intimacy. The kiss stretched out and his cock pressed against mine. He groaned and fingers tightened in my hair.

"I need you, Mac," he murmured when he let me up for air.

"You have me," I promised. I took his hand and led him into the bedroom. A vast, queen-sized bed sat in the middle of another marble room. All a bit much for me but I guessed regular soldiers weren't their usual clients. I'm sure Russians and the Chinese businessmen loved it.

The nerves of the previous night returned. The thought of making love to a man caused the mental scarring my father had managed to produce to gurgle and fester under the surface of my passion. As I lay Jacob on the bed under me, taking great care of him in the process, the fear grew. It reminded me of magma, bubbling just under the crust of the world, ready to erupt and destroy everything in its path. I hated it but I couldn't squash it either.

Jacob's long thick fingers stroked through my hair. "What's wrong?" The words were a gentle prod and after his confession about the women in Syria, guilt added to the toxic mixture in my head.

"I want to make this beautiful for us, but I don't know how." The confession burned my tongue.

"Explain, Mac."

He lay under me with my larger body over his shoulder and pressing against his hot flank. I stroked his chest and belly but didn't touch his manhood. The hairs, not that he had many over his pectoral muscles, were coarse and springy. A much lighter shade than those of his beard.

I shook my head, trying to clear my thoughts but Jacob waited me out, his eyes never leaving my face. "I want you, I really do, but I can't help this awful noise in my head." I tapped my temple.

“Let me guess, it sounds like your father, this voice?”

I nodded and the tears pressed in my eyes making them sting. “He, it, says the most horrible things.” The words were barely a whisper of sound in the large room.

Jacob stroked my grizzled cheeks. “You need to let that voice die inside you.”

“I know.” The tightness in my chest pressed outward and I buried my face in Jacob’s shoulder. Overwhelming emotions made me shudder, but he just lay still and soothed me. So many fears chased around inside my head and heart but the worst one came to me in a flash – what if my fear chased Jacob away? What if I couldn’t make love to him the way he wanted and needed because of fear? What if I broke us because I couldn’t satisfy him?

“Look at me, Mac.”

My instincts were to hide the weakness inside, bury it deep and cover it in layers of stoic denial. Jacob, however, had other ideas and he forced my head up using a finger under my chin. I couldn’t resist the gentle pressure.

“You are one of the bravest and most stubborn men I know,” he said, speaking into my heart. “You will find a way through this and I will be as patient as necessary. I can see your fear. I can feel it racing through your blood. Here’s the thing though, Mac, you can’t live like this forever. You cannot deny yourself happiness because you are afraid of your desires and passions. Not when they are so simple.”

“Making love to you isn’t simple.” I wanted to argue with him. I wanted to justify my fears. I wanted to tell him they had some kind of power over me I couldn’t shatter. Why would I want to tell him these things when they weren’t true? Trying to understand all this made me seem weak.

He continued to watch my face, tracking the emotions if not the thoughts. When he smiled at me the answer to my internal question came to the surface. I wanted to tell him that breaking free of my fears wasn’t possible because it required sacrifice. I carried the fear around inside me because it kept me safe, kept me behaving myself, kept me within the ‘normal’ bounds of society. I didn’t stand out. Didn’t have to be counted among those perceived as weak, immoral or corrupt.

All these lies were a cage around me made by the words and thoughts of others. The casual homophobic references among those I worked with in the army and especially in the SF teams both in the UK and abroad. Language used to turn my desires into something dirty, something to be hidden and denied because it made me perverted.

"How do you live with people's opinions of you?" I asked Jacob.

"Because of my sexuality?" He shrugged. "Most of the time I ignore them. It's not easy though, Mac. When I came out to the team in Hereford the CO had to step in and order them to behave. I longed for you then, even if you didn't want me, the thought of having you at my back to protect me made my heart ache in need. It was a difficult time, I can't lie to you about it."

I wished I'd been there for him as well. I wished I'd been more of a friend in the first place and let him be honest about his life. If wishes were kittens, I'd be drowning in hair balls.

"And now?" I asked.

Again with the shrug. "Most of them are fine. They've moved on to other targets. You know what packs of people can be like if you're different. Soldiers are just the same as everyone else and often worse. Some of them made it clear they wouldn't work with me anymore. The NCOs and ruperts are aware of the problems and try to work around them."

I traced old scars on his belly. "Do you feel safe there?"

"I didn't for a while. Thought I'd get friendly fire in the back at some point but now it's okay. If I fuck up it's the first thing that is thrown at me. It takes a long time to change a culture and the army's culture is always slow to change. How long did it take for men to work alongside women without being idiots about it? How long before the army treated its ethnic minorities with any kind of equality? We're fighting the same battle because we're different, but it doesn't make me any less of an elite operative."

"You're the brave one out of us. I can hardly face the truth even now," I said.

"But I have the support of my family. They didn't want me to hide my sexuality when I joined up and they really weren't happy when I joined the SAS. They wanted me to be honest. Whenever you came home with me on leave, they'd struggle to keep it quiet."

"But all those women when we were away?" I said. "I saw you with them."

He sighed and a faint blush coloured his chest and neck. "I wanted to keep up the pretence. I wanted to do what the rest of you did." He grinned. "Well, everyone but you."

I managed a smile, but it faded too soon. "So you went to bed with those women even though you knew you were gay?"

"Sometimes I was too drunk and horny to care. Sometimes they weren't women at all," he said.

My eyes widened as I thought back to our time in Thailand and other Far Eastern countries where we'd been invited in to train local Special Forces teams. "Oh."

"Yes, oh. The others… I usually just walked them home, gave them money for their time if they were working girls or told them I had to return to the hotel for an early start if they weren't. I was always careful to leave them content, if a little disappointed. Assuming I could please a woman anyway without a road map and GPS."

I laughed. "Yeah, it's not easy…"

"It made me feel like a fraud and I'd often go home from a night drinking via a different route that would take me to a gay bar. It doesn't take long to find a willing partner when you look like I do," he said.

He had a point: handsome, strong, obviously army – catnip to gay men the world over I should imagine. The thought made my guts burn white-hot a growl rose from the darkest part of my body.

"Hey," he said, tugging on my hair, "I've no reason to stray."

"Unless I can't bring my demons under control enough to fuck you," I snapped. The anger in me rose to the surface and broke through. Just the thought of him with another man, any man, who could fuck him into the kind of blissful surrender I couldn't or wouldn't manage, made it impossible for me to stay still.

I rolled off his chest and paced the room to the mini bar. Hands captured mine before I could open the miniature bottle of whisky I'd snagged from the cool interior.

"Calm down, Mac." He put the bottle back in the fridge and pulled me back to the bed. "I'm not going to look for a man to fuck me just because you're having a few squeamish issues."

"Bit more than squeamish."

Jacob arched an eyebrow at me. "I know, but you are squeamish amongst other things and I don't blame you. I'm certainly not surprised by it. Besides, it was me topping most of the time. I'm not a natural bottom as you'll discover when the time is right. For now, can we just get back to cuddling? I like it and I've never cuddled anyone else."

I stared at him in surprise. "Really?"

"What do you think gay men do when they know it's just a onetime thing? Hang around for hearts and flowers? We fuck, we leave. I never spent the night and I never cuddled. You are the only man I've ever spent the night with and that was before we were having sex." Jacob lay back on the bed and patted the mattress where I'd lain just moments before.

"You've only ever spent the night with me?" There were times when my ego could be far too fragile and needy. I climbed back on the bed and lay down.

Jacob sighed in contentment when I returned to stroking his chest. "Yes, Mac. All those nights we were together on missions or training where we curled up to sleep for warmth, I snuggled in for more than just your body temperature. I wanted to feel your arms around me as well."

"What if I can never be inside you?" I asked, refusing to look at his face. "What will you think of me? What if I can't let you fuck me?"

"You're racing ahead of yourself. Some men never cross over that line. Others do but it takes time. We aren't young men, fuelled only by hormones and accepted by our social circle. We are older, with brothers-in-arms not friends as such and many of them will struggle to accept what we have, it takes time. You need to be patient with yourself."

"And you'll be patient with me?" I asked risking a glance at his face. Those honey coloured eyes were full of soft amusement at my internal struggles.

"I'll be as patient as necessary. Now would you kiss me so I can get hard again and we can finish what we started half an hour ago?" He tugged on my hair and I bent over his chest to kiss his firm lips.

Our chests rubbed together as the kiss deepened, the hard and roughened surface of a man's pectoral muscles far more appealing to me than the soft squish of a woman's breast. Jacob groaned and pulled my leg between his so he could rub against my thigh.

I pushed it tighter to his groin and the gentle undulation of his body underneath mine continued to build. We were both hard within seconds, now we were just building the tension, making our balls ache and our cocks throb in need.

The kiss broke apart when I needed to rub against his bearded chin, and I began biting his throat. I held the large and delicate Adam's apple between my teeth, and he arched his back to give me total submission. My hips were now moving in time to his though I remained on my side while he lay on his back.

With lust now spurring me on I murmured, "I want to suck you."

"Fuck, yes, please," Jacob managed.

I kissed down his chest, nipping the places I already knew drew sounds of delighted lust from him. The ribs, the hips, the nipples. Then I detoured his straining cock and nipped the inside of his thigh.

"Hey, I want you back here," he complained, once more using my longer hair as a lead. I'd either have to get it cut or grow it longer so he'd have more to tug because I kind of liked it.

"You said I needed to be patient and you'd be patient as well," I told him, resting my chin on his thigh.

"There's patient and there is cruel."

I licked the back of his knee and he almost shot off the bed. "Don't make me tie you down, soldier."

"I'll tell you anything you ask me, just don't do that again."

I laughed. "If it's that easy to get information out of you how did you pass selection?"

"Interrogators in the SAS don't normally lick the back of their prisoner's knees."

This idea rendered me helpless for several minutes as I imagined some of the hairy-arsed, hard nuts in the PARAs who helped with the SAS selection process licking the backs of the knees of the men they interrogated.

Rather than licking, I nosed at his knee, took hold of his ankles and pushed them up the bed so he lay open to me. The effort it took to override the angry whispers in my head began to dwindle the more I gazed at the body resting above me. Dark eyes watched my quiet contemplation and he smiled at me, reaching between his legs to stroke my hair.

"I love you," he said to me. "I can't believe you're here and we're together like this, it's a miracle." The intensity of his gaze bored into my soul and set it alight.

“I love you as well.” The words were not a difficult confession at this point.

I pushed up the bed just a little more and reached for the prize I’d been denying myself. Jacob’s scent filled my lungs and I licked the soft moveable skin over his scrotum. He shuddered and I took the left one into my mouth, the skin soft, the light smattering of hair rough, and the firm insides something for my tongue to roll.

“Oh, fuck,” Jacob groaned.

I sucked and he arched off the bed, the head of his cock now glistening and a deep red. I continued to play until I moved onto the right side and repeated the process. Jacob reached for his cock, but I smacked his hand. It spurred me on though and I licked the base, the hair clinging to my tongue until I reached his smooth skin. The veins and soft flesh belied the steel and I began to explore.

The smell of him, the texture, the taste, the surrender of his strength, it came as a revelation. When I took him into my mouth for the first time the flavour and texture overwhelmed my senses and I groaned deep in my chest.

“Bloody hell, Mac. Go steady or this will all be over in a second.”

I released the suction on his cock. “Am I doing it wrong?”

He chuckled. “Only if you want me to last longer than a minute. I think we’ve found a new sport you’d be very good at if it went to the Olympics.”

I grinned in pleasure and returned to the task in hand: learning how to give the man I loved everything he could want from me. Jacob groaned and thrashed, bucking off the bed and forcing me to use my hand to control the amount of his cock trying to bury itself in the back of my throat.

During the process my long-neglected manhood decided it had endured enough teasing and the sharp pangs of heated need shot through my body and burned my balls. With my free hand I reached for my cock.

“Oh, no,” Jacob said. “If you get to play so do I. Turn round and give me what I want.”

I pulled back from my ministrations. “What?”

“Sixty-nine, my sex starved student. Get on with it before I flip you over and do it anyway.”

“Um…” I liked the thought, I just struggled with the concept. It would make me vulnerable and expose parts of my body –

“Mac, stop it, it’s perfectly normal. You need to let your fears evaporate and just enjoy the things I know you'll like. This is something you will really enjoy, and I know I will." He tugged on my hair, encouraging me to turn around and swing a leg over his face. "That's what I'm talking about."

I found the position perfect for giving him deeper penetration into my mouth and nudging the back of my throat but when he pushed down on my arse and took me deep in one movement I almost fainted. He tugged on my balls and breathed hard, sucking deep and the rising tide of lust swept away conscious thought. The world came down to two things, the feel of my lover's cock in my mouth and the feel of mine in his.

I couldn't prevent the roll of my hips but with every flex Jacob groaned and bucked up into my mouth. The heat between our bodies made us slick with sweat and I stopped trying to control the amount of Jacob's length filling me. Instead I gripped the backs of his thighs, my elbows on the firm mattress trying to keep my weight off him, while I took everything I could in a frenzy of building desire.

A muffled, "Gotta come," warned me of the impending explosion and I released the tenuous hold I had on my self-control.

Jacob howled around my cock, he pulsed but I didn't pull off. The pressure of the first jet took me by surprise but I sucked it down and groaned as the lightning of my orgasm exploded through me. Flash bright, flash white. Jacob sucked as I licked and he rolled us with great care onto our sides, trapping my head between his strong thighs.

I tapped out. He released me and I turned to scoot up the bed only to find his tongue replacing his cock in my aching mouth. Strong arms dragged me close and he wrapped his leg over my hip nudging my still half hard and very sensitive cock.

After the kiss he gazed at me and a sleepy smile appeared while he ran his fingers through my hair. "I love this," he said.

"My hair?"

"No, you nob, just lying here and being naked with you. I love being naked with you."

"Go to sleep, Jacob."

His eyelids dropped and I watched him slide off the edge of the waking world.

15

UNFORTUNATELY, SLEEP ELUDED ME, DESPITE having Jacob curled up against my flank. His story rolled around inside my head gathering dust bunnies full of bullets and blood. My memories fought to escape the careful control of the boxes I used to capture them before further securing them in a room I kept locked so they wouldn't overwhelm me.

We all joined the army for different reasons, mine were so I could escape my father; maybe succeed at something important; maybe make a difference in a world I struggled to understand as a teenager. No one thought about the consequences of signing up to a life of violence.

It was years before I understood the truth. The army didn't give a shit about me beyond my ability to do my job and the moment I couldn't, it wanted me and the skills I had gone. There were always more people willing to fight. Soldiers had to be young when we signed up, before the world broke our optimism.

I sighed, recognising the wheel of misery I was about to travel. These thoughts led in one direction, just like a donkey having to go in a circle to grind grain, going around in an endless circle and never reaching its destination.

With care I extricated myself from the bed, pulled on some clothes and slipped from the room. A quiet drink at the bar might just be enough to switch me off. When I arrived, I found Brant. She sat, spine straight but eyes downcast, watching the amber liquid in her glass. I almost left the bar, but she turned, saw me and nodded. I walked over and sat beside her on a stool.

"Can't sleep?" she asked.

"Jacob's out cold, at last," I said, nodding at the barman and signalling two of whatever Brant drank.

"How is he?" she asked.

“How much of his service do you know about?” I countered.

“Jacob? All of it.”

“Including Syria?” I asked.

She nodded. “I read the reports. I had to before coming out here. There’s a warning all over his file. They only needed one more reason to boot him.”

I considered the wisdom of my next words, but I had to know more, and Brant held the keys to the lock. “He thinks the men with him lied for him, that’s why he wasn’t tried for murder.”

She drank half the scotch left in her first glass before the second came. “They didn’t lie for him, they didn’t even fucking defend him, Mac. What he doesn’t know is that there was a drone over the site. The footage from that cleared him because it captured the hanging and captured the guns the women did hold. If they weren’t so bent on killing those boys they’d have fired on the patrol.”

A strange sensation of relief swept through me. “So he’s innocent?”

She looked at me. “He didn’t murder them in cold blood if that’s what you’re asking, but innocent? None of us are innocent, Mac. We’ve all killed people we shouldn’t have done for reasons beyond those strictly necessary.”

“Yeah,” I said and sipped my whisky.

“And as for you,” she said into the silence between us, “I will have Lydia and a friend of hers dig through your cloud accounts. If there is anything left of your proof, I want it first and I want to use it, then I might be able to give you back the life you want.”

“Why would you do that?” I asked.

She blinked her large brown eyes at me. “I would do it, Mac, because good and honest men are hard to find. You happen to be both despite the odds. I also want the fuckers who owned Clark. He was just a worm on a hook thinking he was a hawk. I want the fucking eagle. They have no right to use my people or use our Regiment for their dirty work.”

“Thank you, but I don’t want to go back,” I said.

A careful study of me came next and I watched her smile. “You’ve changed.”

I nodded. “I’ve found peace here and if I can convince Jacob to leave, I want him with me. We can’t stay here, I know that, the DRC isn’t safe for…” here we go with the first time admitting it to the outside world, “for gay men.”

Phew, no one died, and I didn't get struck down by lightning. Elation buzzed in my brain along with the scotch.

I refocused on the conversation at hand. "Jacob's not safe, Colonel. I'm not even sure he has all the marbles he needs in the bag. I think a few are running around in the wild somewhere in his head."

She snorted and laughed. "That seems about right. I can see he's on the edge, Mac. You'll keep him straight until I can let you both go. We've a job to do. We have to get the scientist back and her research. If her knowledge falls into the wrong hands it could do more damage than a nuke. Did you know they are currently immunising children against malaria? It kills more people than any other disease, but it's a disease of Africa so no one bothered with it for decades, just like HIV. But now we have a new weapon in our arsenal, a plague carrying bug which breeds and travels like wildfire. As if the world isn't fucked enough."

I sympathised with the woman's frustration. We were just sticking plasters on the wounds inflicted by scientists and politicians, but I also needed to keep Jacob safe. "Colonel, maybe another team –"

"No. No time. Jacob can hold it together until you find Begum and bring her in, that's your job. I'm serious, Mac."

I studied her and had the feeling she saw far more than I did, which unnerved me, but I was a good soldier. "Yes, ma'am." I slugged back the scotch, nodded to her and left the bar. The sudden wash of exhaustion made it hard work to reach my room but when I saw Jacob, sprawled over the bed where I'd left him, I smiled.

"I'm going to protect you, sweet boy, whether you like it or not and we are going to build a life somewhere safe where we can be at peace," I whispered to him, making the promise with more than just words. In my soul I knew my goal had to be preserving what was left of Jacob.

I undressed and climbed into the large bed. The instant I relaxed Jacob mumbled something in his sleep, rolled over me and snuggled. The weight of him on my chest, the soft warm breath on my neck and the rough hair of his leg slung over mine, stirred every instinct inside me. Even sliding into sleep at last, I could think of nothing but Jacob's weight always pinning me into the world.

We made it to breakfast for 08:00 but only just. It turns out showering together doesn't mean we were able to save time. The light of the morning, coming through the large windows of the expensive hotel, made Jacob glitter. His smile brightened the room, the dance in his eyes looked brighter than the sun and the grace of his movements flowed as if possessed of crystal-clear water.

The women were already at a large table in the corner of the room. Miri looked a good deal calmer and when we approached Lydia laughed at us because we weren't quite holding hands, but the joy of our union must be infectious.

"You look better," she said.

"Thanks," we both murmured, placing our food on the table. Buffet breakfasts were a godsend to men like us; we could stuff our faces.

I glanced at Miri, who sat flanked by the other women, and she raised a smile. I returned it and her shoulders relaxed just a little more.

"Right, I think it's time our Regiment boy comes clean about what he knows is happening here," Brant said.

Jacob's light snuffed out. My eyes widened in shock. He became still, the dance gone, and the poise of a savage predator woke within him. I wanted to reach out and touch his hand, to bring the light back, or at least a little of it.

"You're right. I haven't given everything but after what Mac said last night about why he was bumped from the Regiment I think I'm beginning to see the necessity of trusting someone else." He pushed some scrambled eggs around on his plate before glancing at Miri. "Are we sure we want the CIA to hear about this?" he asked the table.

"Miri has agreed to be discreet providing we take Delta off the table," Brant said.

Jacob nodded. "Clark brought the details of the kidnapping of Dilras Begum and the deaths of her team, to the Regiment's attention. The Head Shed sought permission for a small insertion into the DRC to retrieve the scientist and her research or destroy it. We come in, find her and slip out, no one the wiser and no need to inform the government that we were engaging or making a deal with terrorists."

Brant's mouth hardened. "They had no right to sanction such a move, not with you boys. That's what Unit 12 is for."

Jacob grunted. "I know, but, ma'am, I understand now why you weren't called in." He paused to organise his thoughts. "The trouble began the moment we had boots in-country. Clark went AWOL for 48 hours and when he did resurface, he had a wealth of information we'd been lacking – just like that he seemed to know everything we needed to get the mission completed. But he wanted us to sit on it, in Kinshasa, until such time as we could meet with Delta. It was Clark's idea to present as Room 39 but I'm beginning to see things more clearly. He wanted control over the negotiations."

"You think Clark is working for Room 39?" Lydia asked.

"I can't think of any other organisation who could have caused such devastation to my team," Jacob whispered. "No one but Clark knew we were there, and we know Clark wasn't in the building. I think Room 39 are pulling the strings, but we don't know the words to the fucking song they are playing. Delta didn't seem surprised when I mentioned the North Koreans last night. He also didn't seem overly surprised it wasn't a Korean doing the asking. I think…" the pause stretched until I touched his hand. Jacob nodded just once and continued, "I think the North Koreans are using Room 39 and its allies in the world to find people who can help with their weapons programme. While we are all busy looking at the ballistic missiles, they launch into the sea we aren't looking at the people they are gathering, scientists, computer geeks, even marketing experts –"

"Marketing experts?" I asked, confused. Since when were marketing people interesting?

Jacob chuckled, a dark sound. "Mac, you are a great soldier but a dinosaur when it comes to the information age."

I frowned not understanding but Lydia did. "Shit, you think they are either employing or stealing people who can manipulate data points about entire on-line populations."

"I don't think, Sergeant, I know. It was something Clark said just before we left for the first part of the oppo. 'Information is the key to everything, Hayes, I need all the information we can gather then we control the world'. I didn't understand at the time, just thought it was hyperbolic bullshit but Clark kept all this information in his head, he understood the importance of it and it makes perfect sense. Why bother just building bombs when you can control who sits on the throne of any country you target?"

Now I understood. Data mining, the new coal, the new oil, the undiscovered country with wealth just under the surface if you can find a way to tap into it. The scientist we needed to retrieve might be able to help the North Koreans or anyone else, weaponise a virus but data was just as important.

"Okay," I said, "we know it's bad, but we still need to find this poor woman and get her back from Boko Haram. That has to be our priority. Then the colonel can work on controlling Room 39 and its access to the world's data."

Brant nodded. "One step at a time, eh, Sergeant Macalister?"

"It's the only way, Colonel."

Miri spoke up. "I can get back into the general's company. I can find out where Boko Haram are holding the woman."

"No," Brant and Lydia said.

"It would be easier –"

"No," Brant repeated. "We aren't putting you back in there, Miri. I need you as back-up. The boys can deal with the general." She looked at us.

Jacob huffed. "Yep. If we can get to him, we can take him down and find our scientist."

I drew in a sharp breath. "Take down Delta in his own country? If we want to slot him that's one thing but we need him to help find this woman."

"Chinese parliament time people," Brant said. "Let's find a way to make this happen."

We all huddled around the table a little more and began planning. Brant always was an unusual CO, she liked her people to give their ideas, talk through the problems we faced. With all the years of experience and our different levels of expertise, she knew a level of trust from her would push us to reach the best possible results. By the time the waiting staff began clearing away breakfast we had something like a workable plan.

We would return to Delta's lair and simply go through the process necessary to reach Boko Haram's people through the mysterious intermediary they used. Jacob and I would need a sweetener, which meant an arms cache, and we'd need money. Lydia said she could organise both and Brant didn't press on the details. I wondered and almost asked until Brant gave me a warning look to keep my mouth shut. Lydia vanished for a bit to make a call and when she returned the colour in her cheeks was high, but she had an address for us.

Jacob and I returned to our room and picked up the few items we'd left lying around.

“How you feeling?” I asked him.

He shrugged. “Fine.”

“Jacob?” I asked again, pulling him around to face me. “I need to know how you feel, it’s important.”

His eyes didn’t quite meet mine. “Listen, Mac, I know I lost my shit last night and I’m sorry to have put you in that position –”

I yanked on his arm and forced him to press into my body. My mouth sought out his ear, “Listen to me. What happened last night will happen again, and again, until you find some measure of peace. I wish we had time to talk about it in detail, but it wasn’t your fault. Your team didn’t lie for you, there were no charges because there was nothing to charge you with. We will talk about this more, later, but right now I need you in the game and I need you to be honest with me.”

He shivered against me, lips pressing against my collarbone. “Brant knows?”

“She does, all she’s worried about is your ability to see this through without getting anyone in the team dead because you’re vulnerable,” I said, holding his hips. We were curling around each other, touching in ways I’d never done with another person, an intimate carrying of another soul.

His fingers dug into my hips hard enough to hurt. “I can face Delta. I can be Room 39’s lackey. I can make this happen but only if you have my six.”

“Always, love.” The endearment slipped out without thought. Jacob pulled back and my cheeks turned hot, but I couldn’t deny I’d said it, so I just looked at him and waited for a reaction. I didn’t expect the soft smile, the tender touch to my jaw with fingertips, or his warm brown eyes searching my face.

“Then, my *love*, I can do anything,” he said. A soft kiss sealed the deal. “I’m looking forwards to a future with you.”

The colour in my face must have deepened further, if I grew any hotter my skin would peel off, could someone die from blushing? “Good,” I managed with a gruffness that made him laugh.

When we joined the others in the lobby, the quivering strange essence of my new world still held me captive. The soft word, just four letters long, had hit my eardrum as a wave, my brain turned it into neurons so I could understand its meaning, but it caused so many other things to happen simultaneously. My nerves were plucked by the magic of a world-class harpist, while also being stroked by the softest of feathers. Light brushed my skin with a warmth I'd never experienced before and the scent of the roses in the room filled my heart up just as much as the oxygen when I tried to breathe. My entire being became something new, in an instant, as it had when Jacob kissed me that first night. Twice now I'd been remoulded by him, taken as a lump of formless clay no one could love or want, and turned into something else, something magical and beautiful.

Is this why people wanted to fall in love? The sensation felt like falling down and up at the same time. I ached in places I didn't know existed until now and the urge to touch Jacob all the time forced me to stuff my hands into my pockets. I just wanted to inhale his scent and stroke his skin.

"Come on," he said, shaking me awake from my stupor.

16

LYDIA LEANED FORWARDS FROM THE back seat of the truck. "The guns we need are in there," she said pointing.

"That's a government warehouse," I said from the driver's seat.

Jacob shrugged. "Doesn't matter, if Lydia says there's no security to worry about then let's go get them."

I swivelled enough to take in all four of the passengers. Brant looked amused, Miri seemed lost to the world for the moment and Lydia just smiled at me like all this was perfectly normal. "You want me to steal arms from the government I'm currently working for? And how exactly do you know what is or isn't in there and what the security is like?"

"You sure you want to know 'exactly'?" she asked.

"Oh, for fuck's sake, let's just get on with it," Jacob muttered, pushing open the door to the truck. I grabbed his arm to prevent him leaving.

We were sat outside another warehouse in another district of the immense city. Kinshasa covered a vast area and I knew the government had stores like this scattered about, but their locations were secret, and they were heavily guarded. The last thing the DRC needed were more arms flooding the country, forced into the hands of children more often than not.

"I just, I don't trust this," I said.

Jacob relaxed back into the truck. "Explain." As usual he had faith in my instincts. They were honed from years of experience and a sharp mind. Brant also relaxed, waiting me out.

"Places like these aren't ignored or forgotten, even here in the DRC. There should be a full security cordon. If there isn't there's a reason and if we don't know the reason we're walking in blind."

Lydia didn't look happy. "My intel is good and trustworthy."

"Why are there no guards?" I asked her point blank.

She shifted in her seat and scowled at me. "They have something else they need to be doing right now, do you want the guns or not?"

I glanced at Brant, she shrugged. "We need them."

"Good," Jacob muttered, and he climbed out of the car. With a curse on my lips I followed him, and we crossed the quiet road together. The gates were locked but most operatives know how to pick a lock, it comes with the territory of covert ops, so it only took Jacob a moment to gain access. My Glock maintained its reassuring weight in my hand while I scanned the street.

"Brant's driving through," I said.

Jacob opened the gate wide enough for the truck, and I stepped in to help close everything up. We both jumped onto the back of the vehicle as Brant drove around a corner, hiding us from view.

We were outside the warehouse's doors and at some point, guards had been there because I saw cigarette butts everywhere and two small sheds for the men to sit in while on duty. Both were empty. I wondered what emergency they'd been called to and I hoped it wasn't at the museum.

Lydia took something out of her day-sack and attached wire from the console in her hand to the locking system on the door. Within a few seconds a beep and click occurred. She opened the door and Jacob followed her with his weapon raised. I held the rear position until Brant and Miri, also armed with handguns, walked through the small entrance.

"Holy shit," Jacob muttered. "This place is insane."

We all stopped and stared. The warehouse looked to be as long as a football field and probably wider. It contained hundreds, if not thousands of wooden crates, all stacked neatly, some in a shelving system, some too large for that and so were just stacked on top of each other. Each aisle had a letter at the top, big and bold, each section was numbered. An office huddled in the corner of the warehouse, along with a kitchen.

"No fingerprints, children," Brant said. "Sergeant Greenbrook, go find the computer and get us into their systems, I want a list of what's here. Miri go with her. Gentlemen, don't open anything until we know what we are dealing with."

"Yes, ma'am," we said, still gawping at the vast collection in front of us.

"If this is guarded by just two men or maybe a few more, and it holds all this…" Jacob didn't finish the thought.

"Maybe it's been taken from the rebel groups," I said. "You know, before they are destroyed. The government runs arms amnesties from time to time. The DRC also took a lot of arms from Rwanda after the war."

"That's a long time ago, Mac. For all we know this is a stockpile and the DRC are getting ready to go to war with someone." Jacob swept his finger over the nearest box. "There's not much dust on everything."

"Jesus, I hope you're wrong." If this lot was destined to be used for a war, then Africa was in deeper shit than I thought.

Lydia came out of the office with a printout in her gloved hands. "It's a huge inventory and it's all come from China or Russia, within the last 2 years."

"Have you cloned the hard drives?" Brant asked, being practical.

"Yes, ma'am. The information is on a secure server."

"Good, we'll go through it later. I don't want our new friend to know what's in here in detail. Or half of it will go missing before we get the UN in here," Brant said.

"The African Union –" Miri began.

"No. This needs to be flagged outside Africa, but I need to know what it was going to be used for first. We don't need anything complicated for this trade, so let's find a box or two and get out. This place is giving me the creeps," Brant said, looking around with distaste twisting her mouth.

Lydia consulted her list. "Russian or Chinese?" she asked, looking at me and Jacob.

"Russian," we said together. Neither of us had much to do with Chinese weapons.

"I'm not comfortable with this," Miri said making us all pause and look at her. "What if we take the guns and they are used? What if we can't get them back and they end up…" I watched her stuff her hand in the pocket of the jeans she wore. The tremble had not escaped my notice.

I glanced at Brant who shrugged. We had a job to do and few of us had scruples about taking a few more weapons into a place already flooded with the damned things. However, I understood her perspective because I'd lived here, among the people of the DRC and I saw the constant turmoil.

"We can damage each of the guns in such a way as to render them useless. You're right, Miri, we should be careful and make certain they can't do any more harm," I said.

Brant mumbled something to Lydia, but I didn't catch it and Jacob turned back to the list of weapons in her hand. "Oh, those, I like those."

I glanced at Miri to see her reaction but she merely sighed and mumbled, "Men, fucking pricks."

She had a point; we were behaving like children in a toy store the week before Christmas. The ASh-12.7 was the gun chosen by Jacob. A tactical weapon designed for urban conflict to kill only those you pointed it at and not innocent civilians. They would be unfamiliar to Boko Haram and General Delta, which meant they'd be easier to fuck up as well. We'd need the right rounds for the gun and the search led us deep into the warehouse.

Unable to help ourselves we also pilfered a list of other weapons that might come in handy for a rescue mission in the jungle including NV goggles and tactical clothing. Jacob and I found rounds for the guns we already had in our possession and Brant found her favoured sidearm, Heckler and Koch USP. Suitably armed and pushing a large trolley with cases of ammunition and weapons on it, we loaded the truck and left the premises, locking everything up after us. It felt a bit like a trip to a builder's merchant.

"We need to think about how to handle the meeting with Delta," Jacob said while I drove being most familiar with the vagaries of Kinshasa.

"Use one of the big guns and shoot the fucker," Miri said from behind me.

I couldn't help but chuckle. The woman might be in a dark place, but I doubted it would hold her back for long. I'd wondered more than once, having rescued women from slavers while in the Regiment, what was worse – receiving a beating and prolonged torture from being a captive soldier, or being raped. I'd never been raped, and it wasn't likely to happen, but I'd been held and tortured on a mission in Mexico and it still gave me nightmares.

Jacob's hand covered mine on the steering wheel. "You with us?"

I glanced at him, surprised for a moment. "Yeah, yes, of course, sorry." I glanced in the mirror and Brant's eyes watched me but remained expressionless. "I think the only course of action with a man like General Delta is to play the game. If Jacob's up for it, we continue the act that he's working with Room 39. Once we have the connection to Boko Haram we can reassess. My concern is that BH don't just keep people in the north of the DRC, for all we know they've moved her to their base in Borno. We'll have trouble keeping the act up for long enough to get to northern Nigeria."

Brant looked at Miri. “Any thoughts on that?”

Miri sucked air through her teeth. “I think we should try to get this scientist to a mutual meeting place, maybe in Niger or Chad. If we keep her out of Delta’s reach it will make life easier for you because Delta may well double cross you.”

“Even if he thinks we’re working for the North Koreans?” asked Jacob.

“He’s not known for always making friends and being able to keep them. He’s greedy and if he thinks someone else is paying more or he can get this woman to give him more power, he’ll go for short-term interests over long-term plans. He thinks like a European or American politician, mostly short-term and self-serving.” Her bitter assessment didn’t escape anyone’s notice.

“We have to get her back, so that remains the objective,” Brant said. “For now, we continue with the illusion she’s in the DRC, if that changes, we’ll think again but I’m not making plans based on assumptions. Lydia can monitor chatter among the groups, providing they aren’t speaking in one of the local dialects.”

“The general can’t speak most of the languages of the area, it’s one of the things that kept me relatively safe,” Miri said. “I can manage some of them but if we’re talking the languages of Cameroon, Nigeria, and some of the others I’ll struggle.”

Languages were not my strong suit. I could manage enough over a short period of time to keep me out of trouble, but I didn’t have Jacob’s skill and it sounded like Miri was some kind of savant.

“Back to the club tonight then,” I said.

“Joy, can we take Lydia as an extra gun?” Jacob asked, twisting to look at her in the back seat.

She shrugged. “Sure.”

“No,” Brant and Miri said.

“Colonel,” Lydia’s voice took on a warning tone. “Remember the little chat we had about me being a big girl now?”

Brant snorted and her jaw tightened. “Fine, but you’re going in with comms and I want a security detail of some kind as back-up. Mac, do you have some people you can call on or do I need to request manpower from the police?”

I wanted to ask why I couldn’t get the comms unit she offered Lydia but thought better of it and just replied like a good soldier, “Yes, ma’am. I can find us back-up.”

17

STANDING OUTSIDE THE CLUB WITH Danny and eight of the men from the museum made me feel like a colonial prick. We'd gone, all of us, to the museum and I'd rounded up the men I had trained. I explained the mission, or as much of it as Brant deemed wise, and asked for volunteers. No one walked away. We'd been targeted by Delta more than once over the last few months and everyone wanted a little payback. I pointed out we didn't want the mission to go noisy, but I had the feeling they weren't listening with their brains, more likely their assault rifles and they wanted to take the fight to the bad guys for a change.

"There will be civilians in the club. We do not kill civilians," I repeated for the third time.

"We know, Mac," Danny said, hefting his SA80A2. I rolled my eyes.

"Once more for the hard of learning," I said. "Jacob and I go into the building with Lydia. We have four of you maintaining the perimeter that those in the club can see. We have two with the truck and the items for trade out of sight. Danny and Barker will be on over-watch, one at the front of the building, one at the back. Our CO, Colonel Brant will have command. You do as she orders while I am inside the building with Jacob. We allow business to go on as normal. You only act if things go noisy inside and you only open fire if you are fired upon, is that clear?"

A small chorus of, "Yes, sir," came back.

I grunted, not convinced. "We train to preserve life. That is our primary goal. Always." I believed it as well. Despite what people thought, the SAS wasn't in the habit of churning out killers.

I looked over my shoulder at Jacob. The nod he gave me didn't feel reassuring. During the long afternoon, consisting of humidity and therefore sweat, he'd slid back into the man who'd returned to my life a few days ago. The distant chill he exuded might suit the character we needed for the evening's operation, but it didn't reassure me. I just kept circling back to his emotional outburst the previous night and how unstable such a thing made an operator. He needed help, I needed help so I could offer him some kind of peace, but here I stood only giving him more bad memories. At least this time I could hold his back and try to protect him.

Brant touched my arm and I followed her away from the group of people. "Stop worrying about him," she said, her voice low and her eyes glancing at Jacob.

"Can't help it," I muttered.

"I'm serious, Mac. He's trained for this. The headspace he's entering to get this done is something we need. You might think this is cold of me, but Jacob has developed the thick skin a true operator needs and it's something you deprived him of, so let him be the man who gets this done for us. That's management, Mac."

"It's hard, watching him close down," I muttered, fiddling with the lanyard on the SIG516 I carried. The thought of going into the club without it made my stomach churn. I might as well have nothing on me with all the use the Glock handgun would be inside the lion's den.

"Just be there for him when he comes back," Brant told me with meaningful eye contact.

I grunted and wished he'd found me by a strange choice of holiday destination rather than chasing down some scientist who'd gone AWOL from Porton Down. I remembered doing some training there, back when I'd been a grunt in the regular army. The place is surrounded by gentle rolling hills of verdant English countryside and woodland, but its labs and bunkers contain all of the world's worst viral diseases, poisons, bacteria and their cures. Facing an unseen enemy was far more terrifying than facing a true army.

Brant took over command of my men, Jacob handed Danny his SIG assault rifle and I handed mine over as well. Lydia appeared with Miri and we both stared.

Lydia in a combat uniform designed to save lives looked hot enough, even I could admit that, but Lydia in a combat uniform designed to save lives and look sexy made Jacob and I both stare open-mouthed. I heard several uncouth comments from the men behind me and shot them all a look that quelled their enthusiasm for the young sergeant. Her dark hair, large brown eyes and full pouting lips were enhanced just enough to draw attention to her well pronounced cleavage.

"He's not going to be listening to a word I say," Jacob commented.

Miri grunted. "Not my idea, the man is the worst kind of sexual predator, but Lydia wants him off balance and dressed like this, she can function as a bodyguard and your 'beard' if you find you need one."

"I'm not sitting on your lap," Lydia stated for the record.

"Shame, I might be tempted to switch teams again," Jacob said with a wink to me.

For a moment he'd returned and my anxiety eased. "I might let you," I said.

Lydia rolled her eyes. "For fuck's sake, you're all just children and so easy to manipulate, I wonder why we bother with any of you."

Jacob slung an arm over her muscular shoulder. "You just need to keep us in line, Greenbrook."

Her eyes narrowed. "I've broken tougher men than you, Hayes, just remember that."

"I can well believe it," he said.

"All right, you two, stop comparing dick sizes, I have the feeling Lydia is going to win," I said, grabbing their shoulders and turning both of them towards the club's street.

Off the three of us went while the others took up their positions. Some obvious, others less so. Lydia had a concealed ear bud under her thick black hair and a double shoulder rig fitted around her anatomy, helping to give the impression of a warrior woman. I had my Glock at my back, spare magazines in my pockets and another in a shoulder holster. A small revolver sat in an ankle holster under my jeans and boots as well. Jacob carried the same. It didn't feel like anywhere near enough.

We rounded the corner from the side street we'd gathered in for our preparations and strode, arms away from our sides, up the road towards the club. Jacob remained in the middle, I took point and walked a little to his left, Lydia took up the rear and maintained distance a little to his right. By the time we reached the club the huge black guy from the evening before stood in the street.

His sneer said it all and the pattern from the previous meeting continued the antagonism. I watched Jacob grow colder and more distant by the moment, but so did Lydia and I had to wonder – was I like that once? Was I doing the same thing but just didn't feel it? Or had I changed forever when I left the Regiment? I didn't feel like the same man I had been 3 years before, I knew that for certain and the last few nights in Jacob's arms had released something powerful inside me and I didn't know where it would lead.

We walked up the stairs behind the club's main area and women began approaching Jacob; they gave me a wide berth for some reason – maybe I wore the wrong aftershave or maybe it was because I had a better scowl. The first one who placed a hand on Jacob's arms had Lydia in her face.

"Paws off," Lydia snapped, removing the glittering manicured fingers from his shoulder.

The woman's eyes narrowed. "You think you better than me because you have paler skin?"

A nasty smile crept over Lydia's face. "No, I think my guns make me better than you."

The woman hawked and spat on the ground near the sergeant's boots. "Guns don't keep a man warm at night."

"This one does," Jacob said, placing an arm around Lydia's waist and pulling her close for a moment.

Seeing them like that, even for a second, and a wash of memories from Jacob's sexual history burst forth. All those times I'd watched him slope off with some female from a bar in which we'd been drinking somewhere in the world. It added just a little more fuel to the fire of fear burning bright in my belly.

We weren't hassled again on the journey to the room holding General Delta and his men, though it seemed to take even longer than the previous evening. We walked into a twilight zone which could be stuck in time forever, nothing seemed to have changed from yesterday. The same drugs, the same girls, the same glitter and guns. These men and women would never escape this life. They were doomed to repeat each day, each night, until a bullet, a knife, an overdose or AIDs killed them. Maybe a few would escape but they would be as rare as the white rhino.

Jacob took point, Lydia and I at his back. Lydia didn't grace any of the men with so much as a glance, but I caught her eye wandering over some of the women. She glanced at me and flashed a grin.

"White boy," General Delta said the moment we walked into his comparatively quiet area of the large room. "You came back and with some more interesting company than your aged soldier." The general rose from his sofa and approached Lydia.

Jacob and I shifted but the moment Delta reached out for Lydia a knife appeared in her hand. "I don't think so, General. I appreciate the compliment, but I keep this," she waved the large blade up and down her torso, "for him when it's convenient for me." The blade pointed at Jacob.

The general stopped and shook a finger at her. "You are a dangerous woman. I hope he has the leash on you good and tight."

"I let her carry her own leash," Jacob snapped. "Now, if you've stopped harassing my personnel, perhaps we can talk business."

Delta's mouth twisted and the jovial man turned into a warlord. A chilling hardness swept over his entire body and sunlight bent around the violent energy stirring through his veins. I could almost see the evil in the man's soul leap forth to the clarion call of its master, the mind of a murderer. "You bring me no gifts, white boy, so perhaps I take some." Several men stepped forwards and raised their AKs. "Your old man will scream nicely while I rape your girl and give her a real cock."

Jacob didn't move, neither did I or Lydia but the sweat on my back gathered together and raced down my spine. The need to retaliate burned in every muscle but one wrong move and we'd be exactly where Delta wanted us – as victims.

"I have a case of MP5s among other things in a vehicle guarded by two of my local men. I also have others forming a perimeter around your club. There are several snipers who have eyes-on. General, this isn't my first shit show and it certainly isn't my first negotiation. I've been asking around about you and the British and American embassies are likely to come calling after what you did to the spy and the safe house."

Delta assessed Jacob again. "They come into my country and expect to operate without my permission? I have sent a message to the British and the American dogs."

"A message you need to back up with more ordnance," Jacob snapped back. "Stop fucking about and let's get on with this please. I have a report to file with my people and I'd like to give them something positive about your proposed regime change, because if they don't receive my report, be very sure Room 39 will prevent you taking power here."

"You threatening me?" Delta asked, drawing himself up to his full height.

Jacob looked up at him. "No. I am merely stating facts. This posturing will benefit no one. We want an ally in the region. I would like it to be you. I think you have potential, but you need to leave this nonsense behind you," he waved a hand towards Lydia and the other women. "We want to deal with a businessman, not a barbarian."

I thought Jacob had signed our death warrant, but he'd read Delta right, the man laughed. "You have balls of steel."

"More like tungsten," Jacob said. Delta laughed again and the shift in the room went from a war footing to an amicable loathing.

"Have your men bring the gift to the back of the club," Delta said returning to his place on the sofa. The women either side poured their long limbs over his bulk. It made me nauseous.

Jacob flicked me a nod and I rang through to Danny, giving nothing more than the order necessary to move the truck. I sensed his need to ask questions, but Danny knew his role and he stuck to it. Delta waved Jacob to a seat and drinks were provided for him. Lydia and I took up positions either side of his overstuffed chair and watched the men around us. At some point in the career of a killer something happens to their eyes. They go flat, almost dead, as if the weight of the lives they've taken steals something of the killer's soul and drags it with them into the other world.

I know because I've seen it in the mirror. These men had the same look only it went deeper even than mine. They'd seen death in a way I'd never experience, and I wondered which of them cut Clark's face off.

"Now I want to meet the man who can give me Boko Haram," Jacob said.

Delta's brown eyes glittered in the fractured light coming from several sources around us. "Of course."

Something whispered in my hindbrain. I placed a hand on Jacob's shoulder but didn't say anything. He knew though, he could sense it as well. "Wait, General," Jacob said. "Perhaps we could talk to this person somewhere more private?" He waved an arm around the room. "Is this really the place for us to meet with a man who lives for his Prophet?"

We needed to reduce the potential for casualties, and we needed to keep our people safe if possible. Less people, less room for error when this went noisy.

"You make a great many demands," Delta stated. "Anyone would think you are not who you say you are."

Jacob's body tensed further under my palm. "I think you should be careful, General. There is a limit to what I'm prepared to suffer for this negotiation. I came to you out of respect after seeing how you dealt with the Special Forces team –"

"And I don't think you work for the North Koreans, Lance-Corporal Hayes, but I appreciate you showing me the warehouse of weapons you stole from today and the personal delivery." The general's eyes flicked to mine. "And did you really think I wouldn't know you? A thorn in my side indeed, Mister Macalister."

We were cornered and we knew it. Only one way out. Lydia and I drew our weapons and opened fire, moving away from Jacob to give him room and to split Delta's forces. Chaos erupted. Women screamed, tables and their narcotic contents were overturned, chairs thrown, and guns filled the room with noise soon followed by the spray of red up walls and over the floor. The air stank of gunpowder, hot brass, blood and terror. I tuned the screaming out, made sure of each target before I pulled the trigger and my feet operated with the same coordinated instinct as the hand holding my gun.

"Evac left," Lydia yelled. "RV point B, held and secure." She had contact with Brant. The others outside the building would now be fighting to draw the danger away from us.

I glanced left and saw Lydia backing towards a door, two women behind her. A bullet's hot trail scorched over my neck, far too close to my jugular. I dove for a sofa before the next one found its home. Another man lay behind the piece of furniture, which now sent fluff up into the air as bullets began smashing it to bits in an attempt to find me. The man's eyes were already clouding, the huge hole in his forehead evidence of his mortality. One quick look over the top of the sofa and I saw Jacob.

How he'd done it I didn't know but he had Delta in a choke hold, gun to his head and he screamed over the noise. "Ceasefire or your general dies!"

The *thwump* and *snick* of rounds began to stop, I turned, sensing something behind me and released two rounds into the centre mass of a man about to plunge a machete into my back. The hot spray of his life smacked my skin, almost burning in its sudden collision.

"Mac?" Jacob yelled.

"Here," I said and rose, trying to keep a three-sixty perspective.

"To me," Lydia said.

The noise of shouting voices, screaming from downstairs and whimpering from the people in our room sounded distant and otherworldly. I walked, keeping my feet close to the floor, around the dead, many taken out by their own side, and picked up another woman, dragging her towards Lydia. Something chimed as the woman moved, the room growing quieter by the moment. Jacob dragged a silent Delta to our sergeant, the gun pressed into the large man's temple.

"You will die for this," Delta said, almost with a soft cooing to his deep voice. "I will skin you."

"Yeah, yeah. If you'd left my people alone none of this would have happened, all we wanted was the contact to BH," Jacob said. "You did this to your people."

"Western Imperial –"

"For fuck's sake, let it go. The world dumped on you, but you're so caught up in the hate you can't move on," Jacob growled. "I'm Irish, how do you think I feel?"

I finished pulling the woman off the ground. She turned in one smooth movement, catching me by surprise as did the knife in her hand. It sliced not into me but Jacob's upper back. He arched and screamed. The gun in his hand moving away from Delta's temple. She yanked the blade free, turned and I put a bullet into her skull. It exploded all over us, the bone sharp as it struck my skin. I had to blink to clear my eyes of her blood and I could taste the copper burn. Delta turned to attack Jacob. Lydia began firing into the crowd again to keep them back and my gun, already raised, moved the necessary distance to release a round into Delta.

It clicked empty. I hadn't counted the rounds properly. I had only changed mags once.

Delta's eyes were feral as he lunged to take down Jacob who reeled back against the pain near his spine. I surged between them, fist already swinging, just as a large calibre round shattered the window behind Delta, about 5 metres from our location. It covered those nearest in shards deadly enough to add to the chaos. Another window imploded. My fist connected with Delta's jaw and his head snapped back, all his attention on Jacob. Delta was younger, bigger and stronger even than me, a fact that my brain screeched even as I delivered a punch into the hard mass of his gut. It wouldn't be enough to take him down but –

"Drop," Jacob bellowed. No thought, my legs folded. Delta's retaliation against me stopped moving forwards the moment Jacob's gun *ca-cracked* over my head. The hollow point rounds made light work of the flesh and bone monster at close range. The huge body crumpled over me, enemy rounds hitting it, trying to find me. The stink of the corpse made bile surge up my throat and I gagged as I struggled to keep Delta's body between me and the bullets. More large rounds filled the room, taking out random people.

A white hand grabbed at my arm and yanked hard. Lydia. I rose from under the pile of flesh, changed mags in the process and started firing back into the scattering crowd as we headed for escape.

"Mac," Jacob said the word too soft to be good news. I spared him a glance. Blood trailed from his mouth, into the beard. More stained his chest. "I've been hit."

Lydia was out the door. I turned back to the room, with Delta gone men were running from the attack, heading for the exits. I fired at two of the general's guards, both going down and backed into Jacob, scanning the room for more targets.

Jacob almost slumped onto my left shoulder but kept his footing and we moved with care out of the room together. Once through, I slammed it shut and picked up a fallen machete, wedging the door closed.

"Can you keep moving?" I asked, not taking my eyes off the door. Not looking at Jacob and the blood coming out of him. Not considering the consequences of losing him. Refusing to acknowledge the reality of our situation.

"Yeah, just," he growled. "Fuck, it hurts, Mac."

"Okay, fella. Let's just get out of here and back among our people," I said keeping the screaming in my head contained for the moment. I swung around, gave my back to the door and Jacob forced his hand into the belt around my waist, keeping his body behind mine as I took point down the short hallway to the top of the stairs. I could hear screaming behind us, below us, but not in front of us so I assumed Lydia had managed to find a safe way out.

"Stairs," I said. "Eyes right and on our six."

"Roger that," Jacob said, squeezing the words out.

The stairwell on our right went up another layer and down at least two as I peered over the edge. I saw Lydia at the bottom, with Brant.

"Coming to you," I yelled over the edge.

18

THE HARD PLASTIC OF THE hospital chair made my back ache. I listened to the colonel with half an ear as she justified our behaviour to her masters in England. Her plight made me sympathetic, those pricks in London, sat behind their fucking mahogany desks, would never understand what it was like out in the field. Lydia sat on the floor with a computer on her lap and a Bluetooth headset connecting her to someone far away. Danny sat beside me, his wounds long dressed, the white bandage vivid against his black skin. A few of our people were hurt during the skirmish but Jacob had the worst of it.

"He means a lot to you, doesn't he?" Danny asked, his voice gentle.

I rubbed Jacob's blood off my fingers. It flaked and drifted to the ground, the white tiles of the hospital a disturbing grey under our boots. "Yes," I said.

The image came again, one I'd have to learn to live with… *of Jacob collapsing into my arms outside the club. Brant and Lydia rushing forwards to help lift him, then releasing more rounds to hold our position as we realised I needed to stop the bleeding before we moved any further. The women flanking our position down on one knee, Lydia holding her assault rifle to cover one-eighty of our perimeter while Brant covered the rest and called in reinforcements. I pulled my shirt off, the t-shirt underneath wet with sweat, and tried to find the largest hole…*

"Mac, what does he mean to you?" Danny asked, dragging me back to the hospital.

I glanced at my African friend. "Are you sure you want to know?"

Danny blinked twice before his eyes slid away from me for the first time since I'd met him. "No, Mac. I do not want to know." He rose from his chair beside me. "I should return to my family. They will be worried."

My heart ached. My belly churned. My blood screamed. I would never be welcome in his home again, I could see it in his eyes. Feel it rub against my skin. Taste it in the air we shared.

"Love is never wrong when it is consenting," I whispered to his back.

"It is not our way," Danny said without turning to look at me.

Lydia watched me, Brant stopped speaking, both women held still.

I sighed. I had hidden myself for all my life. My father's brutality saw to it. The army's lack of compassion underscored it. My fear compounded it.

"I am sorry you feel that way, my friend. I shall miss you and the family we have but Jacob is the man I love, and I always will. That cannot be wrong."

The tall figure of my friend grew dimmer as he pulled in the shame he felt for me and allowed it to cloud his vibrant world. I could be gay in the DRC but to be gay would be to live on the outside of humanity. I would never be accepted, and I knew my life here was over. If I returned to my job, I would find it gone. If I returned to my home for more than a visit it would be vandalised. Jacob and I could not live together here, and I knew it. I'd abandoned my men when Jacob asked for my help at the museum. There had been not one moment of hesitation for me. Danny found that hard enough to swallow but this was too much.

"Goodbye, my friend," he whispered and the tower of strength I'd loved as a brother, strode away from me forever.

I caught Brant's eye and watched a single tear roll down her cheek even as she looked away and continued to argue our case. Lydia rose from the ground and gave me a spontaneous hug. "We love you," she murmured in my ear.

I managed a throaty chuckle. "Thanks."

"Mr Macalister?" asked a uniformed woman. I rose, bones aching in a way that had nothing to do with too many hours on the go and everything to do with fear for the man I loved.

"Yes."

She looked down at her notes. "You are his… brother?" she asked, glancing at the women.

"Yes, this is my wife," I pointed to Brant, "and this is his girlfriend." Brant nearly choked on her tongue, Lydia managed a smile and a wave. "I work in the DRC. This was meant to be a family holiday."

The nurse's eyes did not betray a single thought in her head, she just nodded. "You can see him but keep it quiet and brief."

"Yes, ma'am," I said, following.

She took me to a ward; the floor was cleaner than the waiting area but the conditions reminiscent of a 1950s British comedy film rather than a modern facility. She opened a white curtain for me, and I saw Jacob for the first time in hours. He looked pale, drawn thin and exhausted but his eyes were open and the moment he saw me, they softened. There were no beeping machines around him, an IV trickled something into his hand, but he didn't need to breathe with a mask and his pupils gave no signs of morphine.

I sank onto the edge of the bed and took the hand free of the cannula. "How are you?" I whispered. The night had been long, but they were dishing out breakfast around us, so we had company in the ward.

He smiled. "Alive. The bullet proved to be easier than the knife wound. The knife nicked a vein, so I lost too much blood but not fast enough to kill me. The bullet must have bounced off something else before entering, *it* shattered rather than my shoulder joint. A miracle apparently."

I stroked his face, longing to press my lips to his, feel his hot breath on my cheek and taste his mouth again. "You passed out in my arms. I thought…"

I thought he'd died, right after we left the building, I thought he'd died. *I screamed in agony. Danny rushed to me as I struggled to stop the bleeding, lifted Jacob, carried him with my help to the truck. We bundled in, raced to the hospital, hot tears, sweat, curses and I remember begging for my lover's life.*

I shuddered and Jacob's fingers tightened around my wrist. "Hey, I'm okay. I'm going to be okay. Once the doctor arrives, I'll be discharged. They stitched me up really well. We can still go and find the scientist."

"No," I said, shaking my head. "No, Jacob. I'm out. I can't do this. I'm not fast enough anymore. I'm too old, too slow."

Jacob tugged on my hand forcing me to meet his eyes. "Every time I've gone out there for the last 3 years I wished it was you at my back and not just because I wanted it to be you, but because you have always been the best for me to work with. You are my friend and the only choice in the field."

"What went wrong in that room?" I asked him. "How did it go so bad so fast?"

"To be honest I don't know," Jacob said. "I think the general had been sampling his stock a little too much. Or he thought he'd catch us, get the guns from the warehouse as well, and hand us over to BH. I don't think he ever believed I worked for Room 39. I think we've been had, Clark told him I wasn't in the safe house. Clark knew you were in the museum. We've gone about this all wrong and it has cost the lives of too many people. We've been chasing shadows."

"What haven't you told us?" I asked him. During the night, the moments I wasn't reliving Jacob lying in my arms, his body more still than it ever was in sleep, I'd been piecing things together.

His eyes slid away from mine and the lies wriggled to the surface.

"Jacob?"

The courage it took for him to meet my gaze warned me to guard my heart. "I… Clark… Mac, I'm sorry."

An out breath, a moment where my eyes closed. "Tell me everything."

"I didn't know you'd been targeted by *them*. Not until you said in the car after our first visit to Delta. Clark offered me a deal. The North Koreans really do want the scientist. They are developing a weapons programme separate to their ballistic missile testing. They want to keep America's eyes on the nuclear programme while they work on WMDs of another kind. They want this woman because she's 'a geneticist of true genius', Clark's words, who can shift the plague bacterium to target only those with specific genes and ensure it's pneumonic rather than bubonic. She works for Porton Down because she's looking for all of nature's worst diseases and switching them up with a new level of genetic understanding and manipulation."

"What was the deal he offered, Jacob?" I asked, a cold lump of something foul in my guts which spread tendrils to my heart.

"You," he whispered. "I didn't know they'd made you leave and when you told me… I… didn't know how to… Mac, Syria fucked with my head. I… Thinking straight, making good calls, seeing the full picture, it's really hard and I just wanted to find you. I didn't take their money. Clark just offered me the chance to find you, to lead a mission here when he found you. He asked for me to lead the mission and although the Head Shed couldn't allow that, they did send me. I think… now I realise the bomb went off too soon. You were supposed to be in the building as well. They want you dead too because I think members of SIS are working for Room 39, for the Koreans."

"You betrayed your Regiment, your country, because of me?" I asked.

Tears welled in his eyes at my tone. "Yes. I should have told you."

I sat. I heard him breathing. Hard and fast. I no longer had his hand in mine. Would I have done it for him? Would I have betrayed everything to find him if I thought I could save him from something? What lies had Clark told Jacob to make him do this? And there was no way on this wide earth Jacob would sanction losing his team-mates for me.

"You didn't know about the bomb?"

"Christ, Mac, what the fuck do you think –"

I glared at him. "I had the right to ask."

He settled, but only because being angry physically hurt. "You going to tell the colonel?"

"Am I going to tell Unit 12 that you've fucked up? That you led us into a meeting with General Delta, one of the most dangerous men on the planet without giving us all the int you had on the situation? No. I'm not going to tell her but so help me, Hayes, you fuck up like this again and I'll shoot you."

"I'm sorry –"

"Save it. I'm too bloody angry right now to accept it."

Jacob snapped his mouth shut.

"How do we fix this because I'm not letting the woman stay with Boko Haram and she's not going to North Korea either. Who else in the DRC knows the Koreans want her? Who else did Clark have contact with? What leads do you have because we just shot the only person I know who could have found her?"

"I don't know, Mac," he said.

I wanted to shake him, growl at him and even punch him in the face for this stupidity, but hadn't I done exactly the same thing? I'd lied to him for years about all the information I'd collected on Clark. Isn't this what men like Clark did? Divide those who were close and keep them separated for as long as possible until they could be wiped from the board. Clark probably had plans for Jacob, who'd have made the grade for becoming an officer once he'd straightened his head out over Syria. The only thing tying Jacob down was me, a man Clark wanted off the planet, so they decided to take me, Jacob and the rest of my old team down.

Commotion on the ward, Brant's voice echoing down the long room disturbing other patients. I rose and opened the curtain. "There you are," she said, striding towards us. "Lydia's found something, time to stop lollygagging, Lance Corporal," she told Jacob, "we have a scientist to catch."

I glanced at Jacob. "I don't understand… How?"

"It's called having friends in low places. Aria has come through and along with another tech whizz at my command, the three of them think they have her location. The deal has already been done, gentlemen and we need to get going because we have to be in Vladivostok in 2 days."

19

Everything moved with dizzying speed and military precision. Which meant Brant took over our lives and issued orders as if she were fighting Rommel in North Africa. By the end of the day we were on a plane from Kinshasa to Paris Charles de Gaulle, then on to Moscow – where we had to keep our heads down because Brant and the Russians weren't on friendly terms right now, and on to Vladivostok on the far eastern Russian coast. A place I'd never been before.

Jacob spent most of the time asleep until we were over Siberia. Aeroflot didn't fill me with confidence so sleeping consisted of a light doze until we hit some turbulence and I gripped the armrests as if they would save my life. The night pressed on the small windows of the plane, the lights were low, and the plane's staff were resting between trips up and down the aisles selling vodka and cigarettes.

"You are angry with me," Jacob whispered in the darkness of the night. The others slept. He shifted in his seat again, his arm and shoulder free of a sling but sitting for hours on planes and rushing through terminals couldn't be easy on his wounds.

"Yes," I admitted, though it pained me to say so.

"Why?" Jacob asked. His fingers stroked the inside of my thigh and I trembled, desperate for more of his touch.

"I shot a woman in the head, Jacob, because she threatened you and we should never have been in that room. All those women. Congolese, Rwandan, Nigerian, desperate women trying to earn money from bad men to send it back to their families. How many of those girls had babies in Kinshasa? Those children will be swallowed whole by the world and spat out with no one to care for them. I've seen their future. It is filled with violence and hate until the world burns in their hearts and turns it to ash, a black coal in their chests incapable of anything good."

I knew this wasn't Jacob's doing. To be fair Delta had more enemies than friends and he didn't have the zealot energy of the fundamentalist Islamic or Christian groups fighting in the jungles far from Kinshasa, at least for the moment.

My frustration rose with Jacob because I had a target. He drew the poison of my futile attempts to help the people of the Congo, my sad efforts of the last 2 years to help a corrupt government stay in power because they were better than the alternative. The information they had on their citizens, all that technology which could have saved hundreds of lives if they'd built hospitals instead of a room full of servers, I kept it all safe so they could remain in power and try to prevent at least some of the deaths from civil war.

And now Danny knew I was gay. I would lose my job. My visa. My home. My dog. It would become impossible for me to remain in Kinshasa for any length of time and yet I wished I'd had more of an impact than some insignificant footnote in an accountant's ledger when he made a note of my wages every week. I had not saved one life and that day our actions had cost so many more, the impact would be felt by every family.

Something wet landed on my clenched fist. "I am sorry."

Jacob wept and my heart ached for him. How could I think he didn't consider the implications of his actions today, or yesterday, or the week before he found me again?

I reached for him, flicking the armrest up and drew him against my chest. "I am sorry, my love," I whispered as he clung to me. "I am sorry. I shouldn't blame you." I whispered the terrible truth of Danny's rejection of our love. It mirrored my father's hate too closely and tainted the bright light being with Jacob shed on the dark corners of my life. I whispered the grief I held in my heart for the Congo and all its sad beauty, stained by blood, violence and greed both at home and abroad.

"Mac, what you did for those men in the museum will save their lives. They have a level of professional training and skill they would never have had without you. Those men are a disciplined fighting force and that will be passed down. You made a difference," he said, his voice low but urgent.

"I guess it's all I can hope for," I said.

He drew circles on my palm, each movement of his finger went in a direct line to my cock, making me shift in my seat. "Did you mean what you said in the hospital? About being too old to fight?"

I closed my fingers over his to stop him moving them. "Yes. I don't have the heart for it, the hunger. I'm tired of the death, the violence, the speed with which everything happens. The decisions. Other than the fights we had to protect the museum, life in the DRC had been quiet for me."

"But you can't go back?" half statement, half question.

I shook my head. "Apparently, I'm gay."

He chuckled and we kissed. "Then we live somewhere we are accepted."

"That excludes a lot of the world," I said.

"How about sheep farming in Australia?" he asked.

"You know much about sheep?"

"What's to know? It can't be that hard, they're everywhere in Wales." It's where I grew up even if I didn't have the accent.

I flicked the end of his nose. "Cheeky bastard. And you have a career, Jacob."

He shrugged. "Don't want to do it any more, not without you."

"I can live in Hereford."

He snorted. "Yeah, you'd go down a storm with the other Regiment wives and girlfriends."

A good point and realistically how the hell would I survive in Hereford? Not like the city needed any more ex-Regiment guys hanging about being useless on civvy street.

"We talked about running a bar once," I said, thinking back to our previous lives.

He lay his head on my shoulder. "Lot of work."

"Lot of late nights."

"Early mornings…"

"Tearoom on the Devon coast?" I suggested.

He laughed. "Cream teas to old dears who will love us because we're the only gays in the village?"

"Bacon sandwiches and cream teas."

Jacob sighed. "We're never going to have the money to buy somewhere in Devon."

I kissed the top of his head. "We'll figure something out. Let's find the Dr Frankenstein of the insect world and maybe something will fall into place afterwards."

"I love you, I missed you every day and I'm sorry I fucked up."

"It's okay and I love you as well," I whispered.

As he slept again, leaning into me, one leg thrown over my thigh and our hands joined I couldn't help but marvel at how things had changed in the last week. I'd lost the world I'd created in the DRC, nothing could change that, and I might not like the homophobia, but I couldn't fight it. However, the things I'd found in exchange were nothing short of miraculous. This physical intimacy, at my age, electrified every fibre in my body. It terrified me but a thousand other words I'd need to describe its beauty flowed through and around me. The shadows of fear about my sexuality, which I'd been living with for so long, had diminished to the point of utter insignificance under the glare of Jacob's desire. I held the future in my hands, one I hardly dared to dream could be real.

The only obstacle to my future lay in saving the Bug Lady from the North Koreans. There would be guns, possibly bombs, and doubtless more dead bodies, but in all this I had one driving force, protect Jacob. It might seem daft, he could do his job after all, but I really wanted us to have a future together and getting us through unharmed had to be high on my list of priorities.

I'd seen it, several times, during my service in the army. A married man who has a child is suddenly unable to go into the field the way he used to and second guesses himself to the point he becomes dangerous. I'd never understood, not really. I'd never had to care for someone. I just followed orders, did the best I could, tried to save those in my squad but it was me, the unmarried man with no family, who went on point most often. I had nothing to lose.

Now though, with Jacob's pulse beating against my thumb where I rubbed his wrist and his heat soaking into my tired body, I knew I had the world to lose and the fear in my guts made it hard to breathe.

Every covert operation in the Regiment layered fear under the determination every soldier had to get the job done. I'd stared it down more than once. That bowel loosening, sweat inducing, foul tasting sense of terror, but this fear was different. An insidious whispering of all the bad shit I'd ever seen inflicted onto a human being could be done to *my Jacob*. How the hell was I supposed to function with this terror gripping my heart and guts?

"I have no fucking idea," I whispered aloud and tried to find some sleep.

"THIS LOOKS LIKE AN APOCALYPSE just happened and no one thought to mention it to the people who live here," Jacob said from the back of the minivan we'd hired at the airport.

Though minivan made you think of children and school runs with perky gym bunny mums. This van looked, and smelt, like it had been reborn after an argument with a scrap yard about where it belonged. The van decided it shouldn't be scrapped. The rest of the world outside Vladivostok would have condemned it to a dignified death. Here it blended right in, but maybe that was because it was hard to see through the fog of pollution shrouding the Soviet city.

"It's nicer further north, the modern Russia is less…" Brant waved a hand at the brutal Soviet world outside.

Once upon a time there'd been a fishing village here belonging to the Chinese Empire, now the Russian Federation had finished what the Soviet Union had started. The place was an industrial warzone. There might well be beauty in it somewhere, but I couldn't see it as I drove. Even the poorest quarters of Kinshasa had more green. There were huge Soviet housing blocks, admittedly with space between them, but nothing green had the good grace to make its presence known. Maybe it was the time of year but from the smell of the air I doubted it.

"I've booked us into the Zhemchuzhina," Lydia said.

"Easy for you to say," I muttered. Her Russian was considerably better than mine.

She ignored me. "It's only three stars but gets good reviews."

"Trip Advisor?" Jacob asked. "I only like to stay if it gets good reviews."

"Idiot," she said. "I'm afraid we've booked in as couples and definitely the more traditional kind."

"I always wondered what it would be like to be married," I said.

"Play your cards right and you'll find out," Jacob announced from the back.

The van jerked in a way that made the steering column shudder in my hands as I stared in the rear-view mirror. Jacob laughed. "You look like you're going to pass out."

"Lance Corporal!" Brant barked. "Not the time."

"Sorry, ma'am."

"If you're going to propose you do it properly. Trust me, my husband fucked it up and I've never let him forget it," she admitted.

"What happened?" Lydia asked.

"Need to know, Sergeant, need to know."

Something electric and modern beeped in the back. "I have a location for the Bug Lady," Lydia said.

"Please stop calling her that," Brant pleaded. "Her name is Dilras Begum and she is the leading academic in her field."

"Yes, ma'am," replied Lydia, distracted by her phone. "The Leer jet has just entered Russian airspace and requested to land at Vladivostok airport in 3 hours."

I glanced in the rear-view mirror at Lydia. "You've hacked the local airport control panel, haven't you?"

Lydia grinned. "I can neither confirm nor deny such an event might have taken place and it wasn't me, governor."

"We have 3 hours to come up with a plan and weapons," Brant said. "We'll also need another vehicle and I need to send a report to Whitehall about where we are with the mission."

"Is that wise, ma'am? We don't know who to trust and if Room 39 do have Ms Begum then we shouldn't alert them to our presence," Jacob said.

"There are still people I trust at MI6, Lance Corporal. Though you are right, we should be cautious, as much as it pains me to say so." She rubbed her eyes and I studied her for a moment while we waited for the lights to change on a junction. Elizabeth Brant had a way of wearing her responsibilities well. They didn't bow her shoulders or make her feet heavy but right now you could see it dragging at her heart and soul. Fighting people you should be able to trust, figuring out the movements of an unseen enemy couldn't be easy for her, and it wasn't a task I ever wanted.

"I have a weapons' stash we can use," Lydia said.

"I take it we'll be owing Aria some more favours?" Brant asked with weary acceptance.

"Money this time, ma'am. The unfortunate truth is, she's better at her job."

"She's not better at her job, Sergeant, she's merely able to sidestep all the rules and laws we have to abide by. A fact I'm rather grateful for right now," Brant said.

"So, we'll get another vehicle and find the weapons?" Jacob clarified.

"You and Lydia can do that, I need Mac with me for the moment," Brant said.

I glanced at Jacob who shrugged. The thought of us separating made the nest of worms in my guts stir like an insecure teenager, but needs must, and we had to stop Bug Lady from reaching North Korea.

When we reached the hotel, we checked in, swapped room keys so Jacob and I were sharing, Brant and Lydia in the room next door. We all showered and changed, still maintaining practical but civilian clothing, and reconvened in Brant's room. Jacob left with Lydia, promising to find a car capable of more energetic driving than the minivan.

20

"WE NEED A PLAN, MAC," Brant said when the others left.

I glanced at the door. "Shouldn't they be involved?"

"We have more experience and we have too few resources to waste time." She had a point.

Sitting side by side Brant pulled up the images of the airport and surrounding roads. "The Leer is due in…" she checked her watch, "two hours thirty-nine minutes. Suggestions, Sergeant?"

I studied the map. "How are they going to get her out of Russia and into North Korea? There's the access using the Friendship railway bridge, over the Tumen River. That's likely to be monitored too closely and the risk of moving an uncooperative female safely is too high. They could put her in a boat and motor over the river but again, too visible, even at night and if they know we're after her then time is against them. They aren't going to want to test two borders by going further north-west into Russia, crossing into China and then down into the Korean peninsula." I pulled the satellite imagery out so we could look at the wider geography of the region. "Coming from South Korea would be beyond stupid. We all have too many eyes-on for them to get away with that."

Brant moved the image around and narrowed it back onto our current location. "There are cargo holds, Sergeant. Room 39 have a great many resources. Smuggling goods is what they do."

"I just don't think they'll have the time to organise it well. I think they're going to want her out of reach fast. If the Russians or Chinese catch wind of what they're up to they'll lose Ms Begum. I don't think either of their allies will want them to have the kind of skills she's able to give them."

"It's not like they can drive her across," Brant said.

A thought hit me. “Bugger, of course. There’s only one sure-fire way of moving her quickly and with relative ease. A helicopter, ma’am. If they have a Leer jet, they have a hel.”

“Why would they leave the airport if they have a hel?” Brant asked. “And if they don’t leave the airport, we can’t get to her. We’re good, Mac, but I don’t want to start a war with Russia because we’ve had live contact in an airport.”

“They have to leave the airport because of flight plans. It’s much harder to track a hel that’s not going to need air traffic control’s permission to take off. They stay low, close to the ground, then the sea and job done, she vanishes into a black hole we’ll never get her out of, and the world will have to start worrying about weaponised bugs on top of everything else.”

Brant smiled. “I like your thinking. We need to find local hel-pads.”

“And flat spaces that could be plausibly used.”

The next few minutes consisted of much muttering and making notes on a pad. When we finished our virtual tour of the city, we had a long list. “Shit,” I muttered. “We can’t cover this.”

“No, we can’t. We have to narrow down the choices,” Brant said.

“Okay, assuming we are right, and they’ll be taking her out of the airport, we have limited access roads to cover.”

“But if we sanction an operation anywhere nearby the Russians will not be reasonable.”

“Why?” I asked. “What have you done to piss them off so much?”

Brant shrugged. “Luke and Sam blew up and killed some high-level Russian mafia and it’s caused a bit of a political shit storm.”

I chuckled. “I liked Luke, he’s a good man. I’m glad he’s happy.”

“There will be wedding bells soon, I have no doubt,” Brant said. “It’s been a long road for them, but they finally have their collective shit together. Talking of which…” She studied me for a long time making me fidget.

I scowled, unused to talking about feelings and relationships, especially with my commanding officer, but Brant ran a tight crew and at least some of her job was pastoral care. The words struggled to come together to describe what I had with the man I loved, but I found them – kind of.

“Jacob and I are… We’re doing okay. There are some issues, we’ve both made mistakes thanks to Clark but it’s nothing we can’t iron out.”

"And your future together?"

I shrugged. "Don't know. I don't want to return to the Regiment, even if they would accept me again. I don't think Jacob needs it either. So we're currently debating the rights and wrongs of running a tearoom in Devon."

Brant laughed. "Yeah, I can see that working for all of 5 minutes. What if I offered you both a job with Unit 12?"

"Considering Jacob's PTSD, I'm not sure that's a good idea, ma'am."

"It is if he promises to attend regular therapy sessions to work through the problems. Let's face it, Mac, he's going to need them regardless of where he works. There are many benefits to working for me. More autonomy, less oversight. More toys to play with and some challenging work environments."

"Like blowing shit up in Russia you mean? That kind of challenging?" I couldn't help but find this amusing, she sounded like a recruitment demon for the devil.

"Just like that, Sergeant. More pay. Better health care. Better pension."

"If we live long enough to retire."

"Fair point. Well, you have my sales pitch such as it is, so have a think about it."

"I will, ma'am and thank you. It means more than you can know that you trust me with this offer."

I meant it as well. To be offered a chance to return to the action? The thought drew me like a moth to the moon. I couldn't help it, despite my words to Jacob, I still craved the fight. The challenges and demands, the chance to use all the training I'd been given over the years for someone like Brant and Unit 12, it spelt nothing short of temptation.

"Back to our task, Sergeant before the others arrive."

We bent our heads over the laptop and studied the access roads, the possible deviations and timings. By the time we'd finished we had a plan and the others had returned. Jacob looked very pleased with himself.

"What have you done?" I asked.

"Got new toys," he announced. "I like this Aria, she knows her guns."

I rolled my eyes at him. "I'm so pleased for you."

"Wish we had time to practice with them though. Do we have a plan?" he asked, handing me a burger and bag of chips.

"We do," I said, around a mouthful of food.

Brant, eating with a little more delicacy than I managed, explained the plan in detail. "There are a limited number of access roads to the international airport on the outskirts of the city." She indicated the map. "They could take several out of the airport providing privacy but only one brings them towards the city and we are surmising they will want to move Ms Begum as swiftly and quietly as possible."

Jacob pointed to the main motorway access to the airport. "So they'll be using the Doroga V Aeroport road?" His Russian was worse than mine.

"Yes. I believe so."

I said, "We don't want to engage the enemy too close to the airport, it'll make life complicated with the authorities but there's a great location here for a staged assault." I pointed to a small road and an industrial area right before the motorway broke off into two major arteries, neither of which we could control with ease.

"We'll be on the wrong side of the motorway," Jacob pointed out.

"Yes, that's a bit of a problem unless you have a small amount of C4 tucked away," I admitted.

"Just as well I'm a good boy scout then," he said with a wiggle of his eyebrows.

"We blow the charge, drive through the barrier, take out the vehicle, remove Ms Begum and be on our way," Brant said. "We return to the city because that's the easiest way to lose the Koreans and any Russian interference. When things quieten down a little we slip out of the city and head to Japan, a simple diversion that should keep them guessing."

"There aren't too many variables," Lydia said. "It's just making certain we have the correct vehicle targeted."

"That will be your job, Sergeant. I need you to get into the airport's CCTV while we're on the road. It's going to take at least 45 minutes to reach the target location."

We stuffed the rest of the food down our necks and drank the soda. The change in everyone's demeanour became pronounced. We were no longer travelling; we were about to engage the enemy and it showed in the quiet but certain movements as we set about our tasks. Jacob took me downstairs and opened the boot of the white Hyundai Santa Fe he'd liberated.

"It's all Russian," he said. "But it's good."

Many of these weapons I'd only read about and never used. The heavy, but awesome looking, Stechkin OTs-38 silent revolver might only carry five rounds, but it really did do the job it was designed for, shooting people with minimal noise. We also had the mythical, NRS-2 which was a knife that contained a single round in the handle and was also noiseless according to the specs. He'd lifted a Vityaz-SN submachine gun and the most exciting toy – a Saiga-12 automatic shotgun. My mouth watered and my fingers itched to be able to play. Childish glee made me want to clap my hands. There were a couple of bolt-action sniper rifles for long range work as well.

"I like this Aria woman," I said.

"So does Lydia apparently." Jacob closed the boot. "We've a small amount of C4 and detonators as well. You happy with the plan?"

"Shouldn't I be?" I asked.

He shrugged. "Collateral damage, Mac. A lot of civilians use that road."

He glanced at me but couldn't hold my gaze for very long and we both remembered the sensation of blood, brain matter and skull against our skin in Delta's room at the club. I gripped his shoulder and forced him to make eye contact. "What we do now we do for the greater good and we will use the minimum amount of force necessary. A few crashed vehicles I can live with. If Lydia can tap into their road cameras, we might even have real time int that can help up minimise the potential for civilian casualties."

He nodded.

I wanted to tell him about Brant's job offer but I needed time to think about the possibilities before I decided what I wanted to do about it. I also needed to consider the impact on Jacob. His mental health had to be a priority. One of the things I'd learned though, since leaving the army, was a simple one – you might leave the army, but it never left you. I still woke with the larks most days, tabbed miles to keep fit, and maintained a high level of awareness looking for potential threats. I couldn't stop being an operator just because I had no government pointing me at a target and I couldn't be a merc.

I closed the boot of the suburban four-wheel drive and leaned against the back. "We need to keep the chaos to a minimum. The less chaos, the less chance for casualties and less sleep we'll lose in the future."

Jacob put his boot on the bumper near my thigh, his amber eyes were bright but calm. "I like to think I'm not trigger-happy, Mac, but when I'm focused on a target it's becoming harder to see the good guys and make the right call. I just don't seem to know who to trust anymore."

"Seeing women murdering those young men is going to skew your world view, alter your perspective. If you find yourself reliving that moment in your dreams, both awake and asleep you're going to have problems distinguishing right from wrong, good from bad. Then you begin justifying the decisions you've made, especially the bad ones, because you have to be the white knight, the good guy. These things place too much weight on your shoulders when they are already under too much pressure." I watched my words sink into him.

He nodded but said, "We should go."

Letting him drop the introspection worried me but I had to maintain the mission's objective, saving Dilras Begum. Saving Jacob would be a more long-term project. When we returned to the operations post upstairs Brant and Lydia were both in dark clothing holding day-sacks. I grabbed my black coat and we left the OP.

I drove through the city, while Jacob prepared the small amounts of C4 we'd need to blow the hole in the barrier. From the satellite imagery we knew that it was a simple double thickness crash barrier, used the world over, separating the lanes of traffic. By the time we reached the site the sun would be setting, local time 20:13 and it would help afford us some cover. Jacob also found two high-vis vests in the car, so we could mask our movements as highway staff, though it would be risky without hard hats.

We now had 142 minutes to reach our destination and prepare for the tactical assault on a moving vehicle. It should take 42 minutes to reach our target location providing we didn't hit traffic on the A-370 or they didn't close the bridge because of high winds. That would leave us with 1 hour and 20 minutes to set the charges, monitor traffic and check our location thoroughly. In theory we had plenty of time.

While I drove, I ran through the SOP, standard operating procedure, for stopping a moving vehicle in traffic or pursuing a hostile vehicle in traffic. I'd done the relevant courses back in the day, but hadn't used those skills in years, unless you counted dodging the traffic in Kinshasa practice.

"Which of us is the most qualified for tactical driving?" I asked the others in the car.

"It's been too long since I did the courses," Brant admitted.

"I've never done close protection training so haven't done the defensive driving courses," Lydia said.

I glanced at Jacob. "I can't be trusted to make the right decisions, Mac." A difficult admission in front of his senior officer. Brant chose to remain silent.

"Me then," I said. "Fair enough, though I'm rusty." I continued to run through scenarios, seeing them as clearly as possible in my head to help me prepare a sequence of decisions in advance of contact. Of course, plans always went to shit once you'd made contact with the target but having a plan never hurt. It certainly helped the nerves that built up during the preceding hours to a possible live fire event.

21

WE MADE GOOD TIME AND when I pulled into the small industrial car park there were no other vehicles in sight other than the ones needed for work. I parked behind a large hedge of trees, on a secondary road, hiding us from the dual carriageway. Jacob and I did a sweep of the area, looking for potential problems but with it being a Saturday evening the site was empty. With rain on the way, light was low and this far from the south of the city there were enough trees and plants to make the place look more like England than I'd been privy to for the last 3 years. It made me homesick for the first time in all those years and I wondered if I'd be able to go back now Clark was dead. Could Brant really clear my name and keep Clark's bosses from depriving me of life outside prison or worse?

"Time to set the charges," Jacob said, cutting off my thoughts.

"High-vis jackets?" I asked.

Jacob looked at the road, checked the height of the sun, and shook his head. "No, we do it dark and hope none of the local police drive past."

We divvied up the charges and crossed the carriageway. I took right, Jacob took left and we placed the charges close to the ground to blow the uprights holding the bars in place. They should just topple over because we also placed a little either end of the section we needed to remove. With the detonators in place we scooted back to the verge and returned to the car.

I could hear Lydia cursing through the open window. "Problem?"

Her dark eyes shot to mine and I took a step back, hoping she didn't reach for the pistol she'd taken from the back of the car. "Fucking Windows update," she growled.

I laughed, which apparently didn't help and backed off until the swearing stopped. "Why have you got Windows on there?"

"Because I didn't uninstall it and the fucking system is still one of the most dependable out there. Right," she said, returning to professional soldier mode, "I'm into the airport's CCTV and I have their comms. Jesus, their jargon is worse than ours." She pressed a finger against her ear piece as if it would help her concentrate.

Jacob and I paced, trying not to explode with the building tension. Until he stopped and looked at me. "I just realised something."

"What's that?" I asked distracted by watching a bird of prey making the most of the twilight over the hedgerow.

"If we die doing this, or one of us does, we die not having had full sex. I think we need to do something about that."

I looked at him now, the bird forgotten. "Are you planning on fucking here and now? I think the women might object."

Jacob grinned. "Pretty sure Lydia would give us scores out of ten."

"Yeah, don't think the colonel would approve though."

He walked up to me, that vivid energy and coiled violence turned to a predator bent on his prey. The gathering darkness and our distance from the vehicle hid our movements from the others. He pressed against me, looking up a little because of our height difference and I gazed into the hungry amber eyes.

"Love you," he murmured against my lips.

I took hold of the webbing vest covering his black shirt and pulled him even closer. Our lips met and the kiss weakened my knees. His hands crept to my backside and those devious fingers dug into the meat of the muscle.

When I let him up for air, he swayed back a little, dazed, eyes wide. "Damn you're hot."

I couldn't help the satisfied grin and smug contentment. "We aren't going to die and when this is over you are going to help me learn exactly what 'full sex' means between us."

Jacob pressed his right hand against the bulge in his pants. "Yeah, that sounds like a plan. You, me, bottle of lube and lots of time." He huffed out a short sharp breath. "Fuck, just the thought of that perfect cock inside me is enough to make me –"

"Gentlemen, front and centre," Brant called from the car.

Jacob groaned and I chuckled enjoying the pride swelling my chest. I made a younger man weak for me – that's an ego stroke. We reached the car and Lydia climbed out with the laptop in her hand.

She set it up on the bonnet. "The Leer jet has landed, and they've come out of the airport on diplomatic plates, South Korean ones the cheeky bastards. They're in two large black Mercedes with tinted windows." She suddenly looked up at us all. "The people of North Korea are starving because of a harvest failure – again – and these pricks are running around the world in Leer jets, with helicopters and luxury vehicles. I fucking hate this world sometimes. Sorry. I just…" she finished her mini rant off with a huff.

"We all feel the same, Sergeant," Brant told her. "It never gets any easier."

Lydia rubbed her face. "Yeah, I know."

"How long before they reach us? Do we know which vehicle Ms Begum is in?" I asked.

"Rear vehicle," Lydia said. "Several metal containers were loaded into the first one, I'm guessing Room 39 are moving something back to their paymasters but I don't know what because they didn't register a cargo manifest."

"So we take the rear vehicle and prepare for the first one to return to back up their comrades," Jacob said.

"Seems sensible," I said. "I don't want to take on both vehicles if we don't have to, they're going to be heavily armed. We'll risk too many civilians if we go in heavy-handed and take on both."

"From what I can see there are six men and one woman, three in each car," Lydia said. "They might change that formation or pick up more people between the airport and here, I can't find any more traffic cameras to hijack until the one that's 50 metres east of our current location. My guess is they'll stick to the speed limit. Everything I've watched them do has been within the law. They are not going to draw attention to themselves."

"ETA?" Brant asked.

Lydia checked her watch. "Eighteen minutes."

"Take your places, gentlemen. We'll be offering covering fire from either side of the junction."

Jacob and I nodded to each other. With the cloud cover it was almost full dark now, so we'd be hard to spot. We took the assault rifles and shotguns with us, checked the traffic and hoofed it over the road. Brant and Lydia would blow the charges and we'd rise out of the ditch, thankfully dry, to take the occupants of the car.

Jacob and I hunkered down. "I hate waiting," he muttered.

"You've never had any patience," I said, flattening a thistle too close to my head with my forearm.

"It's the worst part of any operation," he grumbled.

I glanced at him. "Why?" I asked. We'd been friends for a long time but as lovers I needed to learn about him anew.

In the dark, with the occasional set of headlights sweeping over us, I caught his shrug. "I dunno really. Most of soldiering is waiting, even the training we do is an active waiting, all we really want is to get into the field."

"How are you going to handle the lack of action if you leave the Regiment?" I asked.

"I won't need to be active, so I guess I'll get used to it. You worried I won't cope with civilian life? Think I might get bored and wander off?" His eyes were dark now with the lack of light and I couldn't see his expression. It made me uneasy.

"I wasn't until you mentioned it," I said. "But civilian life is one hell of an adjustment. It's not a smooth transition." I remembered how violent I'd become while living in Spain. I thought the beer and sun, and the easy-going lifestyle would smooth out my sudden departure from active service. It hadn't worked very well.

"You'll be there to help," he said, placing more faith in me than I deserved.

"Of course I'll be there, but you might want to consider whether you're ready to leave the action behind."

He held still for long seconds. "You are though, aren't you?"

"I'm not talking about me. And yes, I'm ready, more than ready in some ways, but I never considered returning to soldiering after being thrown out of the Regiment. They even drove me out of the country, so the job in Kinshasa, as a trainer, suited me."

"You certain you can't go back?" he asked. "I mean, I know Danny isn't very pleased with the whole gay thing but… Well, you sure it's not worth talking him around?"

"Even if I manage to talk him around, I can't talk the rest of the country around," I said.

"Doesn't answer the original question though, Mac. Are you willing to return to action?" he asked.

"Brant's offered us a job, as one of her teams in Unit 12." I admitted this quietly because I still wasn't sure it was a good idea.

Jacob twisted so he could look at me properly, taking his attention away from the road. "Really?"

I nodded. "Yep. Better pay, better general conditions when we're not in the field, better pension if we live long enough to claim it."

"Cool."

The comms unit in my ear crackled to life. "Echo One."

"Receiving, Zero."

"Target 50 metres out and counting. Estimated speed, 60 kmph."

"Ready?" I asked Jacob. We both pulled up our shemaghs to hide our faces and pulled down the woolly hats. Ski masks would be better, but we hadn't found any so this would do for disguises.

Jacob's grin reached his eyes and it gave me all the answers I needed to several questions buzzing in my mind. He still lived for this and I couldn't blame him.

I tapped my throat mic into life. "Moving to intercept point."

"Roger that, Echo One. Detonation in 3, 2…"

Jacob and I rose from the ground but kept our heads turned away and eyes closed to preserve our night sight. The blast made the ground shiver and we both heard the metal screech even above the noise of the explosion. The squeal of tyres and crunch of metal made us run to the road. We both carried our sidearms in to the conflict as the large calibre rounds of the other weapons had more chance of hitting civilians at such close quarters. The SAS developed and specialised the double tap to take down terrorists in confined spaces with a lot of civilians in the mix. We practiced it above all other things, so our urban warfare remained true to our core beliefs – preserve life wherever possible.

By the time we reached the Mercedes it had become entangled in the crash barrier. The other traffic on the dual carriageway had ground to a halt with blaring horns. I scooted around a small Toyota, banging a hand on the bonnet to keep the people trying to leave the car safely inside. Our target vehicle, now at a standstill at almost 90 degrees to the road and crossing both lanes, popped its doors.

“Contact,” Jacob shouted, coming in from my left and loosing three rounds. The first man went down, head spraying a mist of red against the window of the passenger side window, easy to see in the lights. Yellow hazard lights flashed out of beat with each other as people screamed and tried to drive through or away from the explosion of violence.

The driver and other passenger exited the vehicle. I saw the lead Merc screech to a halt, maybe 75 metres ahead of us. Three men debussed from it and lifted weapons in our direction. Jacob, having taken a little longer to move around the cars so he had a better angle, holstered his sidearm and raised the assault rifle. He loosed off rounds and took down one of the men further ahead.

I engaged the other two, moving with a smoothness reminiscent of my youth, and dispatched one as if I were in the kill house at Hereford performing one of the endless practice scenarios. I heard the louder *ca-cack* of Jacob’s rifle against the smaller *pop-pop* of my side arm. The final man I needed to take down confused me for a moment when he threw his gun down and raced at me.

Fighting anyone open handed who worked for the secret service in Korea seemed like a really bad idea. I wouldn’t stand a chance in hand-to-hand combat. They would all be trained martial artists in skills I couldn’t hope to match. At times like this it paid to have a lack of ego. I changed magazines with ease and let two shots go as the man covered the distance between us. Hitting a moving target, even at 10 metres isn’t always a guarantee and the first one missed due to me being unfamiliar with the gun I carried. The second winged him but he wasn’t slowing down, despite twisting to one side.

I took a better stance. Three metres. The man had a knife in each hand. He wanted to cut me to shreds. Fuck. I fired again, hitting the centre body mass and he dropped. Blood hit me from the blowback of the penetration. I ignored him and ran to the vehicle.

22

WITH THE DOOR OPEN I approached with care, my sidearm close to my chest, muzzle pointing down. "Come out with your hands above your head," I yelled. "Echo Two, sitrep."

"Echo Two clear, alternative vehicle leaving the scene, one tango down."

"Understood, Echo Two." I didn't like the silence coming from the interior of the Mercedes. "I am armed, please remain calm. No sudden movements." From the rear of the vehicle I approached, moved into position to fire if necessary and looked into the car.

Blood covered the cream leather interior from the first man down. A small woman now huddled in the back, silent because of the gag in her mouth and hands zipped tied in front of her.

"Do you understand me?" I asked.

She looked at me with large brown eyes, cast in the sickly glow of the car's interior light.

"Nod if you understand me."

She nodded.

"Are you alone?"

She nodded.

"Are you Dilras Begum?"

She nodded.

"We are the British Security Service, you understand? We are here to help you. I am going to reach inside the vehicle and help you exit into our custody. Please do not panic you are perfectly safe," I said, maintaining eye contact and explaining my movements so she could anticipate me, giving her a sense of control. It always helped hostages if you gave them back the illusion of control in a combat scenario. They tended to calm down a lot faster.

I held out my left hand, the right still holding my sidearm and she slid closer to me. She was younger than I expected, her personnel photo didn't do her justice despite her obvious fear and exhaustion. The moment I had her forearm in my hand I pulled her through the car and out into the night. Jacob had now returned to cover our retreat even as sirens wailed in the background.

We took an elbow each and left the road, the other carriageway also a standstill because of the chaos. Brant and Lydia left their positions. We hadn't needed covering fire, so no one knew they'd been present. I should imagine there'd be cell phones taking video but with our faces covered we'd be anonymous.

Within 30 seconds we'd recovered our vehicle, put Ms Begum between Brant and Lydia in the back and I drove smoothly, with my headlights off, down the road we'd parked in so we could take back roads to the A188 and return to the city. We left the scene with no one the wiser, at least for the moment. Providing no one heard us speaking English we should be free and clear of the authorities.

Keeping a watch on the rear-view mirror for any signs of pursuit I watched Brant remove the tape and the wad of fabric in Ms Begum's mouth. Lydia cut her hands free and handed the small woman a bottle of water. She took a long drink, replaced the cap and lunged out of her seat to hit me with the water bottle – repeatedly.

I braked hard and the vehicle juddered to a halt, the ABS kicking in.

"What the fuck?" Jacob snarled, snatching the bottle out of her hand, while Brant and Lydia sat on her. I reached up and switched on the interior light.

"You mother-fucking idiots. You total blithering fools. You nincompoops." A long tirade of what sounded like Hindi burst out of her. Jacob and I twisted in our seats to figure out what the hell was going on.

Brant couldn't get the woman to calm down. Jacob opted for the direct approach, he drew his sidearm and pressed it to her throat. "Shut up," he ordered.

Her eyes widened. I had to admit if he looked at me like that, I'd have shut the fuck up as well.

"Alright, that's enough," I said, placing a hand on the barrel of the pistol and pushing it down. "What seems to be the problem, Ms Begum?"

"I'll tell you what the problem is, you overgrown fucking ape, you left my bugs behind in the other car. Who the hell are you people?" Her rage filled the vehicle. Don't get me wrong, I wasn't expecting a medal for our action over the last few days but a 'thank you for risking your life to save mine' might be nice.

"We work for the Security Intelligence Service, Unit 12," Brant said. "This is Sergeant Greenbrook, Lance Corporal Hayes and Sergeant Macalister. I am Colonel Elizabeth Brant. The SAS were supposed to retrieve you from the Congo but didn't make it, so we stepped in. Why are you talking about bugs? We know why you were in the Congo. We know about Porton Down and your research."

The Bug Lady snapped her mouth shut and glared for several seconds. I could almost see the wheels racing as she built up another head of steam. "When they took down my security detail and my lab technicians they didn't just take me, they took my research. The hard drives. They also took several of the containers carrying my research." None of us had a clue what she was talking about. In frustration at our lack of understanding she almost shouted, "They took my mosquitoes. They have the weaponised mosquitoes in that car! I wasn't taken by Boko Haram. The men who came to the camp were professional soldiers made to look like Islamists."

Silence in the car.

"Maybe you should start at the beginning," the colonel said after a lengthy interval filled with Begum's heavy breaths.

Tears welled in the big brown eyes and they were dramatic enough to make Jacob and I back off. "I can't, I just have to get my bugs."

"I fucking knew it," Jacob said. "Anyone working with bugs is a crazy person. She's a bug lady." He shuddered.

"Why are these insects so important to you?" asked Brant. "If they get out can they really do that much damage?"

"They are vectors, carriers of diseases we're working on, partly to find cures in case anyone else is doing the same thing, but also so we can dominate the market. It's a financial advantage to have the best weapons."

"I don't understand," I confessed.

Begum looked at me. "We've been weaponising insects since the time of the Greeks. Beehives and wasp nests would be catapulted over city walls. Maggot infested pig corpses, thing like that. The Second World War saw an explosion in this research, most of it done by Japan on the Chinese, the

Germans and strangely the Canadians. Everything that can bite or sting a human has been experimented on and used. Even bugs that can destroy crops can be weaponised. I have weaponised the malaria carrying Anopheles genus mosquito to carry the pneumonic plague and I was in the Congo to be close to the source of both pathogens and any local knowledge that might be in the jungle so we can help find a cure for any of these potential diseases. If we are doing it, so are our enemies and we have to be prepared. You must go get my bugs because if they end up in North Korea, they won't need me to turn the world into a zombie fucking apocalypse film they'll have the bugs ready to go."

"You put the Black Death into a mosquito rather than a flea? For money?" Jacob asked. "Because the government told you to?"

"Essentially, yes. It's a bit more complicated –"

"Like we don't have enough problems in the fucking world," he snarled. "We now have to fight insect wars as well. Fuck me."

I put the car back into gear and drove through the quiet suburban area of the sprawling city. This suburb didn't consist of Soviet style housing blocks, modern housing estates were the order of the day and in the distance, I could see the mountains, a darker black against the night sky.

"Do you know how they were planning on taking you into Korea?" asked Brant.

Begum shook her head. "I'm sorry. They only spoke in English to give me orders. They gagged me when I tried to call for help at the airport. I've been fighting for so long I don't know how to stop." She hiccupped and I watched her in the mirror as the defence mechanisms began to crumble. "They shot my security team and took me from the jungle. Murdered the staff I'd employed locally and raped the women before cutting off their hands."

Jacob glanced at me and we both faced front. Another of those conversations Lydia and Brant needed to deal with and now was not the time. We needed int.

Brant took Begum's hand. "Can I call you Dilras, Ms Begum?"

I concentrated on the road and Lydia's quiet instructions from behind my seat whenever we reached a junction.

"You've been through an experience none of us can imagine and survived. Your strength is incredible, Dilras. I just need you to hold onto it a bit longer and get us where we need to go. Do you know how they were planning on getting you out? Anything you might have picked up could give us a clue. We think they'll use a hel – sorry – helicopter but I need to know where from. We have a choice of three sites we've located. We made plans in case we failed to take you on the road." Brant had Dilras's hand in hers and stroked it carefully. Her wrists were chafed and bloody.

I concentrated on the road. The marks I could see, peeking out of clean but ill-sitting clothing, made my heart burn. The sad reality of my job meant I saw this every time we left Hereford and sometimes among the women my workmates called wives – violence. I always thought it was normal for a straight man to feel angry about violence against those weaker than themselves, but it turned out gay men raged at the same injustices. Protecting people from others had been hard-wired into me and the army used that innate need to protect, honing it, polishing it, firing it back out into the world to create havoc among the enemies who would hurt those people I wanted to defend.

Protecting Jacob and the others in the car, then the world outside, drove me ever onwards. If I stopped being that man what would I be? Even after leaving the Regiment I hadn't found any sense of peace until I rocked up in Kinshasa and began training my team. What happened to a person when they were denied the one thing their soul craved? I glanced at Jacob – I knew exactly what happened when someone was denied their soul's duty or love, they turned into shadows and drifted through life until they had nothing left. That would have been me if Jacob hadn't returned to drag me out of the shadows.

"They spoke in Korean most of the time," Dilras said in a much quieter voice. "But one man, he would speak with people in English, sometimes Russian. I think he ordered a helicopter to pick us up from the top of a building near Nikolai's Triumphal Arch?"

Lydia typed with a preternatural speed. "There's a car park nearby with a helipad on the top. It directly overlooks the bay. From there it's a straight run down to the Russian border with North Korea. If we don't stop that hel before it takes off, we're fucked. There's just nothing we can do except get in touch with the American base in Japan and see if they'll lend us a Hellfire missile or two."

"Not really an option, Sergeant," Brant muttered. "You've done well, Dilras. This will be over soon, I promise."

I glanced at Jacob again and he shrugged with one shoulder, the other probably painful after the firefight. How was this going to be over soon? We'd never reach the damned hel in time. Unless…

"Lydia, can you fuck with the traffic systems in the city from your laptop?" I asked.

She glanced at me in the mirror. "You have no idea how a computer works do you?" she asked, the tartness in her voice making the heat rise in my cheeks.

"Um…"

"No," Jacob said. "He has no idea, but can you do it?"

She rubbed her face and picked up her phone, one speed dial later and we heard her talking to another woman. "Hi, honey… Yes, I know… Um… Yes… Well… Aria, please just listen for a second… Yeah, I know, I'm sorry." The ranting on the other end went on for a while. "Have you finished? Good. I need to stop a black Mercedes registered on Korean diplomatic plates from reaching its destination. We have to catch it up. Our registration is…" she reeled off a series of letters and numbers, I would never have remembered. "I can't do it from here I don't have the tech."

She covered the mouthpiece of the phone. "For your information, Sergeant Macalister, I can't actually perform miracles, I merely facilitate them."

"Yes, ma'am," I said.

Her attention returned to the phone. "Yep, that's the one. It just needs slowing down," a long pause, "well, yes, if you can hack the GPS that would be great. Send them all round the houses. We'll be there asap. Thank you. Yes, I promise I'll stay safe."

Lydia hung up. "They are going to find their route changing due to traffic congestion and we should find all our lights are green."

We all focused on the most important thing in our world – reaching the bugs.

23

EERIE, THAT'S ONLY WAY TO describe driving through Vladivostok with all the traffic lights going our way in the dark evening. When it happens by accident on a road you know well, it is a little victory against the bastard who bought all the traffic lights in the first place. This didn't feel like a victory, we were racing against insect Armageddon.

Many people might think that with a little bug spray the world would be saved from a mosquito carrying pneumonic plague, but I lived in the Congo. People died from insect borne diseases every day. Many of the people I knew lived with the long-term effects of micro-organisms racing through their blood and I knew many in Africa still thought the AIDs virus was an escaped genetic test from the seventies and allowed to sweep through the continent as a continued experiment. Even with modern pesticides the efforts to contain mosquitoes failed while animals and birds further up the food chain suffered side-effects from the use of chemicals.

I tightened my grip on the steering wheel as we neared our destination.

"Shit," Lydia muttered.

"What?" asked Jacob, twisting to watch her peering at the laptop screen.

"They're splitting up." She looked at Brant who cursed. "They've stopped moving, two of the men have left the vehicle with two more who arrived on the street. They have a silver case and they are carrying it away to the west."

"The train," Brant said. "They are going for the train. They know we've interfered with the traffic, so they are splitting their resources knowing we'll have to do the same. Unfortunately, they have more resources."

"There's enough virus and breeding pairs in either of those containers to be a problem," Dilras said in a subdued way which made me glance at her.

"Hey, this isn't your fault," I said.

The large brown eyes filled with tears, but she did battle with them and won. "Yes, it is. I've been so wrapped up in my work I didn't stop to consider the consequences of my actions. I know how Oppenheimer felt now."

I didn't have an argument for that one so let it lie, festering. Just considering the implications of Begum's work being as destructive as Oppenheimer's made me feel sick. She was right though; mosquitoes killed many more people than any nuclear weapon had or would.

"We need to split up as well," Brant stated. "Dilras, I'm going to need you to go to our hotel and wait I'm afraid. Jacob, Mac, you two go to the helipad and stop that hel from leaving. Lydia and I will stop the others before they reach the train."

"Boss, I don't think –"

"No, Jacob. You don't. I do. Your job is to follow my orders. Stop that hel at any cost. Do you understand, Lance Corporal?" She held his gaze and Jacob visibly relaxed as her orders soaked into his brain and the training took over.

There is a strange calm to it, when you have an order that you know is right, that you have to carry out, even if it might mean your death, but you know it's necessary.

Brant looked at me as well and I nodded, pulling over to the kerb. "At any cost, ma'am."

"Keep your comms channels open. Good luck, gentlemen and God's speed." Brant, Lydia and Dilras debussed.

Jacob and I were alone again. He guided me through the remaining tangle of streets, we rounded the last corner and he cursed.

"What's wrong?"

"I've just seen a very Korean looking pair in black on foot with a silver case being carried between them, enter the car park," he said, pointing. The sodium lighting of the city streets made it easy to track the targets.

"Do we get out and give chase or keep driving?" I asked.

"They'll be in the elevators by now. Keep driving."

I bumped the car over the kerb and down the pavement so I could reach the entrance to the car park. With a vast array of horns and shouts being hurled at us the car bounced back onto the road and into the black maw of the layered car park, cutting off a silver Jaguar in the process. I floored the accelerator and burst through the white and red striped barrier before slewing the car around the first corner, tyres squealing on the strange green surface of the path we were supposed to follow.

"Fuck, Mac. You know we're going the wrong way?" Jacob asked, hanging onto the 'Oh Shit' handle near his head.

"Yeah. Well. We need to stop the hel. Any idea how we're going to manage that?" I asked, trying to concentrate on the drive and the mission. "You got an RPG in the back there I don't know about?"

"I've half a dozen frags, but I don't think grenades are going to help unless you've suddenly developed a throwing arm to match an Aussie fast spin bowler." He spoke through gritted teeth as I took corner after corner at terrifying speeds. Well, I was scared anyway. Scared but exhilarated as I bore down on a small Japanese Yogo whose female owner yanked the vehicle out of my way with maybe 5mm to spare.

I released a small laugh.

"Not now, Mac."

"Sorry. I love driving."

"No, you love getting into trouble," Jacob said, trying to be cross with me and failing as he chuckled at the fifth layer of parked vehicles as they whizzed by. We hit the sixth floor and I lost traction for a moment, the back end sliding out of control on oil or something. It crashed into the nearest car, metal screaming in agony and the engine roaring as I pushed it forwards, the impact knocking my head against the side window. I blinked back the stars buzzing before my eyes and hit the seventh level.

"How fucking high is this thing?" I asked.

"We've another two to go," Jacob said. "The elevator must have made it by now."

"Fucking hell," I muttered and yanked on the handbrake to take a corner at even more speed. The noise we were creating in the solid concrete block was horrendous and I watched a mother grab two small children out of our path. Layer eight had access to the outside world and natural light filled the almost empty space. Due to the lack of other cars I managed to take the next ramp at 80kph. The moment we hit the straight, Jacob undid his seat belt, climbed into the rear of the vehicle and retrieved our assault rifles. I took the final ramp at a more sensible 50kph and we were at the top.

A Mil Mi-8, known as the HIP, originally of Soviet design but still made by the Russian Federation, sat on the helipad, rotors already turning too fast to see but the car pushed against the turbulence. In civilian colours it looked harmless enough, but we could see two men in black, with a silver case between them on the open door to the hel. The door slid closed as we watched, and the helicopter lifted from the tarmacked roof of the car park.

"Fuck," Jacob said.

"Get ready to jump," I told him.

"What?" he almost squeaked.

"We are overlooking the bay. We get this right we're going for a swim. Get ready with the rifle, Jacob. We're taking out the helicopter with the car," I stated like we were setting up a billiards rack. "By the time we line up a shot, they'll be out of range, we can't risk it."

"What the ever-loving fuck?" He stared at me as I gunned the engine, waiting for the moment I thought this would work.

Everything slowed down, as if I had all the time in the world to make the decision which might possibly kill one or both of us. The hel would take off and move over the sea. The car, with the accelerator jammed down would crash through the wall surrounding the edge of the car park and launch upwards, not downwards. That would work – right? It would go up and not down with enough speed?

"Fuck it," I muttered. "No choice."

"Mac?"

"Yeah."

"You're fucking nuts. Whatever happens I love you, always have, always will," he said as if this was our last moment on earth together.

"We are going to get through this," I ground out. "Ready to jam that gun against the throttle?"

"Yep."

"Let's do this," I said.

The helicopter now sat in the air, drifting upwards and away but not at a sharp angle. It behaved as if the pilot didn't quite know which direction he wanted to go in and I wondered if a Russian flew the beast rather than a Korean. Maybe Brant had managed to contact them, or someone else like the FSB and we were about to be saved…

I floored the engine, kept the revs high in third gear and watched the hel move 20 metres, 30 metres, 50 metres away from the LZ. I popped the clutch and the car lurched forwards, a greyhound racing towards its death with unknowing obedience. The landing zone's surface made a different sound to the concrete we'd been racing over previously, and Jacob thumbed the gun into position, jamming down the throttle with the butt. With our seat belts undone we watched the wall of the car park get closer and the hel slide away. Seventy metres now.

"The car's not going to make it," Jacob said.

"It'll make it. Brace, then jump," I ordered. "The water is a long way down. It's going to hurt."

"Thanks, I feel so much better for your understated explanation," Jacob's voice rose as we covered the ground between us and the wall in milliseconds.

The impact of the wall buckled the nose of the car but we both had our doors open a little to prevent being trapped by the battering. The car rocketed upwards, turning over in a flip as it gained height. I watched Jacob jump free. The hel lurched in the air as if struggling against some unseen force. I threw myself outwards, the air cold, and the sight far below me terrifying in the darkness of the night.

I'd done a lot of jumps into water over the years, even from helicopters, but we had support boats and controlled conditions, especially at night. I'd never done it under fire or from a moving car. I tried to form a locked structure with my booted feet aimed at the water, but the moment turned into a maelstrom of noise and chaos.

The car hit the hel, the tail section. The impact set off the grenades. Even though I plummeted towards the water I looked up. Mistake. The heat of the explosion. The sound wave. The concussion wave.

It pushed me back, destroyed my form and I slammed into the water close to the sea wall.

Darkness and cold stole all thought and instinct. My body tumbled and bits of me screamed in protest. I gasped against the pain. Water rushed in to fill the void. Panic squeezed what was left in my lungs and I struggled to comprehend the confusion surrounding me. Then the training kicked in as items dropped into the water around me and swirled past, dropping into the bottomless darkness which is where I was heading if I didn't do something.

Mouth closed, legs kicked, right ankle in my boot bellowing its unhappiness. Arms moving, both working. Natural buoyancy righting me, and I struggled upwards heading to the pale lights that flickered overhead. Was Jacob okay? What he still alive? I had to find out. I had to know. I pushed with more confidence, the darkness of threatened unconsciousness washing back even as my lungs informed me we were on a failing mission. I pushed harder and broke the surface, only to kick back from a wall of flame only 2 metres from my position. Aviation fluid and burning metal filled the air, covered the water and drifted around.

I coughed up water and turned in place looking for Jacob. Nothing.

"Fuck." Yelling for him over the noise of fire didn't seem a wise use of my resources. The choppy surface, the darkness, and blinding fire didn't help but…

A soft shape floated 8 metres to my left. I didn't think it likely the body would be anyone else. The Koreans and the pilot would be toast. I started to swim. The closer I got the worse things became. Fire raced towards the inert body from the other side and I realised it sat in a puddle of fuel. The hel would have carried a full load. I pushed harder, my entire body screaming in anguish at the movement. I reached the inert form. Jacob lay on his back, unconscious. The fire licked closer heading for his boots. I grabbed his collar, took a deep breath and yanked us both down, under the water. The flames raced overhead and I swam, dragging him next to me, away.

With clear water over my head, I resurfaced, and Jacob spluttered to life, fighting me.

"Stop, you'll drown us," I yelled, coughing from the black smoke and fouled water splashing against my face.

"Fuck… Fuck…" he muttered, stilling, controlling his panic and I released his collar.

"Mac, you're bleeding," he stated.

"We have to get out of this water," I told him.

He swam in a tight circle and pointed, treading water with more confidence than I did in that moment. A ladder rose from the lapping waves about 60 metres from our current location. It might as well have been a 1000 miles for all I could manage.

Jacob made to swim off then stopped. "My shoulder is fucked."

"Leg," I managed.

“Mac?” He moved closer to me in the thick water. “Shit, you’re a mess.”

“Jac…”

“Okay, fella. I got this. Just relax and we’ll take our time.” He padded to my rear and took hold of my chin. I fought the desire to push him away and he lay me in his chest, tipping us both up. “Just hold on, Mac. We’ll get to a hospital real soon.”

24

I WOKE TO WARMTH AND moderated lighting. My brain still in a blurry haze I tried to fit pieces back together. Russia. We were in Russia. My team… No, not mine, Brant's team. We were Brant's team. Jacob was here, should be here.

"Where is he?" I asked, struggling upright, pain bouncing through my head and body like a vengeful gremlin determined to batter me back into oblivion, I could hear it chuckling somewhere in my head. I had to concentrate to maintain focus.

"Whoa there, soldier," murmured a woman's voice. Small hands touched my shoulders and pushed me down as if I were made of feathers. "He'll be back in a minute. He's gone to check on your colleague."

I peered at the woman. "Who?"

She frowned. "I'm Dilras, you don't remember me?"

Deep brown eyes, young, short hair, sensible clothing. "Bug Lady."

Her eyes went from worried, to surprised, to laughter. "Yes, the Bug Lady will do."

"Jacob's okay?" I asked, settling back into the soft comfort of the pillows. I fought to keep my eyes open.

"He's fine except for a few minor problems and ripping some stitches." She looked away and tension filled her small body. "Your friend, the young woman…"

"Lydia?"

"Yes."

"What?" Fear filled the cavity where my heart and lungs should be, throat tightening in response.

"There was a firefight with the other vehicle. Lydia was hit. She's in a bad way. They have her in surgery. Jacob is with Colonel Brant trying to stop you from being arrested. It's all a bit confusing really. I have no papers and apparently all yours are fake."

I had to reach Brant and Jacob. They shouldn't be made to wait for news of Lydia alone. I could see Brant's deep maternal love for Lydia, her protégée, so this couldn't be easy. I knew Brant had two sons, one lost his life in Afghanistan, the other went into business, but losing someone under your command is a different kind of grief. Not that I knew personally about grief, no one but Jacob gave a rat's arse about me, but I'd lost men under my command in the field. A terrible burden.

Levering upright hurt like hell and pain bloomed down my right side, leaving me a gasping, sweaty mess. "Fucking hell," I muttered.

"Apparently your ribs aren't broken but hairline factures in old breaks have led to complications. You'll be in considerable pain for some weeks," Dilras said. In contrast to her panic and care over the killer mosquitoes she sounded bored by my frail human body and its problems.

"Oh good," I said. "I take it the second set of bugs are dead?"

Dilras's face dropped. "All gone." She sniffed. "Months of work gone. Years…"

I looked at her, trying to catch my breath before I pulled the cannula out of my hand. "You really don't see the problem with what you're doing do you?"

She shrugged. "I said I knew what physicists felt like after the testing of the atom bomb." This came in a tone reminiscent of every teenager the world over, further fanning my irritation with the woman.

"Listen, I appreciate the fact that our government thinks we need to stay ahead of weaponised viruses or bacteria but what you people do at Porton Down gives me the fucking creeps. You can stop a man with a gun, you can talk one down who is holding the nuclear football, but you can't stop a plague of weaponised mosquitoes." The anger in me came as something of a surprise. Jacob and I would spend hours debating the rights and wrongs of Western governments interfering in the conflict zones of the world, rarely reaching a conclusion, but this kind of warfare scared me.

"The point is," Dilras said, already sounding bored because she'd had to justify her job to cleverer people than me, "we have a cure."

"Which we sell to developing countries who might be targeted at a massive profit?" I asked, not hiding my sarcasm.

"The British aren't known for being so cruel," she stated.

I laughed at that one. "What's your heritage?"

"Excuse me?" she asked.

"I'm guessing you aren't Anglo-Saxon?"

Her eyes narrowed. "Racism is not –"

"I'm not racist, just tell me."

"My grandparents were immigrants from Kashmir."

I stood and the room swayed. Putting my arse back on the bed and closing my eyes I said, "I bet they fled during Partition because of the fucking mess the Brits left behind, right? Or what about the concentration camps we used in South Africa? You really think American interests won't be served by your research? But of course, they *never* do anything wrong in the world. Even if they have a fucking psychopath at the helm."

Her eyebrow arched and she cocked her head. "He's not a psychopath."

I snorted. I'd lived and worked in the Congo. I saw how decisions made in offices all over the world impacted the people on the ground. The anger fuelled me with just enough juice to make it easier to pull the cannula out of my hand. Blood squirted.

"Your bugs are an abomination, lady. Don't ever forget that. It's people like me who will have to go in and clean the bodies up when they escape into the world, which they will at some point, and start killing people."

"And are we supposed to sit on our hands while our enemies create these things?" she asked, a hard tartness to her voice.

"No, we're supposed to be working towards a world where none of this is necessary but let's face it, that's never going to happen. I just don't like it when people who never picked up a weapon are turned into the victims of war. Your bugs will make ordinary people victims. Men like me will be given the cure so people like you, because you'll be on a government list somewhere, will be protected. Your bugs are the modern equivalent to the atom bomb and some people will have access to the bunkers, some will not. To me, that's wrong." I made it to the door. Fortunately, the hospital gown was a modern wrap around one, so my arse didn't hang out the back.

"You are naïve," she stated.

I couldn't deny she might be right on that score. I had an idealist lurking inside me somewhere.

My right ankle yelled in protest, but I managed to hobble down the hall. A nurse at the station, tutted at me but my halting Russian made her forgive me and she pointed in the direction of my companions. I shuffled along, waves of dizziness making progress unpredictable.

"Dear God, Mac," Jacob cursed. I hadn't seen him coming, he just appeared at my side. An arm around my waist and the world tilted back to the right orbit, so much more comforting and real. "You should be asleep. They gave you enough sedative to knock out a horse."

"That explains the dizzy spells," I muttered. "Didn't like the company."

Jacob grunted in agreement. "Yeah, she's something else, that woman."

"How long have I been down?" I asked as he lowered me into a soft chair. A small whimper escaped because of the ribs.

"Ten hours, maybe a bit more."

"What happened? I don't remember anything after you started to haul me to the wall," I said. He wore clean clothes, but they weren't his and the pallor of his skin, the dark circles under his eyes worried me.

"You passed out. I hit the water before you and resurfaced, the blast lifted you back up and dropped you again. Then something hit me and I lost consciousness," Jacob said, now holding both my hands and staring into my face as if memorising every crease.

"I reached you, pulled you under the fire…"

He nodded. "Then you faded out and I swam you to the edge. From there some dock workers managed to get a harness over you and we lifted you out of the water. They called the ambulance, the local police turned up and we came here. That's when the colonel found me and I… Mac…"

"Lydia, yeah, I know. What happened?"

"The second vehicle had four men in it armed with MP5s. When they picked up on their tail, they drew Brant and Lydia down to a quiet spot near the train station. They took substantial fire, Mac." Jacob's hands were shaking in mine.

"Hey, we couldn't be in both places. She'll pull through."

He looked at me, eyes glassy and nodded. We were soldiers, we all knew the risks. Rubbing his clean fingers, as if they'd been covered in her blood, he said, "She took one to the chest, her vest took the worst of the impact but the bullet still got through. The local police turned up, Brant requested assistance from the FSB and between them they finished off the Koreans. Before the local branch of the FSB could take control of the scene, Brant grabbed the bugs, stuck a grenade under the box and blew it up."

"Good for her," I said.

"Yeah, don't think the Russians are too happy about it though. She's with them and some embassy staff who I guess are actually MI6."

"How long has Lydia been in surgery?" I asked.

"They had to stabilise her first but about 6 hours now." Jacob's hands were still shaking, and I gripped them a little harder despite the pain in my wrist.

"Hey, it'll be alright."

He stared at me. "I can't go to a Russian prison. I can't do that, Mac."

Despite the danger I released a hand and cupped his jaw. "I'm not going to let that happen, Jacob. The colonel will get this sorted. Let's just focus on Lydia for now."

He nodded and turned a little in his seat so he could lean against me. Kissing or holding each other for comfort didn't seem wise, not in Russia, but just feeling his heat against mine, our knees and thighs touching where they could, our arms sharing the arm rest between us and our fingers making the most of the contact, was too good for words. We both dozed while we sat there, waiting for news.

It came in the exhausted shape of our diminutive leader. For the first time I looked at Colonel Elizabeth Brant and saw a woman in her mid-fifties who looked like she needed a hug from someone who cared. I struggled out of the chair and tentatively raised my arm. She gave me a watery smile and folded against my chest, her arms going around my waist.

"You're not as squishy as my husband but this is good," she murmured, relaxing against me for a while.

"Sorry for not being squishy but glad to be of service, ma'am," I told her. I might not know Colonel Brant as well as some of the men and women who worked for her, but I did not mistake this for weakness. I offered a fellow soldier a safe place for a moment among the chaos of an engagement and its aftermath.

When she pulled back, she straightened her spine, tugged down her shirt and lifted those big hazel eyes to mine. "It's good to see you up, Sergeant."

"It's good to be up," I said.

"Well done on the trick with the car. Very inventive, though messy. They're going to be picking bits of that hel up for months along the coast."

"I'm surprised there was enough of it left to float away," Jacob said from behind me. "Are we going to prison?"

"Jacob –" I began in exasperation.

Brant smiled. "That is at least one thing I've managed to square away. No, we aren't being arrested. Though I owe yet more favours in Moscow. I'm going to have to start donating body parts soon to repay my debts."

A cough roused us, and Brant turned to meet a new body in our waiting area, a man in hospital scrubs. "Ah, Doctor Hussein, what news?" she asked.

I guessed he was the one operating on Lydia. Jacob rose and joined us.

The doctor looked serious, his ethnic origins more Far East than Russian and he stood only a little taller than Brant. "Your friend has been saved," he said in his accent like something from a shlock American movie of a Russian bad guy. "She is in intensive care and will be for some time, but she will live if there are no secondary problems. We had to remove part of her lung and repair the ribcage with metal, but we have done a good job. The breast tissue was too badly damaged to save, so at some point she will need corrective surgery."

Bit more information than I needed, and it came as a bit of a shock to realise Lydia was a woman. I mean I knew she was a woman, obviously, but we were a team and gender never occurred to me. Yet another nail in the coffin of my dying heterosexuality I guessed. I felt kind of proud of my lack of gender awareness.

"I'm sure she'll receive the best care possible," Brant said. "Thank you, Doctor Hussein for all your hard work and that of your team."

"That's why she's the boss," Jacob muttered beside me. "Bloody woman can talk anyone into anything."

I grinned; the relief of Lydia's survival made us both flippant. "All she's going to be able to talk me into is a hotel with a spa."

"And food… Lots of food."

With those words my stomach woke up and growled loud enough for Brant to hear. "Go," she said. "We still have the hotel booked and there might not be a spa, but they will serve steak."

"I need clothes," I stated, guessing my previous clothing had been cut off me at some point.

"Sorted, let's go back to your room," Jacob said. "Then get out of here. How long will Sergeant Greenbrook be out?" he asked the doctor.

"You can return during visiting hours tomorrow. She should be conscious by then. I suggest her family is informed because she will need specialist care once she is discharged."

25

THE HOTEL LOOKED LIKE A slice of heaven when we made it back to our room. Brant opted to remain at the hospital but Dilras returned with British Embassy officials to Moscow. My guess – she'd face a full MI6 interrogation on what happened in the Congo, what happened to Jacob's team, and who 'sold' her to the North Koreans. I didn't envy her. MI6 weren't delicate when they thought someone might have betrayed their precious Official Secrets Act. I had to wonder if Brant made certain Dilras ended up in the hands of friendlies in SIS rather than Clark's paymasters.

Clark. Fuck, walking into that warehouse to find him hanging from his ankles, his face cut off, seemed like a very long time ago.

"I'm so tired," I said as I shuffled along to my side of the bed.

"I know, babe, but you need a shower. You still smell of harbour water." Jacob approached me and between us we removed the thick lumberjack shirt he'd found for me. I grunted when his fingers brushed the black and purple mess on my right side. He kissed my lips. "Poor, baby."

"Yeah, poor baby," I agreed, my head hitting his shoulder. I hit the bad one and he hissed in pain. "Shit, sorry."

Jacob laughed. "The state of us."

His scent caught in my throat and my cock took interest. I nosed at his neck, drawing in more of the smell, a dark scent, loam and oak trees, summer wheat and honey bees. Soft kisses made him squirm. "Shower," he whispered.

"Yeah," I agreed.

We stripped and when he saw my cock standing to attention as if on a parade ground he blushed, the colour sweeping up his neck, through his beard and making his cheeks shine. I took his hand and led him to the shower. Where had this new version of me come from? I had no idea, but the steps I'd taken to change my life only led one way, upwards, out of the mire of my past. Just the act of being able to touch Jacob gave me a sense of privilege I hoped never to take for granted.

Pushing sentiment to one side, we entered the wonderful world of modern hotels and their shower cubicles. They tended to be large walk in affairs with solid fixtures and fittings. The hot water rushed from a large shower head and I knew then the hotel would get a five-star rating from me on Trip Advisor.

"Bloody hell, Mac, I still can't believe we can do this," Jacob said, his body not quite touching mine.

I rubbed my bristly cheek against his beard, the friction electrifying the nerves in my lower belly and making the palms of my hands tingle. He twisted his head and our lips touched. These weren't deep kisses, more biting and licking, rubbing and tasting of texture and scent while the water poured over our heads. Jacob's hands cupped my arse and pulled me close to his groin, his cock as hard as mine. His kisses were turning into nips and travelling down my throat. He bit and held my Adam's apple making me groan. At that point I'd done with subtle. I wanted more from my lover. My beautiful male lover.

I plundered his mouth and he gave way under the onslaught, melting into me and becoming pliant, almost submissive. All pain became subsumed by my lust and I pressed his shoulders until he dropped to his knees, fingers digging into my thighs. Most of the water now crashed over my back, soaking into my dark chest hair and trailing down the thickset muscles of my gut. He gazed up at me, water droplets shining on his lashes, eyes a soft demerara brown, dark with desire. The soft pink tongue I wanted licked his full lips and I cupped the back of his head guiding him to my stiff, dark, aching cock.

His lips parted and drew me into his hot, wet mouth. I could feel the stretch of his lips and his tongue a little rough compared to the soft solidity of the roof of his mouth. He groaned and pushed me further into his hungry body. I gasped and cursed, trying to control my desire to flick my hips forwards. His fingers dug furrows into my thighs. He took more, gagged and I pulled back.

"No, Mac, I want this," he ordered, lips already swollen.

"I can't hurt you, my love," I told him, stroking his head, the very short hair dark with water.

"It won't hurt. I want it. Please, let me have control. Then, fuck me."

My heartrate doubled and my chest heaved. "Jacob…"

He rubbed his beard against my balls and shaft making me squirm and tighten my fingers on his scalp. "Fuck me, Mac. I know you want to, and I want it – good and deep. I want to feel it for days." While he spoke, he licked, bit and rubbed against my groin and thighs. I could hardly bear it.

The thought of him under me, spread open for me, willing to take me, proved all the incentive I needed to allow my ruthless side to exact some revenge for his teasing.

I pulled him to front and centre. Pressed my thumb into the hinge of his jaw, his eyes bright with need, his mouth opened with total obedience. This time I fucked his mouth, water spraying over us as I held his head still. I pushed inside with at least some kind of control, watching as I filled him over and over.

"Fuck, you look so beautiful," I said. He gazed up at me. "Oh, baby, keep looking at me like that and I'll come."

He managed to nod and forced me past his gag reflex. I almost dropped to my knees as his nose pressed into my belly. His hands switched to my arse, kept hold with one hand while his other reached for his cock. I watched him give pleasure to himself while he strained to keep me deep. I let him take control, not comfortable with forcing him, and Jacob slid off my cock, releasing his simultaneously.

"Bedroom," he growled, voice burred by his cock-sucking. He rose with his ever-present grace and dragged me out of the shower.

"I haven't managed to wash yet," I said.

"Don't care," he said, turning me and pushing me down on the bed. I struggled up to the top, my cock wilting a little as the pain of my damaged ribs took over.

He snarled something obscene as he rooted through his kit and threw a condom and lubrication at me. "I'm on top, it'll hurt you less and I'll have control. I'm not used to being fucked, so we need to take it slow, I'll need to be in charge."

I could feel my eyes widen at his operational control and just nodded consent. He squirted lubrication on the fingers of my right hand. "I know it hurts but can you manage to open me?" he asked.

After a hard swallow I nodded. "Anything for you, my love."

His smile at my words made my heart stutter. He straddled my hips, leaned over and kissed me deep. With his legs spread I found his tight entrance with ease and circled as his tongue made lazy movements in my mouth. Then I pushed inside him for the first time. Jacob pushed back and groaned, his tongue going deep for a moment before he left off his kisses.

"Fuck yes, Mac. I want more of that. The pain is so good."

"You sure?" I asked. "I don't think I could take it."

He bit my lips for a second or two as I pulled out and pushed in a little more. "You will, one day you'll want it, trust me. When you do, baby, I'll be there, and I'll fuck you for hours while you beg for more."

I groaned at the thought. He was right of course, I'd give him whatever he wanted – always. The sun rose and set with this man. He was my moon, my north star, he was the reason clichés about love existed. He soon coaxed me into giving him a second finger while he kissed me, and rocked deeper and deeper. A vice of hot muscle held me tight, invigorating and scary, obscene and beautiful all at once.

"Enough messing about, I need this," he muttered.

Twisting he took hold of my cock, I hissed out a breath. "Steady, babe, that's the only one I got."

"Oh, poor you. Just try fitting this monster into your arse and see how gentle you want to be," he told me.

I laughed as he rolled the condom on, added yet more lubrication, and turned back. "You need to let me know if anything hurts," he said. "I'll try to keep my weight off you…"

Taking hold of his hands I kissed both palms and placed them on my pectoral muscles. "Use me as you need."

He stared down at me for long seconds. "I love you."

"I love you too."

Lowering himself to my lips he kissed me, took hold of my cock in his right hand, and guided me to his entrance. A spike of nerves on my part threatened to undo all our hard work but he did that rubbing thing against my face which I loved so much, and I gripped his hips, pushing up as he pushed down.

Jacob bit his lips, colour sweeping over his face and neck. "Fuck that's... too much…"

I tried to push my hips down, but he slapped me as I moved. "Fucking stay still, soldier."

I followed orders.

He bowed his back and the hot, tight, damp channel tugged at my cock. I had to remember to breathe and when I realised Jacob had forgotten, I stroked his cheek. “Look at me, love. Look at me. Breathe with me. We want this.”

He nodded, matched my breathing and sank onto my shaft.

“Holy fucking hell,” I cursed. “That’s amazing.”

He rocked and tugged on his balls, already high and tight, closing those beautiful eyes.

“No, love, look at me.”

He did and I saw tears gathering. In awe I watched him rise up, still focused on me, push down, the movement easier this time. He wriggled, eyes widening as I brushed against the magic spot inside his body, before he rose again.

“God, yes, that’s what I want to feel,” he moaned.

Every perfect, corded muscle, every line of his masculine body moved with power and purpose. He took exactly what he wanted from me and I worshiped him as he gave it back ten-fold.

For the first time I had what I’d been waiting for my entire life. A man of grace and power loving all I had to offer. I ran my hand over the flexing muscles, holding his taut hips, tracing the lines of his muscles where sweat trickled as he worked himself into a frenzy. A part of me realised I ought to do something more than gaze at this god-like man but to be honest, I just wanted to watch and experience this gift.

I let my fingers drift down his perfect belly and the tips trail up his shaft. I’d never seen anything so perfect. It leaked and he shivered, crying out each time I swept my thumb pad over the top. When I’d collected enough, I sucked it clean and Jacob growled, leaning forward and licking into my mouth.

The action, the taste of him, flipped a switch. I went from docile to sex addict. “Enough, you want me, you’re going to take me,” I snarled.

I pushed him off me, not confident I could turn us without hurting him, dragged him up onto all fours and thrust into him so hard he braced against the wall of the hotel. With my fingers digging into his flanks I pounded into him hard.

“Fuck, yes,” he shouted. “More, like that.”

So I did it, a blind flurry of movement as he slammed back into me. The tension inside my belly reached critical mass.

"Jacob, I can't..."

"Do it, fuck I need to feel it." The first coherent words we'd managed for long seconds.

I didn't have the experience necessary to grab his cock and make him come with me, but I did have a reward in mind. I allowed the swelling inside me to hit its peak and I held the moment as the internal combustion pushed outward. I cried out, inarticulate with love for my incredible man.

The moment I could draw breath and felt Jacob reach for his cock, I smacked his arse, pulled out, which made him curse, flipped him over and took this cock into my mouth before giving his balls a gentle squeeze.

"Oh, fuck, Mac." His fingers dug into my scalp, hips flicking off the bed and his cock pulsed, releasing his load into my body. I groaned and swallowed, sucking hard, then more gently before reducing him to a shivering wreck with licks at the sensitive tip. He stroked my head where it rested on his thigh.

"Thank you," he murmured, already falling asleep.

I brushed my hand over his thigh and smiled as the thick hair tickled my palm. Who the hell knew body hair could be a turn-on? If I lay there much longer, I'd be roaring for round two.

"You need cleaning up," I told him. I managed to lever my body, now beginning to hurt like I'd been mauled by an alligator, off the bed. In the bathroom I soaked a towel, threw the condom away and returned to a sleepy man looking almost boyish in the soft light of the hotel room.

I wiped the sweat off his back, cleaned up other more sensitive places that made him squirm, and kissed his lean back.

"Wish we'd done that without condoms," he muttered, face still planted in the pillow.

"Why? Less mess," I said.

He looked over his shoulder with one brown eye. "Then I'd have you inside me forever."

I laughed. "Corny much? I'll always be inside you," I said, tapping his heart.

He nodded before pulling me up the bed, to curl around his back and hold him close as we both slept the sleep of the just.

26

I ROSE FROM THE DEEPEST part of slumber with a speed that came from instinct pulling me up from the depths to face danger. It was like rising from the water to gasp at the air. The moment my eyes opened my body moved.

"Don't you fucking, dare," hissed a woman's voice.

Something cold and hard dug into the back of my head. *Jacob*, my first thought. The second took longer as I tried to orientate myself in the hotel room.

"You try anything, and I'll blow lover boy all over this bed," she snapped.

"Okay, you have my compliance," I said, quivering with the need to move because of the hormones dumped into my bloodstream.

"Mac?" asked a soft voice near my right arm.

"Just do as she says," I said, voice tight, body tighter.

Jacob flinched, woke and rose in one fluid movement. He stilled as he saw the guns pointing at us.

"Sit up," the woman commanded, the gun moving away from my skull.

I lifted myself, ribs and back screaming at the effort, off the mattress. It was dark in the room, the lights from outside giving everything a ghastly yellow glow. I sat on the edge of the bed and glanced behind me at Jacob. A second woman with a large revolver kept the barrel tight to his head, just behind his left ear.

"Don't move, babe," I told him. "Don't fight."

"Cute, real cute," the woman said moving back away from me. Too far to go for a direct assault. She held the weapon, a Glock, in two hands, feet shoulder width apart and she watched me, not the barrel of her gun. She knew how to use it. Her finger sat over the trigger.

"He so much as twitches and he's dead," she said. "He's dead anyway, but I'll let you have a few more seconds before I have the deed done."

She was maybe 1.70 metres tall. About 65 kilos soaking wet. Her body mass index would be close to zero by the looks of the corded muscle in her forearms and neck. White skinned with a heavy but natural tan, brown hair, bleached by the sun on the long ends and big green eyes. Her lips were thin, cheekbones and chin sharp. When she spoke, I detected an Oxbridge accent layering something rural, a very English voice. I'd never seen her before.

"Who are you?" I asked.

Her top right lip lifted in a sneer. "What the fuck do you care? You're going to die anyway."

I licked my lips. We were both naked. Jacob had a gun to his head, not a figure of speech this time, and I knew how fast that Glock could take me out. There'd be no walking away with a wound if she shot me at this distance and I'd never save Jacob.

"That seems very final considering I don't know you. I'm guessing this isn't a spurned lover thing, obviously we're gay, so what do you want?" I asked, maintaining eye contact. "The British Government aren't going to give any ransom money for us, and we don't know anything worth selling, so please, tell me how to fix this."

"I want you to watch my friend kill your boyfriend," she said, and her eyes flicked to her companion.

"Get up," growled the other woman in a Russian accent.

"Do as she asks," I told Jacob after his first 'fuck you'.

He moved and she forced him around to my side of the bed. "Kneel," the Russian said, a much larger, blonder woman.

Jacob glanced at me and sank to his knees.

"Hands, *pidor*," she ordered.

Jacob raised his hands and laced his fingers together. He looked at me the whole time as if waiting for the order to action. I shook my head and saw his confusion. The woman placed the revolver, a Nagant M1895 able to hold seven rounds, against his temple. Jacob didn't move a muscle.

I looked back at the smaller woman. "Okay, now what? You shoot him but why? What will it gain? We're just two grunts doing our jobs. We know nothing."

"You killed him," she said and for the first time the barrel of the Glock wavered.

That didn't really help. I'd killed a great many men over the years. "Killed who?" I asked.

"Stephen…" the name came out as half snarl, half sob.

I glanced at Jacob. "Clark," he clarified.

My eyes widened in surprise. "No we didn't. He was dead when we found him."

The movement made me flinch back but that didn't stop the Glock from pushing into my forehead. "No, you killed him. You, the British fucking Government." She made a sound of pure grief and I stared at Jacob knowing this was goodbye, she'd pull the trigger. The kind of grief that drove her to seek us out, break into the hotel room and hold two operatives at gunpoint meant she'd pull the trigger.

The barrel pushed hard enough against the thin skin of my forehead to bruise but she pulled back, stepped back and returned to the correct firing position. The larger Russian woman kept her mouth shut and the gun on Jacob's temple.

I eased myself to upright, ribs protesting, hands up. "We didn't kill, Clark. Why would we? We needed him alive to find Dilras Begum. Losing him cost us dearly. Trust me, we wanted him alive."

She laughed, a tear escaping the corner of her right eye. "Trust you?"

"Bad choice of words," I said. "But I have no reason to lie. I just want to get out of this alive. I want my friend here to stay alive and I'd like you both to leave this room alive."

"Why would you want that?" she asked, eyes like green lichen over granite.

"Because I have no argument with you, and I don't seek death needlessly. Listen to me, please, whatever issue you think you have with us it can be solved." I tried to keep my focus on the woman and not let my eyes stray to Jacob.

"You can't bring him back," she said.

"No, but I can help you understand what happened. We can figure it out," I said.

"They said you killed him," she stated.

I shook my head. "No. Not us, it was General Delta. A man who is dead. An African warlord. We killed him for what he did to our team out there. He took Clark, extracted information –"

The Glock came too close and my heartrate kicked back up as she pressed it against my head again. "No."

I took a short breath. "Yes." A pause. "Please, let me explain what we know then you can make your decision about our fate."

She stepped back. "Talk."

I glanced at Jacob and watched a bead of sweat move around the barrel of the revolver. He gave me a slight nod.

"Okay, from the beginning. I lived in Kinshasa. Jacob found me. We went back to talk to his commander on this mission, the one to save Ms Begum. When we arrived, a bomb took out the team and the building, sniper fire made us flee the scene. We knew Clark wouldn't be with the rest of the team. I've been tracking his movements for years looking for a way through to the men who gave the orders he wanted me to carry out. Kill orders and other things. We went in search of Clark, knowing he had contact with Delta. We found his body in a warehouse. We went to hunt down Delta –"

"You're lying," she stated.

"No, I'm not. Who told you it was us that killed Clark? Who sent you on this mission? Who do you work for?"

I could see the rage building in her, but she lashed it down even as her finger tightened on the trigger. "I'm the one asking the fucking questions."

"Yeah, okay, I know, but please. Before you kill us just think about it. What would we gain from Clark's death at that point and in such a horrific way? Why would we torture him like that? Since when do the SAS need to cut people's fingers off, or their faces for that matter, to extract information? We're a lot more organised than that, you know this. You know what you're doing with that gun so you know how we operate." I spoke with such speed my words tumbled together.

"He suffered so much for *them*," she said.

"Who is *them*?" I asked. "Please, if you want revenge tell us and we'll fix it. We'll take *them* out. We just need names."

She stared at me, her body relaxing by tiny increments while her mind tried to process what I said. The effort it took her to think past her grief and the lies she'd been told almost seemed to hurt.

"Listen, please, just tie us up so we can't follow, and you can go," I said.

The Glock swung away from me. "No, you need to understand the consequences of your actions." The large black barrel centred on Jacob's head and the revolver changed angle just a little so it would fire into his chest cavity and rip his body in half. "I missed you on that fucking rooftop but I'm not going to miss this time."

Jacob shuddered at her words. She'd been there, the day of the explosion that wiped out his team. The day we'd been shot at by a sniper. This woman had been at the beginning of this mess and we were only just finding out about it now. So much had happened since the bombing I'd never spared the sniper a thought, I'd been too interested in Jacob, the mission, the future. She had already tried to kill us twice and I'd not taken any precautions to protect us from a threat made by an organisation that had proved itself deadly to those who tried to stop it or uncover its members and intentions. I had failed.

"No, please, no." I dropped off the edge of the bed and onto my knees, hands reaching for her with no more thought than to beg for his life. "No, please, anything. I can give you anything. I'll work for you to find out who did this to Clark. I swear please, don't, don't hurt him. Please, don't kill him. Please…"

Her finger squeezed the trigger even tighter and in my mind's eye I could see the mechanism click back, the round ready to be struck, igniting with the pressure necessary to rip a life from this world.

I wanted to lunge for her, but I knew the metre between us was too far for me to reach her and prevent the Russian from killing him, then me. Not that there was anything left for me if Jacob died. I couldn't start again after this; I knew it in my bones. He was my only chance at any happiness. Maybe I didn't deserve it for all the death I'd dealt in my life by following orders like the perfect little soldier boy, but if I could just have one more minute with him in my arms, I'd sell what was left of my soul.

"Please… I will do anything for him. Give you anything." The words were the final whisper of a breaking heart. Her finger tightened. I looked into Jacob's widening eyes.

A click.

Nothing.

A misfire.

"Fuck," she snarled.

The Russian woman stepped back. "We kill them both now."

Clark's girlfriend or wife or whatever the fuck she was, looked at me. "It seems you have angels on your side today."

I almost pissed myself in relief. My wrists came together in total compliance. "Just tie us up. Let us live and we'll bring down the men responsible for Clark's death. The real men. Those who control you. Control the lies you've been told."

"You need to stop talking before I change my mind," she snapped.

I closed my mouth.

"Hog tie them," she ordered the Russian.

"I don't think –" the larger woman began.

"No, you don't. I paid you to follow orders. Just do it." The smaller woman waved her gun about now, discipline forgotten, the moment of cold clarity ending on a shivering wail of internal emotional pressure.

I could almost see the rush of control ending. She wanted out. The moment she'd found herself able to kill two men at point blank range had gone and in its wake was confusion. This woman wasn't a natural killer. She normally followed orders and as a sniper she'd been a crap shot. Now she just wanted revenge for the man she loved.

She lifted her gun and tried to stop it wavering. "Find out who got him killed. Find the people who give the orders. Stop them. The things they want to do to the world –"

"Enough," barked the Russian. Did she work for them or for Clark's lover?

The lover might not be able to think any longer, but whatever the pecking order the big Russian was a professional and when she grabbed me, her rough handling made me gasp in pain.

She used plasticuffs after she'd pulled my wrists behind my back. Then she used another set on my ankles, these even tighter and used the simpler zip ties to lace them together. She pushed me over making me cry out in pain. Jacob went through the same procedure. We were lying a metre apart, naked and staring at each other.

The women didn't say anything more. They just left us on the hotel bedroom floor.

27

"WELL, THAT COULD HAVE GONE worse," Jacob said. "Not how I imagined the day starting."

I laughed. "Fuck me, this hurts."

"I need a fucking piss," he said, chuckling.

Things became a bit silly at that point. We both started laughing, the shock of the last few minutes rolling through us. When we calmed down, we took stock and tested the restraints with more purpose.

"Shit," Jacob said. "All I'm managing to do is cut myself." He panted a little at the straining effort.

"Don't do that," I said. "I've an idea."

"I hope it doesn't involve screaming for help. I don't want Colonel Brant or a cleaning woman to find us like this."

I grinned, the laughter just bubbling under the surface. "No, idiot. The knife. The NRS. You took it off your belt. If we can get to your clothes…"

"The clothes on the other side of the bed you mean?" he asked, squirming against his restraints again.

"Hey, Jacob, stop. You're panicking."

"Fucking hell, I hate this." He wasn't listening to me. The laughter of moments ago was slipping away, being chased by the hounds of uncontrolled fear brought to bear by a fear of being tied down. Jacob's PTSD surfaced, I could see it happening in the twitching of his body, the short breaths, the hardness in his eyes and the waves of anger he used to beat it into submission. He'd fail this time because he couldn't move well enough to rid his body of the noxious mix of chemicals generated by his unruly brain.

"Hey, listen to me, listen," I called over his dark muttering and thrashing about. He'd broken out in a sweat.

"What? What possible words of wisdom do you have for this particular problem, Mac?" he asked, voice brutal and sharp.

I didn't rise to the contaminated bait. "I can't move, Jacob. I can't save us. You have to do it and it needs to be quick. I'm not breathing well like this. My weight is on my ribs. Please, help me."

The panic in his eyes made me think I'd missed the mark, but he wrestled with the demons chasing themselves through his head and took a deep breath, one I envied at the moment.

He nodded. "I can do this."

I managed a small smile. "You can do this."

By small wriggling movements to and fro he squirmed past me and the bed. I watched his strong body, the one which had graced me with such desire the night before, now bend to the task in hand. Thinking about the previous night didn't help much because my cock suddenly found the entire situation interesting and decided to grow.

"Bloody hell," I muttered.

"What?" he asked from the foot of the bed.

"I've got a hard-on." The confession set off another round of giggling. Now it knew what it wanted I could control the bloody thing.

"You prick."

"Not my prick. The damn thing is on its own this time," I said.

"Didn't know you were into bondage, Mac."

"I'm not." The firmness in my voice belied the firmness in my cock.

"You old perv."

"Less of the old, you."

"I've reached my jeans," he said.

"Okay, cut yourself loose first. I don't have time for you to make your way back." Which was the truth. My breathing hurt more with each minute that passed. I had the nasty feeling one of my very bruised ribs might have finally given way under the pressure.

I heard Jacob grunt and curse and fight while I patiently waited and concentrated on my breathing. My erection began to fade thank God, but Jacob's grunts weren't helping, and I had the feeling some handcuffs might be in our future somewhere.

"Yes," he cried out. "Thank God for that."

He didn't stop to undo his legs, he bum shuffled to me on the carpet and as he appeared, I saw he had friction burns on his shoulder and hip.

"No fair, I wanted to give you those," I said.

He glanced down as if noticing them for the first time. "Next time, baby, and I'd rather have them on my knees and elbows."

"Christ, Jacob, don't say things like that. I don't need the blood going back to my cock. It's going to get whiplash with all this back and forth."

While I talked, he cut and in seconds my wrists were free, then my feet.

"Ouch."

"Come on, you can straighten now," he said. With care he lifted me off the ground and pulled my legs straight. There is no comfortable way of recovering from being tied in that kind of stress position. I don't care if you're a master of bondage, being tied that tight for any length of time hurts on release.

Once we were both free, we sat on the floor and just breathed, fingers laced together lying on the floor between us.

"What the fuck just happened?" Jacob asked.

"I don't know. Not even sure we should tell Brant."

He looked at me. "Seriously? Don't you trust her?"

"Of course I trust her. I'm just not sure how to explain two of her best operatives were held at gunpoint because we were exhausted after too much fucking, then hogtied before having to cut ourselves loose. And by two women no less. Who snuck into our room without us knowing."

"Fair point well made."

We were silent for a bit.

"I'm hungry," I said.

"I think I'm a bit scared, Mac."

Surprised, I looked at him. "Scared of what?"

"If we can't trust the people sending us into conflict zones what the fuck is the point of sacrificing our lives?" He searched my face as if looking for answers from the one person he knew he could trust.

"I don't have answers for you, Jacob. Our men, Lawson and the others, they shouldn't have died. That was on Clark and he wanted us added to the body count. They have to be stopped though and it's going to be up to Brant to stop them, it's whether we want to be involved or not. That's the question we need to answer."

"Do you want to be involved?"

I thought back to the moment where the smaller woman pulled that trigger. For whatever reason the gun didn't fire, and Jacob remained next to me, not a corpse on the floor, blood and brains… I shuddered, the reality of that image hitting me square in the face. A punch so brutal in its realness the bile rose in my throat.

"I think we have to do whatever is necessary to stop these people. I think whatever vision they have for a new world order isn't one we are going to want."

I'd always been aware of the delicate balance men like me helped to maintain. We worked for a government that didn't lock up the masses when they were angry about something. Didn't send armed troops into the streets to break up demonstrations, at least not on the mainland of the UK, and didn't murder dissenters in their sleep. It gave our government the moral high ground over so many other countries.

The British Government used that moral high ground to force countries who did hurt their people to back down, change their policies, and strive for better human rights. At least our government tried to do those things. We, the Armed Forces and the Special Forces in particular, were used as a tool to make this happen. The broken bits of the world were our battlegrounds and the people our responsibility to keep safe if we could. I believed in this goal. I believed we could make a difference.

I wasn't about to sacrifice the hope I still had in that mission.

Jacob studied me for a while before asking, "How do you know *they* want a new world order? Maybe they just want some money and they'll leave the government alone."

"Since when do people who want power, who orchestrate coups, not want people like us dead? Or at least gone," I said. "They'll come after us and we are the wafer-thin line between *them* and the people we swore to work for and protect."

He frowned. "I don't understand."

"Every dictator, every monarch or baron in history, who wants a change to the order of the world so they can hold power does one thing – they get rid of all those who stand against them. That includes people who can think for themselves, who aren't easy to manipulate. Who chose their faith or way of life over that of the new power. They've all done it: Stalin, Hitler, Mau, Pol Pot, the Romans, even William of bloody Normandy did it."

"You're talking about genocide, aren't you?"

"Not just Jews, Muslims, gays, the Roma, travellers of all kinds. Liberals. The literary elite. If they don't side with the new guys, those that gave Clark and his woman the orders, they get wiped out. Hindus sent back to India. Jews sent to Israel and can you imagine what a true right-wing agenda might do to British born Muslims? It's hard enough for us, as boots on the ground, not to make them guilty by association when we've faced down too many jihadists to count, just imagine the chaos if a government calls open hunting season on them. Under those circumstances how many people in the British Army would you trust not to become the new Storm Troopers?"

Jacob snorted and closed his eyes, resting his head back. "You think too much. It'll never happen. Providing they don't break the law all people in Britain are safe."

"What happens if they change the law, Jacob? What happens if these people get real power, like the North Korean regime has? I'm sure the people who fought the British and French during the Korean War, before the Americans took over, didn't think 60 years on they'd be living as peasants while their leaders have Leer jets and helicopters going around the world kidnapping scientists to create killer bugs."

He watched me again, trying to assess my state of mind. "You're serious."

"Damn straight. Brant is right, we have to figure this out and she's going to need people she trusts to work with her to help. We're staying with Unit 12." I closed my fist over his, lacing our fingers together as if to convince him to come with me. "Leave the Regiment, Jacob. Come work with me and we'll help the team save the world."

The laughter, without the hysterical edge, made me smile. "Okay, young Skywalker. We'll fight the evil Empire even if we don't know exactly who or what it is or what it wants. I think you're taking conspiracy theories to a whole new level but what do I know? I'm just a soldier."

I lifted his hand to my lips and kissed his knuckles. "You're not just a soldier."

"I think you're borrowing trouble, Mac. Then again, I think you've always borrowed trouble."

"Is it going to stop you joining me?"

"No, never. You know that."

I gave him a tired smile and nudged his shoulder. "Shower then food?"

He nodded. "And we'll need a way to explain to Brant what the fuck happened this morning. Why didn't you push for a name?"

Jacob helped me off the ground and between heavy grunts of pain I said, "She had a gun to your head. I didn't want to antagonise her."

"Says the man who made her pull the trigger."

"Christ, don't remind me. I'm going to have nightmares about that click for years."

BY 07:00HRS WE WERE AT a breakfast table with coffee and Brant walked in looking tired but nowhere near as drained as the previous evening.

"Gentlemen," she said, sitting down with us. Her hand whipped out and grabbed Jacob's wrist. "What's this? Sex game gone wrong?"

He pulled his arm back. "Long story and no sex games. Not yet anyway." He winked at me.

"Never with plasticuffs." I rubbed my wrists, the flesh still sore.

"Explain," Brant ordered.

I did, without omissions.

"Naked?" Her eyebrows were raised, and the ghost of a smile hovered over her mouth.

"Yes, ma'am," I said, feeling the heat in my cheeks again.

She broke and laughed. "I'd have paid to see you two trussed up like Christmas turkeys."

"The point is, ma'am," I said trying to distract her from such visions, "we were compromised. Someone told this woman how to find us. Pointed her at us and I didn't think that many people knew we were on an unsanctioned op in Russia."

"You're right, of course, Sergeant. I can still call you sergeant, right?" she asked. "You will be joining Unit 12 on a permanent basis?"

"Yes, ma'am. We are signing up for the long haul."

She looked at Jacob. "Lance Corporal?"

"We're a package deal, Colonel."

"Good. I've informed Sinclair and Locke over a secure network of our unseen enemies' latest movements, they are on standby, but I'd rather not use them unless necessary. They've found a little peace and they deserve it." She sounded almost wistful. I'd seen how close she and Sinclair were when I worked with Luke, while Sam was out of action, and I guessed she missed them. Or perhaps…

"How's Lydia?" I asked, making certain I injected the question with compassion.

Her eyes focused on me. "I managed to see her briefly last evening. I believe the prognosis is good. I've informed her step-brother of her condition, but I think it'll probably be her girlfriend who helps the most."

"The mysterious Aria."

"Hmm. Not the person I'd have chosen for Lydia but there you go. Aria is nothing if not handy when one needs something dramatic to happen."

"Like making sure we get to the bad guys in time to throw a car at a hel?" I asked.

Brant smiled. "Exactly, Mac. I still think it's the most creative way I've ever seen a helicopter taken down."

"Thank you, ma'am. Though I don't recommend it as a way to stop helicopters from leaving the LZ."

"No, not something we'll be writing into the Landing Zone manual for new recruits."

"How long before Lydia can leave with us?" Jacob asked.

"A week I think before I can fly her back to the UK for more surgery. You don't have to stay."

Jacob and I glanced at each other. "Leave no man behind," he said.

Brant smiled and patted his hand. "That's appreciated. Besides, I think you two need some time to make plans as well. What about your house in the DRC, Mac?"

I rubbed my hands over my face. "Christ, I'd almost forgotten about that. I'll have to go back and sort something I guess but I can't stay in the DRC without a job and to be honest, I should imagine they've pulled my visa by now."

"I can get the local MI6 team to sort it," Brant said. "You don't have to go back at all."

"I've a dog."

She shook her head. "There's always a dog somewhere with you lot. Do you want the dog in the UK or homed there?"

I thought about Hound and my shoulders slumped. "He'll be happier there. I'll phone my neighbour, offer to give a donation every month."

Jacob squeezed my knee under the table. "Hey, he'll be okay there. We'll get a rescue dog when we find a place to live in England."

"Is that wise if you're going to be working for me?" Brant asked, tucking into her fried breakfast with healthy disregard for cholesterol.

I felt even more crestfallen at the thought of not having a dog at all because of work.

"Having someone, or something, to come home to is important and with our new remuneration package for working with Unit 12 I'm sure we can afford doggie day care," Jacob stated.

"You want a new pay deal?" Brant asked, her eyes hardening even more than her arteries.

They began to haggle about contracts, and I zoned out. Where would we live in England? Close to London? Close to Hereford? Could we really afford it? Even if I sold my house in the DRC it would be hard to find enough of a deposit to buy a house in either location, especially London. The UK was an expensive country to live in and Jacob had no money.

"A resettlement fee?" she asked with such a level of sharpness to her voice that she brought me back to the present.

Jacob nodded. "I rent a small flat in Hereford. That's no use if you need us in London."

"I might be able to square away a place in Dagenham, or Barking. But not central London," she said.

Jacob grinned. "Done, we can go to Battersea when we get home."

"What?" I asked.

"They're going to buy us a house in London and we can go to Battersea dog home to find a new Hound," he said. "We'll be a proper couple at last."

I smiled at him, the hope in his eyes the most joyful thing I'd ever seen. Three years ago, I lost this man to a world of lies and secrets thick enough to choke. Now I could see a future with him. We could work together, live together, build a world together and make each other happy. I could live with that and I could live with the risks of working with Unit 12.

"A proper couple. I like it, Jacob. We'll do that, all of it."

"Good, but you're in charge of the money."

I laughed. "God, yes, you'll have an allowance, my love."

Brant smiled at us like an indulgent mother duck. "Good. I'm glad that's all settled. I need a full report from both of you. I'll sort you both out with some tech while we are here so we can get you up to speed on what we're doing back in London. It's not all chasing around the world, blowing things up. You might be my blunt instruments on the ground, but I need you both to see the bigger picture. There is work to be done."

"Yes, ma'am," we said in unison.

28

WE MADE IT BACK TO London with Lydia and Colonel Brant in a C-130 air transporter kitted out with a medical bay. Sergeant Greenbrook did well on the journey and managed to maintain a cheerful air until we landed. Being on home turf made the last of her barriers crumble and she wept. Brant ordered us off the plane and I watched a small dark woman run over the tarmac and almost fight her way on board. The mysterious Aria I guessed. I had no idea how she managed to be on a military airbase but interfering didn't seem the safe option.

The offices of Unit 12, a nondescript building off St John's Gardens in central London, felt strange after my time in the DRC and learning to be a small cog in a large machine tested my patience more than once. I had taken for granted my freedoms in Africa with a team under my direct command and no ruperts giving me orders.

Jacob faced a miserable time in Hereford but Brant stuck to her word and pulled his arse out of their firing range. I couldn't protect him from their wrath or politics but I could be there to hold him through the anger Clark's lies had left. When our old teammates found out we were sleeping together we had a mixed reception, some good, some foul, some indifferent. I could wish soldiers were perfect and fully accepted our union, but people were people and change took generations if it happened at all. We just had to keep fighting for our rights.

I did go to my first Gay Pride in full uniform with my lover at my side and we made the papers. The hangover from that day was spectacular.

"Mac?" Jacob called from the office we shared in Unit 12's operational base.

I left Lydia's office and returned to ours. "What?"

"Take a look at this." He pointed to his screen so I came around the back and saw a satellite image.

I frowned. "Where's that?"

He glanced up at me from his office chair and I leaned against his shoulder. "A high pass over North Korea near the Russian border."

I grunted, no wonder it looked familiar, it had only been 12 weeks since our return. "What am I looking at?"

"Troop movements. They are heading towards the coast. Here's a later one." He switched screens. "There's a new boatyard. I think they are mobilising. Could be towards South Korea, could be Japan."

"Could be routine, could be new manoeuvres. Knowing the Koreans it could just be their army out for a jaunt. You shown these to the colonel?"

"Not yet. I'm still nervous about email."

I didn't blame him. If these mysterious bad guys were able to infiltrate the whole of the British Secret Intelligence Service and use its military resources, pen, paper, and face to face conversations were the safest options. Lydia and a few others in Unit 12 were setting up safe places on the internet that GCHQ, Government Communications Headquarters, couldn't track or find and as it was their job to find hidden places it was proving a challenge.

"Alright, give them to Lydia and see if she can send them. Brant should be back the day after tomorrow from the face-to-face with those she trusts in the CIA."

Jacob growled. "Don't see why we can't keep this as a British op."

"They need informing we have cabal threatening our democracy, because if we have a problem like this secret group trying to work towards some goal we don't know about, then so do they. This isn't just going to be a British threat. We know they have people in NATO and the UN, whether it's homegrown, some kind of external manipulation by the Russians, Chinese or Koreans, we need their help."

"Still not convinced." He leaned into me for a moment. "You ready for the weekend?"

"You mean am I ready to attend my first gay wedding?" I chuckled. "Still can't believe Luke and Sam are getting married."

"It'll be our turn one day." Jacob looked up me at with those soft honey-colored eyes I couldn't get enough of in or out of our bedroom.

"Let's make it soon," I said, and gave him a rare peck on his lips. We weren't affectionate in the workplace.

"Is that a proposal, Sergeant Macalister?" Jacob asked me, his eyes bright.

"Could be." The colour rushed up my face again because of my love for this man.

"We were supposed to wait for the perfect romantic moment."

"What about tonight? At home, after we walk the puppies and I'm fucking you?" I whispered into his ear making him shiver.

"I could ask you while I'm fucking you..." he suggested.

I laughed. "I do like it when you're in charge."

He kissed my neck. "Then I'll ask you while I'm deep inside and making you beg to be allowed to come."

I groaned and my head hit his shoulder. "It's going to be a long working day if you keep talking like that."

Jacob's chuckle warmed my heart. The future might be dangerous but we'd face it together.

Find Sarah Luddington at sarah@fictionwriter.co.uk

I don't have a newsletter to join or a Facebook group. However, if you enjoyed this story, or even if you didn't, could I trouble you for a review? They are the life blood of authors and they matter, they really matter.

Many thanks.

About the author

A LITTLE ABOUT ME, I live in a tumble down house in the Southern mountains of Spain with my husband who writes comedy. We have far too many dogs. I'm crap at social media but I try and I'm not good at sharing my life, mostly because I can't believe anyone would be interested.

I love writing, it's my grand passion and the only reason to get out of bed, well, that and the Belgium shepherd that lands on my head every morning. I love reading as well and if you follow my newsletter I'll be posting about other authors I've fallen in love with. I crave stories, so films and TV are a huge part of my life.

I do all I can to support the LGBTQ community. It's important to remember there are many people out there who are victimised for being gay or trans. Just because the law says it's okay to be gay, doesn't mean people don't suffer – we must keep fighting! I'd bang on about all the countries where it's still illegal or you face death for being gay but you guys know about this stuff.

On a lighter note, I also love walking the hounds and trying to keep them out of trouble. I love my swords, bows and pretending to be what I secretly *("Yeah right, it's such a secret." Husband rolls his eyes at me)*, want to be – a knight. I'm a hopeless romantic who would love to rescue the princess or the prince and doesn't really care what gender she is as she's doing the rescuing just so long as the bad guys put up a good fight.

So, that's me. Not complicated, just a human trying to figure out the best way to live. I hope you are to and if you want to share, come and chatter to a fellow traveller through the world and collector of stories.

Also available through Mirador Publishing:

The Prophecy
Vampire
All the following are M/M stand alone or series
Seelie
Unforbidden: A Queer Collection
Chords for the Dead
Men of Sherwood: A Rogue's Tale

The Knights of Camelot Series:
Lancelot and the King
Lancelot and the Sword
Lancelot and the Grail
Lancelot's Challenge
Lancelot's Burden
Lancelot's Curse
Betrayal of Lancelot
Passion of Lancelot
Revenge of Lancelot

Lancelot the Lost Years: The Spear

Sons of Camelot Series:
The Pendragon Legacy
The Du Lac Legacy
Albion's Legacy

Shadow Ops
Fortune's Solider: Alpha
Ultimate Sanction: Bravo
Final Play: Charlie

www.ingramcontent.com/pod-product-compliance
Lightning Source LLC
LaVergne TN
LVHW091144080826
845145LV00008B/2256

* 9 7 8 1 9 1 3 2 6 4 4 3 7 *